Happy Hour at Casa Dracula

Caution:
Upon reading,
hilarity ensues.

Happy Hour at Casa Dracula

Marta Acosta

POCKET BOOKS
New York London Toronto Sydney

POCKET BOOKS, a division of Simon & Schuster, Inc.
1230 Avenue of the Americas, New York, NY 10020

This book is a work of fiction. Names, characters, places and incidents are products of the author's imagination or are used fictitiously. Any resemblance to actual events or locales or persons, living or dead, is entirely coincidental.

ISBN-13: 978-1-4165-2038-2
ISBN-10: 1-4165-2038-4

This Pocket Books trade paperback edition July 2006

10 9 8 7 6 5 4 3 2 1

POCKET and colophon are registered trademarks of Simon & Schuster, Inc.

Manufactured in the United States of America

For information regarding special discounts for bulk purchases, please contact Simon & Schuster Special Sales at 1-800-456-6798 or *business@simonandschuster.com.*

To my fabulous husband, Miguel.

one

the intolerable lightness of being silly

If I had been a rational human being, I would have had a normal job and I never would have gotten involved with any of them. But I was not a rational human being. I was and remain a square peg in a round world.

You would think that a girl with a degree from a Fancy University would have been hired *muy rápido* by some big corporation anxious to ladle on numerous perks and a generous salary. Sadly, my F.U. education did not lead me directly into wealth and fame. All my attempts to become a worthwhile cog in the capitalist machine were met with rejection, the type that has driven many other creative souls to despair and Great Art.

Here are the results of my attempts. No response at all from the many newspapers that should have been interested in a columnist who focused on bargain gardens. A soul-killing stint at an ad agency that concluded when the art director read my sardonic copy for fortified wine. A happy stretch writing a newsletter for a nutritional supplements company that ended abruptly when the FDA raided our warehouse. Miscellaneous temporary jobs, each more wretchedly depressing than its predecessor. Also two entry-level marketing jobs terminated after "improprieties," which were not my fault.

Okay, my mother Regina would have said that they *were* my fault. My mother Regina thought that anyone with breasts as vulgar as my own induced otherwise upstanding citizens to behave badly. My mother Regina had neat, tasteful *chichis*. When she bothered to look at me, an expression of dismay almost came over her immaculately made-up face. "Almost," because medical procedures rendered her incapable of normal facial expressions.

My mother Regina believed my father had wasted his hard-earned cash sending me to F.U. because I was not a serious person. My mother Regina thought thusly because I always referred to her as "my mother Regina" and because I had not dedicated myself wholeheartedly to the reformation and improvement of my garish carcass. "You have wasted your father's money," she said, ignoring the fact that I had worked, taken out loans, and earned scholarships in order to attend F.U.

I now lived in a windowless basement flat of a nice house in a nice neighborhood of the City. My rent was low because I maintained the garden and my landlord found my bosom enchanting. While he never exactly said, "I am captivated by your enchanting bosom," he did stare a lot and that's practically the same thing. The dark flat had a cement floor, a dinky bathroom, and a gloomy kitchenette. At night, I heard scrabbling in the walls, which, I suspected, was caused by fearsome Norway rats.

My income was earned by toiling as a reading consultant to executives and society dames who were book club averse. I garnered extra cash by filling in at a local nursery. My jobs were irregular, sometimes taking only ten hours of my week and other times taking fifty, but I didn't mind. It was better than sitting in an office trying to keep my eyes from bleeding while copyediting training manuals.

I worked diligently on my novel every single possible second that was available after going out, thrift store shopping, spending quality time with my friends, and finding gyms that offered the first month free. In addition to this exhausting work/art/life regime, I tried to improve the world by writing letters to political leaders about Important Issues. I wasn't picky about the issues. The world was full of pain and injustice, and writing the letters helped me keep proper perspective.

My friend Nancy had come up with the reading consultant idea because she knew how much I liked recommending books to friends. She had given me business cards on lovely ecru stock with "Bennett" hyphenated to my last name. Underneath was "Reading Consultant," with my phone number.

"Why the Bennett hyphenate?" I had asked.

"Like Eliza Bennett, you have a fine posterior," she had said. Nancy had been my F.U. roommate freshman year.

Despite her unfortunate WASPier-than-thou perkiness, we had become friends.

"Eliza had fine eyes, not a fine fanny, you cultural barbarian. You never even finished *Pride and Prejudice.* I wrote that paper for you."

"And now I am showing my tremendous appreciation for your scholarship. Also this gives you credibility with Anglophile aspirants, my little brown *amiga.*" This is how we talked to each other. We thought being silly was the height of delightfulness.

Speaking of which, my name was outlandish enough without the Bennett hyphenate, but I took the cards and thanked her.

I filled my days, but there were times when I awoke in the middle of the night, listened to the scratching in the walls, and felt afraid and lonely. I missed rooming with Nancy and hearing her gentle snoring at night. Nancy did not miss me; she had moved into her boyfriend Todd's condo and was a happy camper.

People can be divided into two distinct groups: those who desire constant companionship and those who prefer calm solitude. The unnecessary crowding in *The Brady Bunch* repelled me, but I longed for an Eliza Bennettish existence: a house filled with family and friends, the agreeable conversation of a kind and compassionate sister, and the promise of dances and engagements.

Instead I had my mother Regina, rats in the walls, and boyfriends who were like beach reads, momentary fun but nothing you'd ever bother to buy in hardcover. I worried that perhaps I, as a nonserious person, was only a beach read as well. I had just reread *Middlemarch*, and I had a deep and sincere desire to be a deep and sincere character.

Nancy had connected me with most of my reading clients, but one of my former beach reads, a Russian artist named Vladimir, introduced me to Kathleen Baker. Kathleen was one of *the* Bakers, known for their famous sourdough bread: "Did a Real Baker Make Your Sour Round?"

Kathleen was fiftyish and very chic. Like my other clients, Kathleen wanted me more for company than guidance. Sometimes she patted my head as if I was a pet and I half expected her to toss biscuits to me and say, "Good girl, catch!" I had to constantly steer the conversation back to her reading and remind her that we had a scholarly purpose.

In her enthusiasm for literature, Kathleen decided to host a reception for hot new writer Sebastian Beckett-Witherspoon. She was absolutely thrilled when he accepted. I know because she said, "I am absolutely thrilled that Sebastian Beckett-Witherspoon has accepted my invitation to hold a reception for him. Are you familiar with his work?"

In a word, yes. In three words, all too familiar. In a few more words, why wouldn't Sebastian B-W die, die, die a grisly and humiliating death? I pulled my lips into a simian grimace that I hoped Kathleen would interpret as a smile. I told her that we had met at F.U. "Marvelous!" she said. "Of course, you will be at my reception. I'm sure he'll be delighted to see you again."

"Perhaps you overestimate my delightfulness," I demurred. I had taken up demurring like mad. I thought demurring was the last word in refinement, right behind murmuring, deferring, and suggesting.

"Don't be a silly goose," Kathleen said. "This will be a good opportunity for you to meet other literary people."

So here I was at Kathleen's soirée for Sebastian Beckett-Witherspoon, the highlight of a lackluster season of morose poets, grimy novelists, and patronizing essayists. Kathleen had a magpie's fascination with all things shiny, so the room gleamed with polished floors, glittering mirrors, and lustrous furniture. I was afraid that if I moved too quickly, I'd skitter and crash down on my sincere and serious *colita.*

I wore a simple linen shirt-dress that I'd bought at a thrift store, cream sandals, and fake pearls. My straight black hair was pulled back into a low, Grace Kellyish ponytail, and I'd used a light hand with my makeup because I wanted to look good without looking like a good time.

I did what I always do at gatherings: an initial scan of the room for people of hue. One Asian man in a pinstripe suit, an African-American couple in earth-toned natural fibers, and a mixed-race woman. No obvious Latinos except for me and one waiter. I sent him the silent message: "Right on, *mi hermano.* Power to the people."

At a real party or in a club, I knew what to do or say, but here I felt as awkward as I had my first day at F.U., hauling cardboard boxes to my dorm while almost Nordic-looking people strode confidently forward with matching luggage. The other guests seemed to know each other, but their eyes slid over me and moved on to others more important.

I was all too aware of the ecru business cards in my small pocketbook. Sometimes you seek guidance in nineteenth-century heroines and other times you find inspiration in nineteenth-century hucksters, such as P. T. Barnum and his Feejee Mermaid. If Barnum could shamelessly peddle a monkey head sewn on a fish body as a sea nymph, then surely I could try to promote my novel to an agent or publisher.

Then I saw Sebastian B-W, scion of one of the most powerful families in the country. He stood by a window, and most people would have thought it was merely a lucky accident that a shaft of light from the setting sun glowed on his golden hair. He smiled and nodded as he talked to an older man. Sebastian's skin was evenly tanned with a slight, marvelous blush of pink on his cheeks. His teeth were as pearly as ever, and he seemed to have aged very little over the last several years. He was just over six foot, slim and graceful in a navy jacket and a soft blue shirt that brought out the sea-color of his eyes.

I had thought, la, la, la, that I would come here and Sebastian would see that I had moved beyond the past, that I had matured into an urban and urbane woman, a fellow scribe, and that we could have a civil, even friendly association. But just looking at him made me panic like a hemophiliac in a pin factory.

"Yummy," said a voice nearby.

"What?" I was startled and turned to see a small, wiry redheaded waiter with a tray of petite pastries.

"Would you like something yummy?" The waiter held the tray toward me and winked. He was as gay and pleasing as a posy of Johnny-jump-ups. He had a wide smile and big green eyes to go with his shock of red hair.

"I always enjoy something yummy," I replied suggestively,

unable to stop my chronic flirting mechanism. Nancy said that my need to flirt was directly linked to the lack of a strong paternal figure in my life and the dominating presence of an unloving mother. I thought it was because boys were so dang pretty.

"I certainly didn't mean him," the waiter said, tilting his head toward Sebastian. "That novel was offensive."

Of course I had read Sebastian's novel, looking for secret clues to his character in every word. "I thought I was the only one who didn't like it."

"Please, girlfriend, it was pretentious as hell," said the waiter. "His school churns them out like that." He saw my expression and said, "What's the matter?"

When I admitted that I had gone to F.U., he grinned and said, "Well, present company excepted. You aren't involved with him, are you?"

"Me, involved with him? Ha-ha, you make the funny," I said flippantly. "Does he turn your engine?"

"Not my type. I like them less evil incarnate," he said. "And also hairier."

Before we could continue our fascinating conversation, the headwaiter angrily gestured for my new friend to circulate. It was time for me to circulate, too, and the first person I had to talk to was the guest of horror. My heart was pounding faster than a flamenco dancer's feet. I grabbed a flute of champagne off a tray, downed it quickly, and grabbed another.

Moving through the crowd, I noticed that everyone was surreptitiously peeking at Sebastian, all awaiting their chance to have a clever or insightful exchange so they could relate the story at their next dinner party. He caught sight of me and his smile froze. I tried to calm myself as I walked to his side.

He continued his conversation with the older man. "Naturally," he said, "I only write about perversions to expose them to the condemnation they deserve. I am not a voyeur, not one who is titillated by the steamy, I mean, seamy underbelly."

Seamy underbelly? I guess that was my cue. "Hello, Sebastian."

He turned his head fractionally toward me. "Hullo," he said tersely without meeting my eyes.

"*Hullo?* Are we suddenly British? Lord love a duck." I didn't know what that expression meant, but I'd always wanted to use it. "In America, we say 'hello' with the accent on 'hell.'"

The older fellow said to Sebastian, "I enjoyed talking with you," then edged just far enough away to eavesdrop.

Sebastian held out his hand and actually said, "I'm Sebastian Beckett-Witherspoon. And you are . . . ?"

He won tonight's P. T. Barnum award for even trying this. I wanted to stab him repeatedly with a tiny cocktail fork until he leaked all over like a sieve. "If you don't cut it out, Sebastian, I swear I'll make your evening here one of undiluted misery."

He blanched and spoke in a low whisper. "Undiluted misery! You have no idea how much you've caused me. What are you doing here?"

"I'm a very close and special friend of Kathleen's. In fact, I'm her literary consultant," I said, trying to sound important.

Sebastian was confused. "You mean you suggested that she have this reception?"

"Oh, be real," I snapped. "Did I like your incest-fest novel? I did not." It occurred to me that this was not the most politic thing to say if I wished to resuscitate our association.

"*You* are criticizing me? You, who write political horrors!" He snorted. "Blood and gore and monsters and tedious left-wing diatribes. Utter swill."

Why were my feelings hurt when I had no respect for him? "You said you liked my stories," I said before I could stop myself. I pushed away a memory of the early weeks of our acquaintance and how I felt seeing him strolling across campus toward me, smiling as the wind blew back his hair.

"I may have said it, but I didn't mean it."

"Did you ever mean anything you told me, Sebastian?" It was as if no time had passed since our last encounter: I was flooded by unnameable emotion, wanting to cry and shout and say all the things I'd never had a chance to tell him. I hadn't done anything wrong, yet he had cast me out of his world. What was worse, he'd done it when I was taking a course in Milton, so I'd become obsessed with finding the answer to my misery in *Paradise Lost.* I'd received an A on my term paper, but my time would have been better spent getting advice from *Cosmopolitan.*

"Why are you here, Milagro?"

The whole history of our relationship was in the knowing way he said my name. It felt too intimate, as if he knew too many of my secrets. "I'm here to make contacts. Introduce me to your agent or your publisher."

"You are still out of your tiny little mind."

Before I could retort, wheedle, or threaten, Kathleen began speaking on the other side of the room. Sebastian moved away so fast, it was like he had been teleported.

"Your feminine wiles leave something to be desired," said a deep voice so close to me I felt warm breath on my neck. I stepped away reflexively. Beside me was a somewhat fabulous man in a strange suit. Now, Nancy would tell you that I often see fabulous men, that I think more men are fabulous than not, and that I am overly generous in bestowing the description of "fabulous" on a man. Her comments have caused me to doubt my ability to judge fabulousness, and I was feeling particularly insecure right now.

I focused on this man just to center myself. Rich brown hair brushed straight back, gray eyes, a strong nose, pale, perfect skin, nice cheekbones, and a lovely, rosy curved mouth. He was medium height, lean and muscled. He smiled crookedly, which either added or detracted from his charm, depending upon your point of view. "Aren't you going to say anything?" he asked.

"As you have noted, my feminine wiles have eluded me this evening." I was still trying to figure out what was wrong with his suit. It was well made, but the cut was about fifty years out of style, give or take a century. And the smell . . . under the light, clean scent of a good aftershave was cedar. My guess was that his suit had been hanging in a closet for ages.

His smoke-colored eyes took a leisurely journey up and down my body, causing my trampy internal gears to shift of their own volition. "Perhaps I misjudged," he said. His voice was as sexy as a funky bass line on the dance floor.

My recent encounter with Sebastian had made my nerves buzz, and I had no idea if this man was flirting with me or insulting me. "So kind of you to offer your criticism gratis to strangers," was my utterly pathetic retort. Who said "gratis"? Pretty soon I'd be uncontrollably uttering "pro forma," "ipso facto," and "carpe diem" in conversation ad nauseam. As a tactical maneuver, I moved through the rapt audience to the other side of the room before I said anything else idiotic.

Sebastian was now addressing the guests, droning the usual glad to be here, happy so many devoted fans, et cetera, and opening a copy of his novel so that he could read a chapter aloud. Had I ever enjoyed his writing or had I been so flattered by his attention that I convinced myself I liked this drivel?

The other guests seemed enthralled by Sebastian's stream of blather. He used words like "luminescent," "tumescent," "iridescent," and "transcendent." Perhaps they handed out *New Yorker* vocabulary lists at every graduate writing program in the country. I wouldn't know. My mother Regina had convinced my father that liposuction on her "problem spots" was more critical than helping me through grad school. Listening to Sebastian now, I began to think that maybe she'd had a point.

The carrot-topped waiter returned and whispered, "Warm chèvre with tapenade," as he offered his tray.

"No thanks," I said.

The waiter gracelessly deposited his tray on a side table. "You seem to be attracting the attention of some of the gentlemen here," he said chattily. I wasn't surprised at his unprofessional interest in me. I have always had a symbiotic relationship with the waiter species.

"If by that you mean I imposed my company upon the guest of honor, then I guess, yes."

"No offense, but these guys aren't your type. I know what I'm talking about." Coming from someone else, his statement would have sounded like a *West Side Story* stick-to-your-own-kind, but I assumed he was offering his assessment of sexual orientation.

I wasn't going to insult his obviously flawed gaydar, so I said, "Thanks. I'll take that into consideration."

The waiter winked at me, then slipped away. I wondered why he left the tray of hors d'oeuvres. He was a nice guy, but a very bad waiter.

Sebastian finally concluded his yammering. There was hearty applause, and then I saw the fabulous man smiling in my direction. Sauntering to me, he said, "This joint is a bust. Let's scram."

Though I had come to the party to hawk my wares, this was not what I had in mind. But the room seemed too close and too crowded. I was still fantasizing about stabbing Sebastian, and I thought it was a good idea to get away before I did something legally prosecutable in front of numerous witnesses. "I don't suppose you're connected to the publishing world?"

"Why else would I be here? You're a writer?" His lopsided smile inspired parts of my body to attempt mutiny and throw themselves at him. "We'll go somewhere quieter where we can talk about your writing. I can tell you are an interesting writer, unique."

"Excuse me, but exactly how dumb do you think I am?" Men seemed to think there was an inverse relationship between bouncy bazooms and brainpower.

His laugh carried to his eyes and he said, "That did sound like a bad line, didn't it? But I'm right, aren't I?"

"Every writer wants to think that she's unique and interesting. That doesn't mean it's true." I hated the idea that Sebastian had out–P. T. Barnumed me tonight. Would Barnum have rejected a potential investor? "You haven't introduced yourself," I murmured, as if I was a proper young lady.

The fabulous man took my elbow and led me through the crowd. He escorted me down the marbled hallway, through the wood-paneled foyer, and when we were away from the chatter of the party, he said, "I am Oswaldo Krakatoa."

His name was patently absurd. I was strongly tempted to question its veracity. "I'm Milagro De Los Santos." Judging from his expression, I had just won the ridiculous-name contest.

"Miracle of the saints?"

"It's a sad little story. I'll tell you sometime when I'm feeling particularly full of self-pity. You can call me Mil."

"All right, Mil." We stepped outside. The fog had rolled in and the damp Pacific air was refreshing after the packed, overperfumed room.

My bus stop was far down the street. My options were: talk to this handsome fellow, track down my pals for a whine-and-wine session, or go home and cry a million tears because my business cards were still in my handbag and Sebastian had frazzled me to the utmost.

A limousine pulled up and the driver stepped out, opening the passenger door. I wondered who the lucky bastard was. Yes, I knew every drug dealer and prom kid rented these, but those tiny bottles of liquor were so amusing. Oswaldo said, "I'm staying at the Hotel Croft. We could talk there in the bar."

I loved the Sequoia Room at the Croft. They had silver bowls of salted cashews and the waitresses let you nurse one overpriced cocktail for hours while you listened to the pianist play Gershwin. It was one of the City's great old hotels, and I always liked to imagine the passionate trysts that took place there, the corrupt business deals, the after-theater dinners.

"I'm not . . . ," I began, and then I saw Sebastian rushing out of Kathleen's house. He looked outraged and he was heading my way. "Sure, let's go, *now.*"

Oswaldo waved to the limo driver, who said, "Good evening, Doctor."

Doctor? Perhaps he had a PhD. Personally, I felt that if someone couldn't prescribe entertaining pharmaceuticals, he shouldn't use the title of doctor socially. I slid into the backseat of the limo and the driver closed the door. Sebastian was in such a rush to get to me that he stumbled on the curb and fell. Through the dark window, I could see his features contort, more in rage than in pain. What in the world was the matter with him? He should have been relieved to see me go.

My escort leaned forward and said, "The Croft, please." I liked that he said "please" to the driver. Turning his clear gaze on me, Oswaldo asked, "Are you a colleague of Mr. Beckett-Witherspoon?"

I supposed that technically I had been his colleague. College, colleague, and all that. "I was, but we had aesthetic differences."

He said, "Tell me about your writing," when I was busy noticing how nice his knee looked in his ancient trousers. Why had I never noticed men's knees before? I was amazed at how quickly the torment from encountering Sebastian was dissipating in the company of an attractive knee.

"Hmm?" I said cleverly. "Why don't you tell me about what you do?" I wanted to know what he did so I could decide whether to tell him about my novel or my short stories.

"This and that," he answered. "Handle documents, read things, ensure they get to the right people."

Was he an agent, an editor, or a mailman? "What genres do you prefer?"

"Fiction, nonfiction, theology, philosophy," he said. "Prose, poetry." Well, that about covered everything from the Koran to dirty limericks. I wondered if I was being taken for a ride in more than one way. It didn't matter. At least I could grab a cab or a bus from the Croft.

"Excuse me for asking," he said, "but how well do you know Beckett-Witherspoon?"

I could tell this was a trick question. "How well do we know anyone? How well do you know him?"

"Oh," said Oswaldo, "I know him more by reputation."

"So, are you a real doctor?" I didn't think so. He looked too carefree.

"The driver likes to make people feel important." He added, "I've often thought that I would like to be a veterinarian."

And I would like to be the Princess of Mars. I didn't bother to make small talk the rest of the way, which left my mind vulnerable to totally unwarranted images of mad lovemaking in limos.

I was so unevolved as a human being that I thought it was cool to get out of a limo in front of the Croft. One of the doormen recognized me and winked as he held open the heavy brass-'n'-glass door. "Just one drink," I murmured to Oswaldo. I needed just one drink before I could face going back to my dark and dismal abode.

We crossed the cushy burgundy carpet to the entrance of the Sequoia Room, where we were assaulted by raucous voices raised loud over a hearty band. It was that traditional matrimonial celebration song, "YMCA." The concierge rose from behind his desk and glided to us. "I apologize, but we've had to move a private party from another room due to a damaged carpet. Perhaps you would like to relax in the Hamburg Room?"

A bar had to be bad in multiple ways to earn my disfavor; the Hamburg Room was one of the City's few watering holes that achieved this classification. It was a dim, uncomfortable room decorated with truncheons, shields, and suits of armor. I had had a particularly unpleasant evening there after ingesting some hallucinogenic mushrooms purely for research purposes. (I was creating a character who returns to her shamanistic roots after discovering she can shape-shift into a mountain lion to avenge a polluting chemical plant.) I said, "I don't think so . . ."

"Or if you like," said the concierge obligingly, "the Croft will send drinks to your suite, Doctor. Complimentary, of course."

The odd doc turned to me. If Oswaldo had suggested drinks in his room, I would have said no. If he had tried to urge me or in any way lure me, I would have said absolutely not. But the offer had come from the concierge, so I said, "Fine."

"What would you like?" Oswaldo asked.

"Something tropical in a coconut with little parasols."

"Send a pitcher," said Oswaldo. Ordering too much booze was not necessarily a mark against a man. Most of the published writers at F.U. were drunks.

We silently rode the elevator to Oswaldo's upper-floor suite. He unlocked the door and held it open for me. Judging by the size of the rooms and the view of the City, he was either successful or profligate. The lights glimmered charmingly in the night. The sitting room was all coffee tones: mocha armchairs, an overstuffed espresso-covered sofa, thick latte-colored carpets, and the walls were a nice steamed milk shade. Okay, I'm making that up, but they were a creamy white. There were no obvious signs of literary business: no manuscripts on the desk, no books piled on the coffee table, no Post-its stuck to the walls.

I dropped into the armchair closest to the door. "Are you really in publishing, Oswaldo?"

"Not major publishing, but I've got a little publishing side business."

"Answering personal ads is not considered publishing."

He laughed. It was an honest, warm laugh from inside. It washed over me like spring rain and I relaxed and started laughing, too. "Really, I have been published," he insisted. "Articles and research papers."

"Why the ruse?"

" 'Ruse'? You have a strange vocabulary."

"Books have always been my consolation." I said it mockingly although it was true.

There was a discreet knock at the door. Oswaldo opened it and a waiter wheeled in a cart with a frosty pitcher and two drinks in coconuts with pink parasols and pineapple garnishes. They were so perfect I wanted to take a picture of them.

When the waiter left, Oswaldo handed a coconut to me and sat on the sofa.

I took a sip of the frozen concoction. It was sweet and fruity. Only an hour ago, I had felt out of place and insecure, but now I congratulated myself for my admirable sophistication, enjoying the attentions of a fabulous man in swanky digs. "I'm pretty sure this is what the Lost Generation drank," I said.

"You haven't told me what you write about yet."

Still stinging from Sebastian's criticism, I answered blithely, "Fiction, stories with political implications."

Oswaldo leaned forward, looking at me intently. "Political thrillers, then? Like le Carré or Cruz Smith?"

Although I had not read either of these authors, I doubted that their novels featured zombies. "Not quite. I use the supernatural to represent the manifestation of various life forces, good, evil, the unconscious, the id, et cetera."

Now Oswaldo grinned broadly. He had a generous mouth, a sensual, facile mouth, and I found him more attractive by the second. "You mean horror stories?" he asked. "Do you believe in those things? Monsters, ghosts, vampires?"

I didn't want to waste my time defending my writing to someone who preferred more conventional literary fiction, so I said, "I'm not superstitious, but myths do serve a purpose. They symbolize and explain fears and anxieties in a way that science cannot."

"Do you think so?" he said. "What purpose does the Loch Ness monster serve?"

Now he was teasing me. "Do you like Sebastian's latest novel? Because if you do, you may as well know now that my style is very different."

"I would have guessed as much," Oswaldo said. "I was there because I was curious about his work. I've heard a great deal about him. I haven't had the chance to read his book yet."

"The critics love it," I said, thereby not committing one way or another regarding Sebastian's work.

"So they do," said Oswaldo. "He seems rather businesslike for an artist, so establishment. Is that how he always is?"

"You're assuming that I know him well," I said.

He sipped his drink. "Um, yes, I got that general impression."

I suddenly had a shift in awareness. "I thought you invited me here because you were interested in me, my writing. But all you really want to know about is Sebastian." My breasts practically slumped in shame. I swallowed my drink quickly, feeling momentary brain freeze, which seemed appropriate for the situation. I would have bet Oswaldo was a heterosexual, but that dang waiter had been right. "That's the icing on the cake for this evening!"

I stood up and grabbed my bag. The evening could yet be redeemed. I'd go to the lobby, phone my friends and find out where they would be tonight. "Ask Kathleen," I told him. "She knows where Sebastian's staying. A man of your means can surely schedule an appointment or an interview or a tryst or whatever it is that you want."

Oswaldo jumped up. "No, no, that's . . ." He grabbed my arm. His lovely fingers were warm on my flesh. "I *did* want to know about him, but, you, there's something about you and I didn't expect to meet anyone who could make me feel . . ."

I could have huffed, "What kind of girl do you think I am?" But the truth is that I'm the kind of girl who can be picked up by some fake doctor bozo in a weird suit at a posh party, go to his hotel suite, become insulted, and then realize that she's never been so attracted to anyone before. I'm the kind of girl who impulsively tugs him close and kisses him like there's no tomorrow.

I felt as if there was no tomorrow and no yesterday and nothing but *this* moment and *this* moment and *this* moment. My need to touch him went beyond coconut drink–fueled desire. My mind shut down entirely and turned control over to my nervous system. I lost sense of where my body ended and his began. I felt an arm stroke a back, but could not tell if I was stroking his back or he was stroking mine. Our tongues slipped into each other's mouths, our legs tangled in an effort to meld our bodies. We pushed together carelessly, wildly, and crashed against the coffee table before tumbling to the carpet, his body beneath mine.

I felt as if a door had opened and I'd stepped into light and open space. I felt truly happy in a way I had never felt before. It was like I had been living in black and white and suddenly I could see in color.

I became aware of a warm mineral taste in my mouth and I broke away from Oswaldo. I put my fingers to my face and discovered that my lower lip had been cut. My fingers came away glistening with blood. Oswald's lip, too, had been cut in the fall. A gleaming red drop beaded at the corner of his mouth.

"Milagro," Oswald said softly. He didn't pull me toward him or push me away or laugh about our clumsiness. He just stared at me with his smoky gray eyes, his chest rising with every slow breath, the red, red drop of blood exquisitely balanced on the edge of his pink lip and his creamy skin.

I knew the dangers of exchanging body fluids, but an inexplicable compulsion rose in me. Irrationally, unreasonably, I didn't try to repress it. The caution I had always taken seemed insignificant compared with the desire that now enflamed me. I lowered my lips to Oswald's and put my injured mouth to his, tasting him, hungry for every drop, every part of him.

He tasted like the ocean; he tasted like the earth; he tasted like the sky; he tasted like life itself. I heard him say, "No, we can't," and his argument convinced neither of us. He grabbed me tightly and rolled our bodies over until he was on top. Our hands were fumbling with each other's clothes and I became aware of a banging, a loud insistent banging, but it wasn't us, not yet, and then the door flew open and someone shouted, "Stop!" Turning to the door, I saw Sebastian, who looked furious.

I was about to tell him to get lost, to go to hell, wondering why he had decided to bother me, when some tiny part of me became aware that I felt strangely disoriented. And while I wanted to stay with Oswaldo forever, the core of me that was Milagro De Los Santos, miracle of the saints, ordered me to get up, to grab my bag, to get away now before I lost all will and control.

Shoving Sebastian aside, I rushed down the hall. I was aware of the men shouting at each other. Then the walls began to waver and the floor roiled under my feet. I stood still, thinking that it was an earthquake. None of the pictures on the walls fell, though, and the flowers were still in their vases.

The elevator doors were open. I stumbled inside, punched the lobby button, and leaned against the mirrored wall. My mouth was red and my eyes were wild. I noticed that my dress was partially unbuttoned, but I didn't care. When the elevator doors opened, I nearly collapsed into the lobby. The redheaded waiter was standing there and he caught me. "Are you okay?"

"No," I said, but I was thinking that it was an awfully big coincidence that the same dang waiter was in the Croft lobby. And that made me wonder how Sebastian had found me in the hotel room. Why were we all at the Croft? Was someone having an after-party for Kathleen's reception? Had I come here for an after-party? My thoughts were slipping and sliding around in my brain like eels. I couldn't hold on to any of them long enough to make sense out of the situation.

"Come sit down here," the waiter said, and he helped me to an enormous ottoman by the entrance. It was scarlet, like Oswaldo's blood. I rubbed the dark leather with my thumb and licked at my lips, my tongue searching for a last drop. The waiter's deft fingers buttoned my dress to my neck. "Stay here and I'll take care of you. I have to do one thing. *Stay here,* okay?"

I may have nodded or my head may have just dropped.

"I'll be right back." He ran off and left me.

two

rats in the walls, bats in the belfry

I waited an eternity, but it may have been only a few seconds before I forced myself to stand up and step carefully toward the entrance. My favorite doorman, a towering, middle-aged black man, opened the heavy door and said, "Hey, babe, you okay?"

"A taxi. Please, don't tell them where I've gone." He blew on his whistle and a Yellow Cab swerved to the curb. "My friend is at My Dive," I said to the doorman. My knees began to buckle and he grabbed my elbow to hold me up.

"My Dive," the doorman told the cabbie, "and make sure she gets there." I saw him pull out a bill from his pocket and slip it to the taxi driver. "Make sure she gets there *safely,*" he said threateningly to the cab driver. The doorman had always been nice to me and I was glad I'd often let him pat my bottom. Now I was so grateful, I brushed my breasts against him as he helped me into the cab. "Pay me back next time, okay, babe?" he said gruffly.

"Yes, next time. Thank you." I tried to speak clearly even though my voice seemed to be coming from far away.

Neon signs vibrated with color as the driver wove in and out of traffic on the crowded streets. Transvestites seemed painfully beautiful and the air around junkies hummed with sorrow. The cab driver jerked to a stop and barked, "Twenty dollars," even though it was only a few blocks and the doorman had already paid him.

I tried to focus on the meter, but couldn't. "No, too much," I said. I fumbled with my pocketbook and handed him a few crumpled bills. I was damned if I was going to let a cabbie treat me like a tourist.

I opened the cab door. The curb looked impossibly far away from the solid black front door with the tiny magenta lettering reading MY DIVE.

Then Lenny, the bouncer, was there, holding me up. "What in hell . . ."

"Mercedes," was all I could say. Lenny threw me over his shoulder like a sack of potatoes.

"You're a handful," he grunted. I decided to take it as a compliment.

I knew I was safe, so I didn't care if I was panty-flashing anyone. It was either very early or very late, because the club was empty as Lenny trudged through the run-down dance room to the right of the small raised stage. My head banged against the wall when we went down the dingy narrow hall covered with old posters and black-and-white photos of musicians. A few seconds later, I remembered to say "ouch."

Lenny used his foot to push open the pea-green office door, eased past boxes of bar supplies and files, and dumped me on an itchy old mustard-colored sofa. I heard Mercedes say, "Milagro!" and I closed my eyes.

"A cab dumped her here. She's toasted," Lenny chivalrously offered.

"Am not," I said. "Drugged."

I felt a warm thumb on my eyelid as Mercedes pulled it up. "What did you take?"

Shaking my head made everything worse. "Suspect I was drugged. Kindly let me sleep."

Mercedes released my eyelid and sighed. I didn't need to see her to know what she looked like now: sweatshirt, basic Levis, her frizzy auburn hair pulled back with a giant barrette. She was a big, solid girl who had her Scottish father's build and her Afro-Cuban mother's coloring. Honest, cheerful, hardworking, thrifty, and brave, Mercedes was the antithesis of cool and, therefore, the hippest person I'd ever met.

She started hauling me up. "If you've been drugged, we'll get you to the hospital."

I just wanted to sleep, so I struggled against her. "No need to alert Scotland Yard, lassie. Let me be. I'm hokay."

Mercedes had dealt with a lot of drunks and overdoses in the course of her work. She threw a blanket over me and made a phone call. I was trying to sleep when a man came in and bothered me. He took my pulse and looked at my pupils and asked me questions. He told Mercedes to keep me hydrated and to make sure I didn't choke on my vomit, which was so disgusting because I had never, ever vomited in my life.

I fell into something that was Not Sleep.

Have you ever had nitrous oxide at the dentist's or temporarily died and floated outside your body? There I was, hanging over myself and watching Mercedes make phone calls, work at her computer, and shuffle through papers. I saw the neon beer-company clock ticking away the time and heard the music playing loudly in the club. I heard people fill up the club, shout conversations, and stomp around on the dance floor. I listened to the sound guy chatting with the lighting guy and the band warming up. The clink of change at the bar was as clear to me as the hiss of matches and laughter from a tipsy girl. I heard the melodious tinkling of ice in drinks and toilets flushing and rain beginning to patter on the sidewalk outside.

Throughout the night Mercedes checked on me, listening to my breathing and putting her comforting hand to my forehead. Although only a few years older than me, she seemed ages more mature and experienced. She'd started state college at barely seventeen, then left after a year to take a computer geek job. She'd scrimped and invested so she could buy this club when it was in foreclosure. She had gravitas. Why couldn't I have gravitas, I wondered as I lay on the ratty sofa in my crumpled linen dress.

Mercedes forced me to drink glass after glass of water. The beauty of having friends in the nightclub business is that they always remember to put a twist of lime in your drinks.

At about four in the morning, long after the club had closed, I realized that my body was trying to keep me out of it. Like hell if I was going to let that happen. I would not go quietly into the good night. I dropped down from the ceiling and my body tried to push me away. When I shoved myself back into my flesh, my body jolted with the shock.

Mercedes looked up from her desk. "About time. How you doing?"

My mouth tasted like a wino's armpit. I remembered the evening, but did not have the energy to sort out the facts now. "Not terrific, but I'm still alive."

Mercedes plunked a pile of letters and file folders into her outbox and stood up. "You said something about taking drugs."

Had Oswaldo drugged me? He'd picked up the drink from the waiter's cart and handed it directly to me; I'd focused on the cute little pink parasol the entire time. I couldn't even tell if I was on drugs. When I shook my head, something other than the usual idiotic thoughts rattled inside. "Maybe I've got the flu."

Putting her hands on her broad hips, Mercedes said, "What do you want to do? Do you want to come to my house?" I adored Mercedes's house, especially because she could afford to pay for heat and always had lots of good food and music and strong, sweet coffee in tiny cups. However, I had a mortal fear of being sick in someone's house.

My mother Regina had frequently said that nothing is more disgusting than a sick child. Not wanting to give her one more reason to resent my existence, I had made it a point to never ever get ill. "I think I'll go home," I told Mercedes. "Can you give me a lift?"

My recovery was brief. As soon as I got inside my dismal flat and closed the door behind me, I was taken by the chills. I was shivering so violently that I could barely manage to brush my teeth and almost blinded myself when I removed my contact lenses. My blankets weren't enough to keep me warm, so I took all the clothes out of my closet, piled them on the bed, and crawled beneath the heap.

three

wherein our heroine loses her fashion sense

I fell into some sort of delirium. While that sounds *muy romantico* if you go for repressed Victorian heroines, my condition was not so marvelous. Instead of wearing a lace-trimmed white cotton nightgown, I struggled to creep into flannel pajamas that my father, Jerry D, gave me as a college graduation present. The large red and black penguin print detracted considerably from the drama of my condition.

When I was alert enough, I'd make a cup of tea or a bowl of ramen, but I couldn't take more than a few sips. The food and drink tasted revolting, and I had an almost painful craving for meat that I was too weak to satisfy.

Time meant nothing to me. I shifted in and out of consciousness, seeking sleep to release me from my aching bones and alternating fever and chills. Sometimes I imagined Sebastian as I had last seen him, condescending and cruel, and other times I remembered him as he had been, as beautiful and radiant as an angel, smiling at me from a distance, holding out his arms. That vision would dissipate and Oswaldo with his brushed-back chestnut hair and clear gray eyes would appear, irresistible and insatiable, his lean limbs wrapping around me, his full mouth grinning in mischief, draining me of all my energy and filling me with pleasure.

When the phone rang, I didn't answer it. A few times I got up and listened to my messages. Clients wanted to schedule appointments, and the nursery harangued me to come in right away to substitute for a sick employee. Nancy called and wanted the gossip about Kathleen's party. I pulled myself together enough to call her back and say that I was sick and would share the grisly details later. She offered to bring over lobster bisque, but I pleaded with her to stay away so I wouldn't infect her.

Maybe I'd caught the illness from Oswaldo. I remembered how he'd pushed me away from his cut lip. In my agitated state, I yearned desperately for the taste of his mouth and skin and blood again. Once, I imagined I felt his itchy wool suit against my skin, and I awoke drenched in sweat on the floor. I had gruesome dreams, too, vile visions of carnage and sex that shocked me.

The scrabbling in the walls began to sound like Morse code. I thought they might be messages about Sebastian. If I listened hard enough, I could learn the pattern and understand his secrets.

Once I hallucinated that my *abuelita,* my grandmother, had come back to me. I could smell *canela,* the cinnamon tea she loved, and feel her small brown hands stroke my hair as she recited the silly consolation for a child's injury: "*Sana, sana, colita de rana. Si no sana hoy, sanara mañana.*" I could hear her voice murmuring prayers in Spanish and the soothing click-click of her rosary beads. I would have endured much more suffering to have those few moments with her again.

One day I awoke and was able to sit up. I toddled slowly to the bathroom, pausing whenever dizziness overcame me. Something was wrong with my vision. When I put in my contact lenses, everything was blurred worse than without them. My old glasses were just as bad. I saw better without either, although there were disturbing flashes when objects would suddenly come into almost three-dimensional focus only to fade into fuzziness again.

I carefully stripped to take a shower and observed with uncharacteristic detachment that all my charming, decorative fat had vanished. My bones stood out sharply on my hips and my wrists. I leaned against the shower wall until the hot water ran out and then I stood under the cold water. I didn't feel clean. I didn't feel right.

I glanced at the clock. It was 3:00 a.m. I pulled on sweatpants and a sweatshirt over my pajamas and slid my feet into worn suede loafers. A man's tweed overcoat completed my ensemble. I found a few dollars in change in the coat pocket.

As I left the house, I caught sight of myself in the mirror. My wet hair clung to my skull and my eyes were dark hollows over jutting cheekbones. My full lips looked as oversized as

Mick Jagger's and my skin was as sallow as bacon fat. I pretended that I was fashionably punk.

There was a twenty-four-hour supermarket only a few blocks away. I walked slowly, counting each step, seeing my breath in the chilly air. My need for protein, for red meat, was so strong that it propelled me into the harsh glare of the store's fluorescent lights.

At the meat section, I selected a pound of ground beef swimming in bright red liquid. Eager to get home, I rushed to the one open checkout. The clerk had seen worse than me, so she just raised her brows a bit as my trembling hands counted out the coins for my purchase.

Honestly, I had planned to fry up a burger when I got home, but I was agonizingly hungry and so weak after days without food that I thought I would pass out. I made it to the corner before I took out the package and tore a corner of the plastic wrapping. I lifted the Styrofoam tray to my mouth and sipped the blood. Then I sipped again. In seconds, I was sucking at the raw meat, trying to extract every drop of liquid and telling myself it was no different than eating steak tartare.

When I heard the footsteps behind me, I tried to hide the packet of meat, embarrassed to be caught. I turned to see a rough-looking young white guy approaching. The glint of a knife in his hand sent a jolt of fear through me. But before I could do anything, the predatory expression on the man's face suddenly dropped away. I used the only weapon I had, the package of chewed hamburger. I threw it and the man hollered in terror and bolted away.

I must have looked worse than I thought. Sure, men had

run from me before, but it was usually after we'd dated for a while.

As I trudged home, I forgot the attacker and fretted that my unsanitary eating habits would probably result in a raging E. coli or Mad Cow infection. I shuddered to think of all the rude comments my mother Regina would make at my funeral if I died of the latter.

My body must have needed the protein, though, because I felt much stronger. I entered my flat and surveyed the horror. It smelled like the men's locker room of hell. I opened windows and gave the room a few spritzes of Ô de Lancôme. My sheets were rank, and I yanked them off and put them in a laundry bag. My next duty was washing up the mugs of moldy tea and bowls of congealed ramen that I'd been unable to eat.

Now I had to call the local health clinic. After determining that this was not a life-threatening emergency and being quizzed by someone at a call center, I finally got through to an advice nurse. I told her I was sick, that I'd had an unsafe exchange of bodily fluids, and that I thought I'd exposed myself to E. coli or Mad Cow.

"What's your temperature?" she asked.

I put my palm to my forehead. "Hot."

"Have you had any vomiting or diarrhea?"

"That's disgusting, no."

"How do your lymph nodes feel?" she asked.

I didn't exactly know what lymph nodes were, but I thought they were somewhere around my throat. I searched around and noticed the swelling on both sides of my upper neck. "Tender and swollen."

She told me that I could come in that night but that I'd have to wait in the emergency room. That could be hours, what with gunshot victims and heart attacks getting priority. I promised to come in if I felt any worse and made an appointment for the next morning. She recommended that I contact the man with whom I'd swapped body fluids.

I was torn about Oswaldo. I was jonesing to see him, but not when I looked like this. I needed to talk to him to make sure that I had only contracted an ordinary flu and to find out if he felt as madly attracted to me as I did toward him.

It was almost five in the morning, which seemed like a reasonable time to catch Oswaldo in his hotel room. I phoned the Croft, and as the phone rang, I imagined his warm laugh and the knowing, greedy way his hands had moved over my body. The front desk clerk said they had no Dr. Oswaldo Krakatoa staying there and couldn't disclose if one had ever been there. "We at the Croft respect the privacy of our guests," said the snooty clerk.

I assured the clerk that Dr. Krakatoa was totally desperate to find me and that he would appreciate the clerk's disclosing his whereabouts. The clerk was intransigent and rudely hung up the phone when I suggested that he was a servile minion of hell. I would find Oswaldo later when I looked and felt better.

Now I forced myself to sort through the pile of old mail I'd been neglecting on my desk. A lefty flyer informed me that a group called Corporate Americans for the Conservation of America, or CACA, which purported to be an ecofriendly alliance was actually the front for a shady multinational consortium. The flyer urged readers to write to their representatives to support an international workers' rights bill that CACA was trying to quash.

I would have done this immediately if not for the incessant scrabbling in the walls. Virginia Woolf wrote that women artists need a room of their own; she should have specified a *ratless* room of their own. Also, I couldn't invite fabulous men over for a romantic evening if there were rats running around the place.

I located the nexus of noise, a few feet to the right of my bathroom door. I got as far as using a screwdriver to carve a hole in the drywall before exhaustion overwhelmed me and I collapsed on the unmade bed fully dressed.

four

raticide (not the punk band)

I didn't wake until sunset the next day. I had missed my doctor's appointment. I did a cursory physical check before I attempted to sit up. I didn't feel sore or cold, but I was weak and hungry again. My vision had improved, I guess, if I defined "improved" as seeing everything clearly but with a heightened sense of dimension.

I checked my answering machine. I was shocked to hear Sebastian's voice, tense and edgy, leaving me a message. I listened to it again and again: "Milagro, this is Sebastian. Call me right away." He left a local number.

Going into my closet, I pushed through the bright clothes to a box hidden in the back. I dropped onto the floor and rummaged through the evidence of our friendship: theater ticket stubs, museum programs, restaurant matches, and other sad little mementos. The voice on the answering machine was not the boy who had sent me these witty postcards. I deleted his message.

On the way to the bathroom, I was horrified by the sight of four dead rats lined neatly in front of the hole I had made in the wall.

A memory stirred, the image of myself squatting by the hole in the wall and waiting, screwdriver in hand. I tried to repress it, but could not. I had been filled with rage. I could not and would not tolerate vermin reducing my modest circumstances to utter squalor. A girl had to have some standards, and if that meant stabbing rats to maintain those standards, then pass me the screwdriver.

A pity that I wasn't still consumed by the kind of anger that gets you through really icky situations. I tried not to look as I used newspapers to shove the small corpses into plastic bags. I drenched the floor with disinfectant, scoured like an obsessive housewife, then threw the sponges and the screwdriver into another plastic bag. I washed my hands in scalding water, scrubbing hard to get off any contagion. Only when I had deposited the bags outside in the bin did my hunger reappear.

I called the health clinic again and was told I would have to wait fifteen minutes to talk to the advice nurse. My stomach rumbled loudly so I hung up. Tomorrow I could try to get a walk-in appointment.

After an extended search, I discovered a few dollars in the pocket of a vintage velvet shawl. My newfound wealth gave me a surge of energy, and after my shower, I did all those girly grooming things I'd been neglecting for days, like brushing my hair.

I pulled on my tightest black pants, which now bagged in the seat, and a stretchy white shirt. Tragically, my tatas lacked their usual bodaciousness, especially since my bra was too loose around them. While changing into a nubby sweater that would hide the wrinkles in my bra fabric, the phone rang.

"Hola," I said.

"Milagro, it's Mercedes."

"Hey, *chica,* I was just going to grab a meal and visit you at the club. *Bailaremos y cantaremos* and all that."

"What is going on with you?" she said in a very unamused voice.

"What do you mean? I've been sick."

"I *know* that. Something else is going on. Some people have been asking for you lately."

I ignored her ominous tone in the excitement I felt that Oswaldo was trying to find me. "A fabulous man, quirky dresser, hair the color of a sienna Crayola crayon, silver eyes, lithe as a cat . . . ," I began.

"No," she said. "These guys didn't look interested in dating you. Have you done anything wrong?"

She caught me off guard. "It depends on what the definition of 'wrong' is. Morally wrong, legally wrong, ethically wrong, a sin of omission—"

"*Cállate la trompa,*" she said brusquely. "Wrong like something a cop would be interested in. Any dead bodies, any bank robberies, any forged currency?"

"Mercedes, you know me better than that," I said, all

huffed up while at the same time wondering if I'd let any criminal behavior slip my mind. "What did they look like?"

"It happened a few times. One was a redhead, friendly, skinny little guy. That was maybe Tuesday or Wednesday. He was asking Lenny and the bartenders if we knew who you were, where you were. No real alarms going off with that one. Way gay, but with you, I never know."

What can I say? Gay men liked me, and sometimes they *really* liked me. Nancy said it was because I radiated strong and confusing pheromones, like those used to bait insect traps.

"He seemed harmless, so Joe said that yeah, you came around sometimes," Mercedes said.

"Gay, redheaded, and skinny?" I knew two gay redheads and one sexually ambiguous strawberry blond, but I had a strong instinct it was that chatty little waiter again. Which made me wonder, why did he keep showing up?

"The other *gavacho* looked Ivy League, blond, handsome in an establishment way. Totally The Man. He tried to give Lenny money for info on you. I didn't believe him and I didn't like him."

Why was Sebastian so interested in me after all this time?

Mercedes said, "Don't tell me you're involved with drug selling, Milagro. The Man gave us some bogus story about being interested in your writing."

I was irked that my friend assumed bogusness from anyone who expressed interest in my writing. "Mercedes, if I was dealing, don't you think I'd pay my drink tab? I know who you're talking about, and, believe it or not, he's a critically acclaimed writer." I didn't add that he was also a horse's ass. Perhaps

Sebastian really did want to talk to me about my writing and I'd deleted his phone number from my machine. "Did he leave a number?"

"No, we told him we didn't recognize you because slutty Latinas all look alike."

"I wish you were here so I could slap you upside the head." I was rewarded by a brief chortle on the other end of the line. "What did you *really* say?"

"I *really* said too many people came in the club and that you weren't anyone we recognized. That's it."

"Thanks for the warning, but you don't have to worry about them." I was profoundly disappointed that some oddly dressed nutcase calling himself Professor Pompeii Eruption hadn't asked after me. My stomach rumbled loudly. "Who's playing tonight?"

Mercedes launched into high praises for the country rock band she'd booked. I hadn't seen them before, but she swore "they're hotter than my *mami's* stove for Easter dinner."

"Country rock? Probably country crap," I said snippily to cover up the fact that I intended to grovel at her feet later for money. She got suspicious when I was too nice.

"You are such an ignorant bitch."

"Yeah, well, if you insist, I'll come by."

"Whatever," she said, but she said it cheerfully.

Since I was going to My Dive later, I dolled up my outfit, adding dangly earrings, a jangle of rhinestone bracelets, and a delightful cropped fake leopard-skin jacket. Fake leopard is one of those timeless classics. I slipped my feet into funky red sandals with sexy little straps. I plastered on extra makeup to hide the circles under my eyes, and I finished my look with scarlet lipstick.

I was jittery as I left my flat, and I tried to delude myself that I was just excited to go out, to be well again. Well again? My knees were practically buckling, and the hunger I felt was so intense I almost cried out as I clattered down the street to the market. I stumbled and kept myself from falling by windmilling my arms.

The supermarket meat section glowed in a red-tinged light. First, I grabbed the family-economy package of ground beef, but then I noticed that there was much more liquid in the smaller amounts. I shuffled through the packages and calculated the totals. Blood dripped from one package onto my hand. Without thinking, I licked it off and felt an exquisite tingling through my body. It was because I was starving. Looking up, I saw a butcher behind a glass display window staring at me. As I sashayed away, I thought I must be looking pretty good.

The night clerk at the checkout was the woman I'd seen before. I placed my packets of ground beef on the counter along with my money. She glanced at me and her eyebrows went up a little higher this time.

I hurried out of the store even as she was picking up my money. Down the block, most of the small shops and boutiques were closed. The door to a spice shop was set far back underneath the second-floor overhang. I moved into the darkness.

A girl should always look her best when going out, so I tried to be neat while I slurped the liquid from the Styrofoam trays and sucked the raw meat until it was gray and dry. Energy flowed through me like a current. I would see a doctor tomorrow. I'd find out what was causing this abnormal craving.

I threw the remnants of my meal into a trash can by the metro stop and descended the broken escalator steps to the trains. As my train racketed its way downtown, I remembered what Sebastian had been like at F.U. Everything about him had been golden—his hair, his reputation, his family—and when he introduced himself to me at a visiting professor's talk, I had been dazzled. His grandfather was Frederick Beckett-Witherspoon, a magnate who had guided more than one president in international affairs, but Sebastian wasn't interested in economics or politics. He liked the arts, lectures, dining out, and books. He was invited to faculty parties, not because of his family's donations but because he was pretty, charming, and bright. Women flocked around him, yet he wanted to spend time with me.

Was it possible to revive that friendship? I certainly wouldn't have thought so by my last encounter with Sebastian, and yet I felt a small flutter of hope somewhere deep inside.

After scrounging through my purse, I found an old, hard piece of gum. By the time I rode the escalator out of the metro, my mouth felt fresh and minty. The crowd of people milling around outside My Dive cheered me. Lenny was at the door. He smirked lasciviously when he recognized me, but his smile fell away as I approached. "Hell, babe, what happened to you?"

This is not the sort of thing a girl on the town wants to hear. "What do you mean?"

"You're a little, uh, you eating okay? You're not smoking your meals or nothing?"

"No, Lenny, I had the flu. I'm better."

Lenny didn't look convinced. "You make sure you start eating right. Only a dog wants a bone."

"But every guy wants a boner, right?"

Lenny guffawed and slid his arm around my waist. It didn't feel like the usual friendly cheap grab; it felt like a medical exam as he searched around my rib cage.

I twisted away from his inquisitive fingers. "I'm going to find Mercedes. Later, gator."

The club was packed and music was blasting from a quintet onstage. What the hell were they playing? It sounded like a mix of Willie Nelson with garage metal and soca thrown in, but the whole was much more rocking than the sum of its parts. Instead of looking for Mercedes, I pressed toward the stage. You know how you listen to a song and you think, this is the best damn song I've ever heard? That's how I always felt at Mercedes's shows. Some loser had the nerve to grab my diminished ass and yank me to him, as if he had a chance. I had to kick him and leave the dance floor, which was fine, since the first set was over.

Mercedes was upstairs talking to the sound guy. She wasn't as subtle as Lenny. "You look like hell. I thought you said you were okay."

"Whatever happened to 'You can't be too thin or too rich'?"

She dragged me to a stairwell where the light was so painfully bright I could see her dark freckles on her caramel skin. "You look bad. I would have taken you to the doctor."

I smiled and shrugged. "I had the flu. I'm better now."

"You sure?" She kept her hand on my arm.

I felt a wild desire to confess that I was drinking hamburger blood, I had killed rats that were scrabbling in coded messages, and that I dreamed about the kisses of the man who might have infected me. I wanted to rest against her sturdy frame, feel her comforting arms in a big *abrazo* around me, and have her tell me that everything would be all right.

Instead I said, "Actually, I'm broke. I wasn't able to do any consulting or garden work this week." I guessed that I'd been sick for about that long. "And I don't have money for food."

"*Tonta.* All you had to do was ask."

"I'll pay you back as soon as I can."

"You better," warned Mercedes. She thought I didn't have a strong work ethic. She was the child of immigrants and she had an unwavering belief in hard work. My own family's drive had taken a detour in their second generation here, when both my father and my mother Regina had directed their energies toward worshiping her existence.

I watched the rest of the set from upstairs. Mercedes brought me a Virgin Mary with an extra celery stick and a bowl of Goldfish crackers. "Just as good as tomato soup." After years of working in clubs, Mercedes knew how to make a meal from typical bar supplies.

The drink and the crackers tasted wonderful. I got seconds and I felt like a regular person for almost forty-five minutes straight. Mercedes offered to give me a ride home if I waited until they closed, but I'd asked for enough favors already.

She counted out several twenty-dollar bills into my hand.

It seemed like a fortune, except that my rent was due tomorrow. I still didn't have enough to pay my landlord and I hoped he would understand if I needed a few extra days to get the money.

"It's too bad we can't do something to make you normal enough for a regular job," Mercedes mused as I pocketed the money. "You're like a Monk tune—not everyone appreciates those discordant notes even though that's Monk's genius."

"I could always marry rich," I said, and we both laughed so hard we were gasping for breath.

five

an old flame burns down the house

Even though it was late, I decided to take public transportation instead of paying for a cab. The underground metro stations were closed, so I walked down the empty street to a well-lighted bus stop. Under the odors of exhaust, coffee beans roasting, and sewage, I could smell the first trace of spring. The fragrance came from the blossoms of the street trees, Victorian box. The sturdy, dull-leafed trees had blossoms with the most amazing fragrance: it smelled like falling in love.

The heady scent made me think of Oswaldo. I had never felt so out of control with a man before. I wanted my feelings to be real, not merely a prelude to my flu delirium.

I was contemplating my solitude when a big, dark Bentley stopped at the curb. I shook my head, one of those city motions for "Get lost, creep," when the back door opened. Sebastian Beckett-Witherspoon leaned out with a picture-perfect smile. "What a surprise to see you!" he said.

What surprised me was his friendly expression. "You would be more convincing if I didn't know you've been stalking me." I stepped back, wary of him.

He ran his hand through his shining blond hair, a gesture so deeply familiar to me that I felt an ache inside. "I was looking for you, Mil. I just wanted to . . . just wanted . . ."

He got out of the car. My emotions hopped around like a frog in a blender, which is not as pleasant as it sounds. Being with Sebastian had defined me by what I was and, just as important, what I wasn't. I wasn't a man. I wasn't a WASP. I wasn't old money. I wasn't conventional. I wasn't connected. I wasn't anything that mattered to Sebastian. And yet he had thought I was marvelous. At least that's what he'd said.

He stood in front of me and I saw his expression alter as he got close. "You look . . ."

"I think I look wonderful. I've been on a purifying water and yoga regimen."

"I'm sorry, Milagro," he said softly. "I was so shocked to see you again. I behaved like an ass at Kathleen's and . . . before. Is it possible for us to move on, to salvage what we once had?"

Of course I had fantasized about this moment. My fantasies had included tears and a devastating dress, but reality outdid my fantasy, since I hadn't imagined a dark Bentley or that Sebastian would be an acclaimed writer or that he would ask for forgiveness just when I was so artistically fragile and destitute.

"I don't think I can trust you again." Even as I said this, a part of my soul hoped he would revert to the Sebastian I had first known. Another, more selfish part of me hoped he would help me find a publisher for my novel.

"Mil, you're one of the few people who truly knows me." He looked deep into my eyes. "I apologize for the other night. I was just so shaken. I know I didn't handle things well then . . . and before." He swallowed. "I was jealous, Mil. You're the better writer and I was immature and jealous and threatened."

Was he telling the truth or feeding my ego? "What's the big rush at reconciliation now, Sebastian?"

He smiled sadly. "I've missed you."

"What were you doing at Hotel Croft that night? Why did you come to the room?"

He reached out and touched me tentatively on the arm. "You were so upset when you left that I followed you. I was worried about you."

"I can take care of myself," I said as I was running my hand up my throat to feel for telltale swelling. "But I have been a little under the weather lately."

"I thought you looked unwell." He gestured toward the car. "Let's go to my place and talk." He told me he was staying in a town nearby. "It's a beautiful house in an apple orchard. There's a guest room."

What city girl hasn't dreamed of staying in a house surrounded by apple trees? Well, I hadn't until he mentioned it, but then it became unspeakably romantic, in a Laura Ingalls Wilder sort of way. You know, *Little House in the Orchard,* only with indoor plumbing and sophisticated repartee. Did Sebastian want a friend for the night or something more?

I was suddenly nervous, not knowing what I really wanted from him either. "I have things to do tomorrow," I said, thinking about going to see a doctor and trying to get a few hours at the nursery so I could earn some money.

"I'll bring you back whenever you want. I promise."

Would it be more personally rewarding to tell Sebastian to go to hell and take the bus to my depressing flat or accompany him to some groovy house, laugh over old times, have him introduce me to his literary crowd, and swear eternal allegiance to our whatever-it-was? "I'll give you another chance."

He hugged me and I was overwhelmed. Even his clean, citrusy cologne was the same. It felt like coming home—that is, coming to a normal welcoming home, not an antiseptic display house inhabited by my mother Regina.

Sebastian held open the car door and I slid into the seat behind the driver, who was not visible through a dark glass partition. Sebastian got in and closed the car door. He pressed an intercom button and said, "Let's go."

I noticed that he didn't say please.

The windows were so dark that I could barely make out the glow of the streetlights. Sebastian held my hand and smiled at me. My fingers slid between his just like they used to.

"You look tired," he told me. "Why don't you rest?"

I felt invigorated, but closed my eyes so I could savor the moment and remember the past. I had been thrilled the first time he took me along to a room filled with acclaimed academics. And the most exciting thing was that they seemed to enjoy talking to me, Milagro De Los Santos from the provinces.

With Sebastian by my side, I'd felt clever and beautiful and talented. Although he was only twenty then, he'd carried himself with charm and grace. He'd tried to polish me and succeeded to some degree. We'd talk late into the night about plays we'd seen or essays we'd read. He'd gently correct my pronunciation of words I'd learned from books and encourage me to study more diligently.

I had known something was wrong even at the best of times. At elegant functions, my inner idiot had compelled me to make inappropriate wisecracks. Sebastian had discouraged my affection for rock-chick clothes and criticized my appreciation of women writers as "naively sentimental."

If his girlfriend, Tessie Kensington, had found his interest in me odd, she'd never said. Sebastian had joked that she was relieved not to endure events she found tedious. We had been able to go on this way until I started dating an oblivious pothead engineering major named Bernie. "Dating" is perhaps inaccurate because Bernie, highly unreliable at the best of times, had conducted our association like an extended series of one-night stands. At least it kept the relationship fresh.

Sebastian and I had fought about Bernie, absurd but fierce battles, since we'd both known that Bernie wasn't worth the trouble.

Now I let the minutes pass, conscious of Sebastian's cool hand in mine. When I opened my eyes, I said, "Do you remember Bernie, my dope-fiend beau? I gave him up just to please you." Bernie had bravely covered up his anguish by shrugging and mumbling, "Wherever the tide takes you, dude."

"Did he even notice?" Sebastian asked.

"He was completely torn apart, utterly devastated. I only hope that he recovered. Did you ever give up anything for me, Sebastian?"

"Only my self-respect," he said as he released my hand.

His sharp tone set me on guard. "What do you mean by that?"

He turned away. I suspected that we were traveling in the wrong direction and not just emotionally. I couldn't see well through the car's tinted window, so I pushed the button to lower it. It didn't work. "Please ask the driver to lower this window," I said, but Sebastian ignored me.

I pressed my face against the glass and saw grassy hills, not our destination's dense woodland. "Where are we?"

"We'll be there in a little while."

"There *where*?" I suddenly sensed something very disturbing about Sebastian.

"Tell me about your rendezvous at the hotel," he demanded.

"That's none of your business. I thought we were going to be friends again."

"What did he say to you? What did he do to you? What is his name? I need to know."

I couldn't believe that Sebastian was kidnapping me because he was interested in Oswaldo. I said so loudly as I pounded on the glass partition.

The window behind the driver slid open. "Sir?"

"It's all right, Peters," Sebastian snapped. He turned to me angrily. "I am not kidnapping you, you melodramatic slut. I am taking you into custody for questioning."

Calling me a slut was one thing, but calling me melodramatic was going too far. "I hate you, you pompous jerk! Let me out of this car right now." I kicked the back of the driver's seat. "If you don't let me out right now, I'm pressing charges!"

"Cease that commotion right now," Sebastian said, "because you're not getting out, especially since you're quite probably infected." When I stopped kicking the seat, he said, "Oh, so I finally have your limited attention? Did you think that I wouldn't recognize the signs of your contamination? How have you been living lately, Milagro? What have you been eating? And, more significantly, what have you been drinking?"

His words chilled me. How did he know about my illness? What *was* my illness? "This is why you were looking for me?"

"There is no other reason I'd ever want to see you again. I thought I made that abundantly clear in the halcyon days of my youth."

The bastard. "You can deceive yourself, but you're not fooling me, Sebastian. I know how you felt about me once." I saw something behind his eyes, a flicker of hurt.

"Perhaps I did succumb momentarily to your cheap allure," he said. "I didn't realize then that I was nothing to you but a way to grasp at everything I was, everything I had. You used me, Milagro."

His accusation stunned me. "That's not true, Sebastian. What I felt for you was real. You know how I felt."

I saw the confusion on his face before he turned away. "I don't believe your lies anymore. Every day, I give thanks that my family and friends helped me escape from your avaricious ploys and, unpleasant as it is to deal with you again, perhaps you can be useful to my organization."

"Organization?"

"Don't be any stupider than absolutely necessary," he said, regaining his composure. "I'm a member of Corporate Americans for the Conservation of America. We want to rid the country of a vile infestation."

"CACA?" I pronounced it *caca.* "CACA *is* a vile infestation and you aren't even in a corporation. You're running around pretending to be a writer."

"Still a practitioner of the childish rejoinder, I see. We say the initials, C-A-C-A, not the acronym, and I am on the board of two major corporations."

"Still the arrogant bastard, I see. Let me out of the damn car now."

"Or what?" He pushed me and I fell back against the door. "You're weak. You always thought you were the strong, independent one. Look at you now—you're pathetic."

Unfortunately, he was right. I wasn't strong enough to go *mano a mano* in the back of a speeding Bentley or even a really slow Hyundai. "What do I have to do with anything?"

"You'll be our guinea pig. Frankly, we're astonished you're alive. This may be related to your peoples' cockroach-like ability to adapt and withstand toxins. We'll use you for testing, and if you cooperate, we may only sterilize and monitor you."

I was missing pieces of the puzzle, but I was pretty sure

they added up to a really ugly picture. Okay, I was infected with something, Sebastian thought I should be dead, and Oswaldo was the carrier of the infection. "You're so majorly loco. What have I been infected with?"

"'With what have I been infected,'" he corrected.

I wouldn't kill him quickly. I began imagining Ian Fleming–type torture devices for Sebastian.

"You were swapping blood with a vampire, you fool," he said sharply. "You've been infected by a vampire."

"Are you living in the Dark Ages?" I shouted. "At least tell me a plausible lie."

"Do I look like I'm kidding? Would I be here with you otherwise?" His face flushed red. "I wanted to leave you so far in the past that I could forget you entirely, but here you are again." He paused and closed his eyes. "You seduced me with your base animal appeal and you tried to drag me down to your level. I reject you, Milagro, I reject you and all creatures of darkness."

"Is that a swipe at me for being a Latina?!" I snapped.

"Spare me your politically correct outrage," he sneered. "I was referring to your vampire-tainted flesh."

Fear flooded through me, but I steeled myself by thinking of my mother Regina. I hadn't lived this long only to quiver in fear of an F.U. snob, albeit a completely insane F.U. snob.

I had a flacon of Jovan Musk cologne in my purse. Yes, it was retro, but in an amusing disco way, and besides, I could spray it in Sebastian's eyes once we stopped. I had a pen, too. I would spray him, then jab him in the jugular with the pen.

"You are so completely deluded," I said, attempting to distract Sebastian while I waited for an opportunity to attack. "Vampires were based on Vlad the Impaler, who was a murderous sadist, but a *human* murderous sadist. Vlad, vampires, look up the etymology of the word."

"I know damn well that Vlad wasn't a vampire, but that doesn't mean vampires don't exist. I'm talking about medical fact. I bet you're wishing you could bite my throat right now." His voice lowered. "I bet you're thinking of sinking your teeth into my flesh and clamping down, sucking out all my juices, sucking my very being into your voracious, scarlet mouth, your full lips opening wide, and swallowing me down . . ."

"Keep dreaming, Sebastian. I am so not interested in sucking any part of your repressed anatomy," I said disdainfully. "Excuse me for asking the obvious, but exactly why the hell do multinational corporations care about vampires? Hate competition from other bloodsucking parasites?"

"You've reached the point, Milagro, where you're no longer naive, but tediously ignorant," he said. He reached into his pocket and pulled out a compact little weapon.

"That looks like a gun, only smaller. Did you order it from the Sharper Image Spring Paranoiac catalog?" I was surreptitiously fishing in my pocketbook.

"Don't tempt me."

"Tempt you? That's what this is all about, isn't it, Sebastian. You can never get over the fact that you were tempted by me."

"Shut up! Shut up! Shut up!" he shouted, and pointed the gun at me.

six

survival of the fabbest

Suddenly something crashed into the car and the Bentley jerked hard to the right. I jabbed the butt of my hand up hard and hit Sebastian in the nose. He cried out in pain and another jolt bashed the car off the road entirely.

We were bumping roughly down a slope, and I didn't know how far we would go. Sebastian screamed time-honored Anglo-Saxon obscenities while holding his bleeding nose with his left hand. I grabbed the gun and twisted it away just as the car rocked over on its right side.

Sebastian wasn't moving. I unbuckled my seat belt and tried kicking the door. Suddenly it opened and a pair of huge hands attached to size-appropriate arms hauled me out of the car onto a slope covered with scrub brush. The moon was full, and the gorilla holding me didn't look happy. "You godless vermin, you godless vermin," he snarled. He had an unappealing snub nose between pale piggy eyes, and his neck was as thick as his head. He looked like an accountant who'd attended wrestling camp.

"Let her go!" cried a strong, lilting voice.

I twisted my head and saw that damn redheaded waiter scampering down the hillside toward us. Unfortunately, he was not accompanied by armed bodyguards and ferocious Rottweilers. However, he was wearing really cool jeans, a khaki shirt, and a leather bomber jacket—very Indiana Jones Goes to the Castro.

"Demon!" shouted the driver.

Although I wasn't in fighting form, a kick to the groin was still a kick to the groin. I didn't connect solidly, but Peters automatically dropped me. Just as I regained my balance, he moved to grab me. I pointed the nifty gun in his direction. I assumed that Sebastian, filled with righteous fury toward me, had removed the safety or whatever.

Peters smirked. "You wouldn't kill a God-fearing American, would you, girlie?"

How clueless was this goon? "Nope, but I will kneecap you." He lunged toward me and I pulled the trigger. While I *did* aim for his knee, the shot went off course a considerable distance north. Peters buckled over, holding the injured part of his body and shrieking worse than a spoiled *niña* who finds her favorite Barbie decapitated.

I didn't have time to contemplate the result of my first gun-firing experience because the waiter had reached my side.

"Milagro, I have been looking everywhere for you! Thank God you're alive. We have to get out of here."

I instinctively liked the waiter because he was a cute Froot Loop. Nonetheless, I pointed the gun toward him and said, "Let's pause here for a moment. Why are you always showing up wherever I go? How do I know you're not in league with CACA? How do I know you have my safety and best interests at heart?"

He threw his hands up and shouted, "Please, girlfriend!" He pronounced "please" as if it had about twenty vowels in it.

It was a very convincing argument, strengthened by the fact that Sebastian's blood-smeared head popped up out of the car door like a hideous jack-in-the-box. "Milagro!" he shrieked. "Milagro, you bitch!"

I shoved the gun into my pocketbook, and the waiter and I scrambled up the embankment. He held my hand and pulled me along, showing surprising strength for a small guy. My right foot slipped on a rock and I fell, breaking a strap on my sandal and tearing the knee of my pants. I began to slide, but the waiter held tight until I got my traction back. Coyote brush and brambles scratched us and snagged my hair.

A huge, shiny Ford truck was parked with the engine running and techno blasting from the sound system. We slammed the doors, and the waiter drove like a soccer mom late to pick up her Valium prescription. I tried to catch my breath, and he handed me a quart bottle of organic raspberry protein drink. I gulped it without thinking. When my heart stopped pounding, I said, "Who are you anyway?"

"My name's Gabriel." He kept checking the rearview mirror. "The raspberry juice is the right color. Your craving can be satisfied by a food with a color trigger. Cranberry juice, a good zinfandel, anything that's red works. In the summer, gazpacho is great when you can pick tomatoes off the vine."

I held up my hand. It had almost stopped shaking. "As much as I'd love to discuss chilled soups with you, can you tell me why you've been following me, where we're going, and why everyone is hunting me?"

Gabriel turned down the music. "We're going to a safe place, a ranch out in the country. You've been infected by, well, it's hard to explain." He gave me a concerned look. "It's a miracle you're alive."

"Yeah, I hear that all the time. Miracle, that's my name." I don't know if he thought I was kidding. "Oswaldo?"

Gabriel nodded. "Yeah, Oswald. He said it was an accident, the blood exchange."

"It was, I don't know . . . Wait a minute. You were at the party with Oswaldo?"

"Oswald," he corrected me. "He's my second cousin."

My heart was still racing, but now at the idea of seeing Oswald again. I thought that maybe I shouldn't be so excited to see the man who had infected me, but my desire for him was stronger than common sense. "What were you doing at Kathleen's?"

"I help our family with security."

I was going to say something sarcastic, but Gabriel *had* run Sebastian and his thug off the road.

Gabriel continued. "Oswald went because he wanted to check out Beckett-Witherspoon. I was sent along to keep things in line."

"Oh, good job," I said dryly.

"I *tried* to warn you away, didn't I?"

Okay, so he had. "What's Sebastian got to do with your family?"

"CACA, or *caca,* as you call it, is the latest project of a ghastly group that has its origins in an ancient crypto-mystical organization. They've been building their wealth and power for ages. They hold on to some of the absurd superstitions of the past, but they're really all about the money." He shrugged one shoulder. "I guess it makes them feel special, the ritual and exclusivity. Try getting into *that* club."

If Gabriel was telling me the truth, his comments solved a few mysteries in my life. But not all of them. "What's wrong with me? What do I have?"

"It's a genetic condition, like sickle cell or Tay-Sachs. Oswald and, well, me too, we have it."

"If it's genetic, how could I have contracted it?"

"You don't really have it, I think. But I'm not a doctor."

I mulled this over, then said, "Sebastian is under the lunatic impression that you're vampires."

Gabriel jittered to the music for a minute, letting my comment hang between us. Finally he said, "People are so uninformed. They believe in folktales and have these crazy prejudices."

"Uh-huh. Your point being?"

"It's not like we drink human blood! That's like believing in the boogeyman or something. It's just that contact with our blood has consequences. Like mixing AB positive with AB negative."

I didn't think I was getting the whole picture. "And?"

"We don't process protein like most people. We require more protein in our diets, and it causes us to crave, uh, meat. You know, like those pregnant women who eat clay because of a mineral deficiency."

"With the difference being that pregnant women eating clay sounds wacky and quaint, while bloodsucking creatures of the night sounds grotesque and depraved."

Gabriel turned onto another highway, heading north. "I told you, we don't 'suck blood.' I would think that a woman of color would understand prejudice."

That shut me up.

Even in the middle of the night, there were plenty of cars speeding by, no doubt going home from the swing shift at work, heading to their drug dealers, or slipping away from affairs. I guessed that I was the only one on the road who was heading toward Count Dracula's country hacienda.

"You know," Gabriel said calmly, "lepers were hated and exiled before modern medicine came up with treatments for the disease."

"I'd be pretty irritated if a leper had infected me, too."

"If you had bothered to practice safe sex, this wouldn't have happened," he retorted. "We have to practice safe sex our whole lives! You have no idea what it's like to fall for someone who will never accept you because you were born different!"

"Ha," I said, "and ha again. One, I did *not* have sex with Oswald, and two, I think I know what it's like to be outside the norm. And besides, being a vampire is completely different from being an ethnic minority."

"We are *not* vampires," he snapped back. "At least your people can intermarry and be open about who they are and share their culture."

As we sped northward, the landscape gave way to black hills silhouetted against the cobalt sky. Stars became more visible. The rush of our battle against CACA and my desire to see Oswald dimmed considerably at the realization that I might be terminally ill. My life had been like my favorite dresses: cheap, frivolous, and too short. I began to cry quietly.

"It isn't all bad!" Gabriel said consolingly. "There's an upside. If you live, your life span might be extended. With really good skin for most of that time."

"I already had really good skin," I blubbered. All I could think of was "if you live." How had I gone through life not knowing about these creatures? "How many of, um, *you* are there?"

"Not many," he said sorrowfully. "Certainly not enough for us to amass any political power." He was silent for so long that I thought he was done talking, but then he added, "Part of me thinks that's okay, that our time is almost over. Another part hopes that someday science will help prevent our bloodlines from becoming extinct."

We drove in silence past miles of vineyards, and then took a winding road over a mountain. Huge trees crowded over the road, obscuring the sky. Reflecting road markers were our only guide. On a stretch where the hillside beside the road dropped off into a gully, I took the gun out of my pocketbook, wiped off my prints, and tossed it out the window down into the darkness. Gabriel watched me without saying anything. Maybe I felt safe with him or maybe something in me just shut down. I fell asleep.

When I awoke just before daybreak, we were driving on a bumpy narrow lane. Gabriel must have stopped somewhere, because he was drinking coffee from a paper cup. The sky was growing lighter and I guessed the majestic trees along the road were ancient live oaks. Somewhere nearby, a rooster crowed. Birds sang and called.

Gabriel turned off the lane and stopped the truck in front of a white gate. "We're here," he said, and reached through the truck's window to a post with a security box. He punched in a code and the gate swung open. As soon as we drove through, the gate swung shut behind us. Ahead I could see the dark shape of a large house set back among the trees, lights on the first floor glowing warmly. "How many people die from—what do you call this anyway?"

"Usually we just say 'our condition.' "

"And the mortality rate?"

"I'm not qualified to answer your question. I'm not up on that stuff."

"Right," I said skeptically.

A pack of mixed-breed dogs came rushing up to the truck, barking out an alarm. Gabriel slowed down and parked the truck behind the house. "They won't bite." He hopped out and began petting the animals as they jumped excitedly around him, wagging their tails.

I exited the vehicle more hesitantly. Up close, I could see that the house was a squarish structure made of pale sandstone. I followed Gabriel to the front porch. He opened the front door and said, "I don't know if anyone's up."

Hesitating at the door, I wondered what sinister scene

lurked inside. Satin-lined coffins, suits of armor, endless marbled halls that echoed with mad laughter? My expectations for a Transylvanian theme were undermined by the foyer's California Mission decor, terra-cotta pavers, and a stairway with a wrought-iron banister.

To my right, an arched doorway opened into a spacious living room with white plaster walls and unscary brown leather furniture. "You'd think vampires would go for more drama," I commented as I turned back to Gabriel, who had paused in front of the mirror and was trying to smooth down his hair.

He glared at me. "You're really funny—*not.* And, yes, we have reflections. Let go of your tired old prejudices."

"Did you chant that at the gay vampire day parade? 'We're clearly here, we're queerly undead, get it through your badly coiffed straight head'?"

Someone cleared her throat in a decidedly critical way. Turning toward the sound, I spotted a petite silver-haired woman on the landing of the stairs. Despite the early hour, she was dressed in neatly pressed jeans and a tailored pink and white gingham blouse. Her soft brown moccasins matched her brown leather belt. She stared at me with exotic, emerald-green eyes, and I felt like a deer caught in the headlights of an eighteen-wheeler.

Gabriel flushed and croaked, "Grandmama!"

As the woman descended the stairs, I became somewhat self-conscious about my silly *zapatos* with the broken strap, my torn pants, and my leopard-print jacket.

"Who is this, Gabriel?" Her voice was precise and icy. She was comfortable being openly hostile, little knowing that if there's one thing I'm used to, it's being unwelcome in a home.

When in the presence of an alpha female, one should never show fear or she'll attack like you're the slow gazelle at the watering hole. Stepping forward and extending my hand, I smiled in a blatantly insincere manner and said, "Milagro De Los Santos. Pleased to meet you."

She ignored me and said, "Gabriel." It was a reprimand.

"This is the girl Oswald told us about," he said as if he'd been caught cheating on a test.

"She's alive, then?"

"Why don't you poke me with a stick and check?" I said.

She turned her luminous green gaze upon Gabriel. "You know I disagree with your cousin's decision to bring her here."

"Excuse me," I interrupted, "but 'her' is standing right in front of you."

Gabriel put his hand protectively on my shoulder. "I barely managed to get her away from Beckett-Witherspoon. This is the best place for her . . ." Under his grandmother's stare, he faltered and added, "For now."

"We'll have a meeting to discuss this further." The woman turned to me. "Young lady, I will not pretend to be happy about this situation. I cannot stress how unfortunate it was that my grandson encountered you and succumbed to your unsafe overtures. Your lack of wisdom indicates that you are not a person to be trusted. Frankly, I am not comfortable having you here."

It had been a long night and I was tired. "If you're going to trash me, at least introduce yourself. I'd like to be able to refer to you by name when I cuss you out later."

The corner of her mouth twitched, but the movement was so brief that I couldn't ascertain whether she had smiled or sneered. "Edna Grant. When you do cuss me out, refer to me as 'Mrs. Grant' or 'Edna.' Either will suffice."

"It will be my pleasure, Edna," I responded. Gabriel looked as if he wished the earth would swallow him whole.

"Gabriel, show this person to the extra room."

"Yes, Grandmama."

Gabriel opened one of the doors on the left and led me through a spacious dining room and into an enormous kitchen all done up in cheerful undead colors of blue and yellow. Pots and pans gleamed from a rack. There was a long trestle table and a restaurant-quality range with six burners. The vampire business must be pretty profitable these days.

Gabriel was saying something about importing the kitchen tiles from Tuscany.

"Gabriel, what about the sun? Does this mean I can never go out in the sun again?"

He sighed. "I don't know. No one from outside has been infected in . . . in my lifetime, at least. And, no, sunlight doesn't make our flesh spontaneously combust."

"I didn't mean . . ." Who would have guessed vampires would be so sensitive?

He sighed. "It's okay. Some of us are more photophobic than others. You'll probably be okay if you wear sunscreen and a hat."

"Is that what you do?"

"Hello?" he said, pointing to his head. "I'm a natural redhead. I always protect myself from the sun's damaging rays."

He led me into a short hallway behind the kitchen and opened the door. "Here's the, uh, here's your room."

Despite my limited experience as a guest, I knew what it

really was. "It's the maid's room. You're sticking the Mexican girl in the maid's room."

Gabriel looked a little embarrassed. "Really, we all use it." I followed him a few steps into the room. "Believe me, sometimes you don't want to be too close to Grandmama." He pulled open the shutters to the murky, pre-dawn light and flipped on a lamp.

"Fine, whatever." The room looked more like a college dorm than a maid's quarters. There was a bed covered with a blue spread, a navy recliner, and a large wooden desk by a bay window. An old bicycle with a basket leaned against a bookcase filled with paperbacks.

"You've got privacy and your own bathroom," Gabriel said, opening a door to a spacious all-white bathroom with a claw-foot bathtub. It was one of those bathrooms that made you want to sing show tunes while soaking in bubbles.

When I stepped back into the bedroom, Gabriel slid open the closet doors. "There are some spare clothes here. You should be able to find something to wear and there's usually an extra toothbrush in the—"

I realized that I was going to collapse. "I'll just go to bed now. Thanks."

As he left the room, he said, "Milagro, I really am glad that you're okay."

"We don't know that yet, do we?"

"Good night," he said, and left before I was able to ask him where Oswald was.

seven

wherein our heroine considers her options

Although I was exhausted, I was also uneasy and nervous in this strange house. Intending to rest for only a few moments, I lay down on the bed. But as soon as I closed my eyes, sleep overcame me.

When I awoke, a soft breeze came in though the slats. Had someone come in and closed the shutters while I was sleeping or had I done it myself and forgotten? I listened. No rats scrabbling in the walls. The clock radio said it was 10:17 a.m. Had I slept for only a few hours or over a day?

I got out of bed feeling grimy. After searching through the dresser, the best outfit I could find was a flannel shirt, baggy gym shorts, and tube socks. My shoes were beyond repair, so I looked in the closet and found purple flip-flops. They were several sizes too big. In order to keep them on my feet, I had to do a graceless clomp-shuffle, clomp-shuffle.

I locked myself in the bathroom and double-checked the lock before I stripped down. I decided against a shower because the theme to *Psycho* kept playing in my head, so I made do with a quick splash. After dressing in the clean clothes, I braided my hair and ventured back out to the bedroom.

Glancing in the mirror, I decided that I didn't need to see Oswald until I looked better.

My mother Regina would have been more horrified by the way I was dressed than by the fact that I'd been infected with vampirism. I was having problems thinking clearly, but I felt surprisingly okay, considering the situation.

In the kitchen, a place was set with a croissant, a bowl of strawberries, and a red beverage. I tasted the drink cautiously: it was red orange juice. Fancy schmancy. I poured a mug of dark roast coffee from an insulated carafe and added cream. A newspaper was folded on the table. I scanned it looking for a report about a brilliant and spectacular young woman who had been kidnapped by villains.

Through the window, I could see fields of tall grasses that spread across to a band of trees at the base of green mountains. The house was in a stand of beautiful old walnuts and live oaks that were just leafing out. An unhealthy climbing rose framed the window. A plot of land that must have once been the kitchen garden was now in an awful state of neglect.

"I see you're up," said a pleasant, manly voice.

I practically jumped. "Yes, um, yes, I was just admiring the view."

This man resembled Oswald, but his features were more regular and balanced. His polite smile was even and his light brown hair was brushed in an unsuccessful attempt to subdue the natural waves. His eyes were brown, too. Slim and neatly groomed, he looked like a really sexy mathematician unaware that he was a prime number. I wanted to unbutton his shirt, muss his hair, and exclaim, "Good heavens, Professor Dracula, you're stunning!" I despaired over my own state of severe unfabulousness.

"I'm glad to see you looking well," he said. "How do you feel?"

Danger comes in nice packages sometimes, so I was contemplating the damage my butter knife could do to this man if he suddenly sprouted fangs. "Okay, not bad, actually."

"It's quite a relief to hear that, Miss De Los Santos."

"Call me Mil. And you are?"

"I'm Sam Grant, Gabriel and Oswald's cousin."

Now, Sam may seem like an ordinary name, but I loved it because I loved Sam Clemens. My fear seemed completely unwarranted in light of his pleasing manner and this positive association.

"Please don't let me rush your breakfast," he said, startling me from my contemplation of his nice jawline, "but we would like to have a little talk with you about this situation."

"We?"

"Yes, my grandmother, Gabriel, and myself."

Oswald was conspicuously absent from this group.

Sam continued, "We think it would be highly desirable to work out a resolution to this situation." His voice was as comforting and formal as a mortician's. "If you're ready . . ."

I wasn't, but I found myself clomping after him through a door adjacent to the living room and into a masculine study. Edna Grant and Gabriel sat on a loveseat. "Milagro," said Sam, "you've met my grandmother, Mrs. Grant."

She nodded curtly, but Gabriel smiled and said, "Morning, Mil."

Sam gestured to an armchair. "Milagro, why don't you sit here?"

"Should I have my attorney present?" I said, joking nervously and wondering if an attorney could actually help me in this situation.

Sam laughed politely and said, "It's nothing like that. We'd like you to tell us in your own words what happened the night you met Oswald."

"Which begs the question, where *is* Oswald?"

Edna spoke up. "Oswald has been asked to remain in his shack until this matter is resolved."

"Shack?" I said.

"It may as well be a shack," Edna said, "considering the mess there. You expect that a grown man will live like a decent human being."

I had no idea vampires had such high standards of housekeeping.

Sam explained, "He's not here because we want to hear your side of the story."

"First, I need some answers. Am I going to die?"

"Death and taxes are certainties," Edna snapped.

Sam looked at his grandmother and she shrugged unapologetically. "Mil," he said, "you told me that you're feeling okay.

That's wonderful." He looked genuinely pleased. "There's a chance you haven't been infected at all. Perhaps you've only had a common virus that coincided with your encounter with Oswald?"

I thought about the hamburger blood, the fever and chills, my enhanced vision, and shook my head regretfully. "What's my life going to be like, medically speaking?" I asked.

"You have to understand that this is a unique situation," Sam explained patiently. "There hasn't been another incident of accidental blood contamination in generations. We can only make educated guesses about your health after we've performed a few medical exams."

I immediately pictured a large slab, boiling test tubes, and demented lab assistants. They were going to examine me over my dead undead body.

"I've scheduled an appointment for you this afternoon with our family physician," Sam said. "She can answer all your questions about your physical condition."

"Can we move on?" said Edna tersely. "I have things to do."

Sam nodded to his grandmother. "Certainly. Milagro, please describe the events of the evening you encountered Oswald."

I could tell from Edna's attitude that she was on a blame-the-victim mission and it really ticked me off. "Fab food, impressive floral arrangements, lackluster guests, and a deplorable literary reading."

"We asked for what happened, not a review," Edna said.

My mother Regina had often said, "I'm sure you won't be making smart remarks on your deathbed." I wanted to call her and tell her she was wrong, but then I'd have to talk to her.

"Milagro," Sam said calmly, "you were at Sebastian Beckett-Witherspoon's reading. According to Oswald, you and Beckett-Witherspoon were already acquainted."

"'Were' being the operative word," I said. "We knew each other in college."

Edna looked surprised and asked if I had attended F.U. I told her that yes, I was an F.U. alumna.

"Where have the standards gone?" she said, and I wanted to tell her where she could put her standards.

"How well did you know Beckett-Witherspoon?" Sam asked me.

"That's inconsequential."

"I'm afraid it is important since he kidnapped you in order to get to our family," Sam said.

"We were mere acquaintances," I said. "We'd lost contact." This was as much as they needed to know. "Oswald introduced himself, told me he was in publishing, and suggested we continue our conversation about my writing at his hotel."

"Anyone with one iota of common sense would not go to a hotel room with a man she had just met," Edna said.

Things were bad enough without this old bloodsucker maligning my iotas. "I saw no harm in a conversation about literature." Also, he was fabulous.

Edna let out a derisive snort. "Oh, I'm sure that's just what you wanted."

"Yes, it was," I said defensively. "When we were at the hotel, Oswald kept asking about Beckett-Witherspoon. I realized that was the real reason why Oswald wanted to talk to me and decided to leave." Here's where my noble authoress tale got tricky. "I tripped against the coffee table and Oswald attempted to catch me. We collided and cut our lips."

Edna blew out a breath as if it was a preposterous story.

"You didn't stop contact once the cut occurred?" Sam asked.

"Of course I did." Sure, eventually. Why should I mention the whirlwind of sensations I'd felt when Oswald kissed me when I didn't understand it myself? "Sebastian barged into the room and I left."

"You are aware that body fluids can transmit diseases, aren't you?" Sam asked as he fiddled with a pen.

"I am certainly aware of the normal diseases that can be transmitted," I said tersely. "When Sebastian abducted me, he claimed that I had been infected by a vampire."

This word got their attention. "That's ridiculous," Sam said. "However, I do understand how harrowing this experience has been for you."

"Utterly harrowing," I agreed. "Incredibly harrowing. Exceedingly harrowing. Mind-bogglingly harrowing."

"Thank you, Milagro," Sam said, placing a calming hand on my harrowed shoulder. "Your story generally corroborates Oswald's."

"Good, because that's exactly what happened."

"If I may have a word with Milagro privately." Sam looked at Edna and Gabriel. They both stood and left the room.

When the door closed behind them, Sam came close to me and said, "I sincerely hope that you did not find our questions too rigorous."

"No one expects the Spanish Inquisition," I mumbled, trying to hide the fact that I suddenly felt foolish and embarrassed.

He was kind enough to smile. "You must understand that we are reacting to the concern that you might have died. It's incredible that you are doing so well—I mean, amazing, according to what we know from folklore."

"Yes, it's always a miracle when I'm alive," I said matter-of-factly. I couldn't help admiring his sweet brown eyes. The observation threw me into a new despair. Here I was, sick, an unwelcome guest of vampires, despised by Sebastian, my pathetic existence suddenly more deplorable, yearning to see Oswald, and yet I was so trivial that brown eyes distracted me.

I pulled my thoughts away from his pretty eyes and said, "Now I'd like a few answers. Like why is Sebastian so hot and heavy to get to your family? And how does he even know about your, um, condition?"

Sam twirled his pen. "Sebastian's organization and our family have a long and complicated history. We think he might have guessed that Oswald was one of us because of Oswald's strong resemblance to our great-grandfather, who was an industrialist. We fear that CACA has obtained one of the few daguerreotypes made of him."

"But why does Sebastian harbor such hatred toward people with a genetic anomaly?" I was trying my darnedest to be polite about the bloodsucking, undead angle. "He is not an unsophisticated thinker."

"I can only offer my own theories." When I nodded, Sam went on. "I suspect that Beckett-Witherspoon is looking for a legal avenue to quarantine us in order to get the patent on our DNA. His organization has controlling interests in numerous bioengineering firms. How much would some people pay for an extended life span or increased immunity to disease?"

I thought about women like my mother and Kathleen Baker. "A fortune," I answered. "And I'm in the middle of all this because of Oswald."

"While Oswald shouldn't have been with you, particularly since he is engaged . . ."

I couldn't have been more stunned if I'd been hit upside the head with a cast-iron frying pan.

"Milagro," Sam said quietly, "I was surprised when I heard what happened. I truly believe that Oswald would never knowingly endanger someone else. And certainly not for personal reasons, when his fiancée is such an astonishing, accomplished, and extraordinarily beautiful woman."

"It's not as if Oswald is the only man who has thrown caution to the wind for the pleasure of my company."

"I'm sure many men find you attractive!" Sam said generously despite my current state of hideousness.

"Well, it's been real, and it's been fun, but it hasn't been real fun." It was a dumb thing to say, but what did it matter at this point? "Please tell me where Gabriel is, so I can get a ride home."

Sam shook his head. "Beckett-Witherspoon surely knows where you live by now and without our protection, he may well harm you. You have to stay here until we find a way to defuse CACA."

"Now that I know he's dangerous, I believe I can take care of myself on my own turf."

"I am not just speaking of Beckett-Witherspoon, but all of the CACA and their willingness to act violently in order to achieve their goals," Sam said. "The owner of the daguerreotype of our great-grandfather, a confidant of the family, was found hanged, his home ransacked. The police said it was a suicide, but he had no history of depression, no personal crises, and the note appeared to be forged."

My little brain went ticking through the information I had recently received. "You said that your family has a long and complicated association with Sebastian's organization, yet you plan to defuse them. How long is that going to take? One millennium? Two?"

"We're fine-tuning a plan of action. I believe a resolution is imminent," he said.

"You better be right about that, Sam."

And that is how I came to be a houseguest at Casa Dracula.

eight

to snooze, perchance to hallucinate

After the inquisition, I felt disoriented and weak, so I went back to my room, locked the door, and lay on the bed. Staying here meant that I would eventually have to face Oswald, I felt too angry and humiliated to deal with that, but CACA thugs could be lying in wait for me at my hovel.

My muscles throbbed and ached and no matter how I turned, I couldn't get comfortable. After a few hours, I got up and went back to the study, where Sam was talking to Gabriel.

"I accept your invitation to stay," I told them. "But I need my clothes and my writing things. Also, I need to make phone calls. People are probably very concerned about me."

The vampires said they would provide me with writing supplies and pay for new clothes since they didn't think it was safe to send anyone to my apartment. Sam said, "You can make calls, but I must ask that you not disclose our phone number or location. Corporate Americans for the Conservation of America has long arms and deep pockets."

Gabriel glanced at Sam before saying, "I haven't been able to find out the condition of Beckett-Witherspoon's guard, but they'll use that against you if they can."

I hadn't been the least bit bothered by shooting that gorilla, and I said so, adding, "They kidnapped me! Sebastian pulled the gun on me!"

"Milagro," said Sam, "we all know what happened, but the criminal justice system will give a certain amount of credence to Beckett-Witherspoon." Sam gestured toward the phone on his desk. "You can call from here. It's a safe line."

I waited until the men moved their conversation to the doorway and then I picked up the phone and called Nancy. Our friendship had really developed after F.U. when we both moved to the City. I'd had a lot of time on my hands because I was frequently unemployed, and she'd had a lot of time because she lived off her trust fund. She answered on the second ring, trilling, "Todd!"

"No, it's the anti-Todd," I said. I'd never met anyone named Todd until I went to F.U. The name still cracked me up. "Hey, Nance."

"Mil, I am so wanting to talk to you. What is going on with Sebastian? He left three messages here looking for you."

"I talked to him at Kathleen Baker's party. He behaved very badly and he looks like hell."

"I don't believe it!"

"It's true. He was very rude." This was not the time to tell Nancy about the vampires. One, she'd never believe me, and two, I wasn't sure I could make a convincing argument for something that seemed so insane.

"I mean I don't believe that he looks like hell," Nancy said. "I always thought he'd age beautifully. If he behaved so badly, why does he want to see you again?"

"A natural perversity," I said.

"That sounds intriguing!" she said. "He's always been such a gentleman to me."

Of course Sebastian had been nice to Nancy. She was his kind of people: old money, the right pedigree, the right schools, the right clubs. I said, "I absolutely never ever want to see him again. Promise me you won't tell him you talked to me."

"Mil, he did call *un-deux-trois* times. Maybe your strong and confusing pheromones finally had an effect on him . . . ," she began.

"Nancy, never in a million years. Promise, not a word." After she swore on a stack of Italian *Vogue*s, I said, "Anyway, I met some marvelous people who invited me to stay at their ranch in the country, so here I am. I'm looking at it as a writing retreat."

Nance made a high-pitched girly sound and asked me where I was staying. I named a fashionable town on the other side of the mountain and said, "Kooky Pescatelli invited me. They've got these incredible vineyards." Kooky Pescatelli was a character in one of my short stories. "I'm just going to hang out here for a while. Kooky is delightful. She collects pewter mugs."

"Pewter mugs, my sweet pink ass! Is there a cute guy there?"

"No! Well, yes," I said, glancing at the cute guys in the

doorway, "but that's not why I'm here. I really need time away from the City, time and quiet and a place without rats in the walls, to reflect and work on my novel."

Nancy was satisfied with this vapid explanation. She then described in grisly detail various types of trim on wedding gowns. "You haven't even set your wedding date, Nance," I said.

"Oh, but I have just decided to have a bridesmaids' tea and you have to come. You have to wear something puce."

We spent a few minutes arguing about what color puce was and then she blithely said, "I'm having it at the Croft." When she told me the date, I realized I had no idea what day today was.

"I'll try to come," I said.

"You better come, Milagro De Los Santos, no ifs, ands, or big butts. Promise me you'll be there."

We debated over how I should give my oath and finally decided that I should swear on an annotated collection of Shakespeare's tragedies.

I was relieved when my call to my landlord went to his answering machine. "Hi, it's Mil. I just wanted to say that I've been called out of town on a personal emergency." I dropped my voice and added, "I know I'm late with the rent, but I promise I'll pay you soon. Please don't forget to deep water at least once a week. *Really* deep." I tried to sound suggestive so he would be inclined to be lenient with me.

Mercedes was next on my list. She seemed to think time in the country would do me good. She lectured me about working hard for a purpose and said that being an artist was not all parties and pretty boys, but actually strenuous labor and dedication. I always felt a personal obligation to Mercedes and I promised not to slack off.

By the time I hung up, Gabriel had left. Sam asked, "Don't you want to call your parents and tell them you're away?"

I shrugged. "Not especially." I looked down at my ugly *chancletas* and said, "Clothes."

"We'd like you to have a medical exam first to ensure your continued health," he said. "Then you can buy some clothes."

I envisioned a gala shopping spree à la *Pretty Sick Woman.* Sam would sip an espresso and nod with approval while I twirled around in designer gowns. Clerks on commission would smile approvingly at my style and capacity to spend someone else's money.

Edna suddenly materialized in the doorway. "You aren't going like that, are you?" she said brusquely.

It was funny because my mother Regina had said exactly the same thing to me on numerous occasions. "If you could lend me something, maybe a skirt or—"

"Never mind," she snapped. "Let's go."

"Thank you, Grandmama," Sam said.

I hesitated. "But shouldn't we be worried about Sebastian's group?"

"Oh, you're safe enough with me, young lady," Edna said, and patted her handbag.

"You have a gun?"

"No, I have a phone and common sense. I'm sure you don't know what that is." With that she walked away.

I shuffle-clomped after her. There was the satisfaction of knowing that no matter how embarrassed I was, Edna would be more so by being seen with me. Which shows how very little I knew.

It was late afternoon when we stepped out of the kitchen through a mudroom/laundry room. Edna took a straw hat from a row of hooks for herself and handed me a ratty, olive-colored canvas baseball cap. Then she picked up a bottle by the sink and squirted sunscreen into her palm. She gave the bottle to me.

"No, thanks, I don't get sunburned."

"Ha, suit yourself," she said in a way that suggested that she'd be delighted if I sizzled like a *chorizo.* I put on the sunscreen just in case.

We walked to the back driveway, where a parking area was partially hidden by a fence. The dogs bounded up to us, and I was surprised to see Edna slipping biscuits to them. Probably fattening them up for a night when she wanted *barbeque de perros.*

The fields were the vivid lime of new spring growth. In the distance I could see a silver ripple of a stream. Looking down the lane, I spotted a brown barn. I was so busy admiring the scene, I didn't notice that Edna had gotten in a dusty green Jeep until she started the engine. I would have pegged Edna for the luxury sedan type.

I hopped into the Jeep. "It's very beautiful here."

"Your powers of observation are dazzling."

I probably would have said something snappy, but I felt snap-impaired. The closest neighbors lived in a small white cottage to the left. It was protected by a vine-covered fence. Oswald's ramshackle shack must be elsewhere on the property.

As we drove to the gate, Edna veered clear of a rider on a roan horse. He was wearing faded jeans and a pale blue shirt, and sat upright in his saddle, one hand loosely holding the reins. I only had a second to see his face under the shadows of his cowboy hat: it was Oswald and he had been gazing right at me. How was it that a man could look so fabulous and yet be such a scoundrel?

Edna glanced my way and I felt as if she was daring me to mention Oswald's name. "Edna, how long have you lived here?"

"Too long," she said tersely. When I asked where her family was from, she named a town that sounded like it was spelled with nothing but x's, z's, and k's.

"How do you spell that, Edna?"

"You can't," she said.

I remembered that a good interviewer asks open-ended questions. "Why don't you tell me a little about your family?" I asked. "How are Sam and Gabriel related and where are your children?"

"Has no one explained human biology to you, young lady? The boys are cousins in the usual way and my children are off in the world as they should be. Now, may I drive without your incessant chattering?"

We took a road that wound through hills with groves of fruit trees and vineyards. After about thirty minutes, we reached a more urban area. Edna parked in the lot next to a small office building and got out of the Jeep. A sign said LOWER SKY COMMUNITY CLINIC.

She walked to the front door and I shuffle-clomped after her. The lobby was clean and bright plastic chairs lined the wall. "Sit," Edna ordered, so I plonked myself down near the table of magazines and Edna went to the reception desk. I was thoroughly engrossed in a tabloid magazine when I felt a bony claw on my shoulder.

"Come along, young lady."

"You say 'young lady' as if it's a criticism."

Edna hmphed at me. I shuffle-clomped behind her down a hall with health posters on the walls, including "The New Food Pyramid!" The smiling sphinx did not indicate that blood was one of the primary food groups. Edna led me to an exam room and said, "Make an effort to behave. Dr. Harding understands your situation. You're supposed to put on the gown."

I decided to wear the perplexing paper gown with the opening in the back, because the sight of my shrunken bazooms made me terribly sad. I sat on the exam table and gave them a tender squeeze. "I'll fatten you up, my darlings, I promise," I was assuring them, when there was a knock on the door.

A tall, willowy young woman entered, a doctor, I assumed by the stethoscope and also her name tag, which said Winifred Harding, MD. She looked about my age, which I found disconcerting.

She was pretty in the way that girls who've always had everything are pretty: blond hair fell smoothly to her shoulders, pale blue eyes, clear skin, nice cheekbones, a small, neat chin, and a good forehead. Her nose was a touch too long to be ordinary; the nose is what made her interesting. She gave me a cool appraising gaze, like the sorority girls at F.U., a gaze that seemed to say "Not quite up to our standards, Sissy."

"Ms. De Los Santos," she said curtly. "I'm Dr. Harding."

"Good afternoon." I sat up straight and stopped swinging my legs. "I was told that you understand my condition."

She pressed her lips into a narrow line. "I've been told that you've been infected. However, we don't really know what the effects will be. It's been so long since an outsider has come into contact with the condition that we have no reliable scientific data."

"You're one of them, right?"

Dr. Harding nodded and said sharply, "Yes, some of us even go to medical school."

"I wasn't implying anything," I said.

She performed all her little doctor activities, such as bashing my knee with a rubber mallet, jamming her cold stethoscope on my chest, strangling my arm with a blood pressure cuff, and blinding me with a penlight. She asked me to describe my symptoms. I mentioned the chills and fevers, exhaustion, weight loss, change in vision, and a sense of ennui like in those Danish movies where the characters smoke and complain for two hours. The doctor showed profound indifference to my apathy.

Her cool, thin fingers explored my throat and felt under my arms. I winced. "Your nodes are a little tender and swollen. I'm more concerned about your nutrition. What have you been eating lately?" she asked.

"Cranberry juice?" I offered. "Um, berries?" I was always good at multiple-choice quizzes.

"You may find that your metabolism runs a little faster."

"The Transylvanian body beautiful plan? Thanks, but no thanks."

She gave me a chilly look from her undead blue eyes. "Unwanted weight loss can be a serious problem. You need to make sure you eat a balanced diet, perhaps five to seven small meals every day with lots of fruit, vegetables, and whole grains. Have you been eating anything peculiar?"

Now, like most people, I like to keep my peculiarities secret. Gabriel had claimed that the vampires didn't drink blood, so I didn't want to repulse her by confessing to my bovine beverages. "So where did you go to medical school?" I asked.

She named an acclaimed university in Europe. Great, she was not only a medical professional, but also cosmopolitan and multilingual. "Have you ever heard of pica?" she asked.

"You mean that craving for weird foods? Gabriel already told me that red foods and liquids help."

"Yes, they do. Pica's most common in pregnant women. Some children exhibit it, such as eating lead paint chips because of the sweet taste. There's generally both a physiological and a psychological component to these cravings. As I was asking, have you been eating anything peculiar?"

"Steak tartare," I lied. "Oh, and some carpaccio. The day before last, I think. Usually I keep away from uncooked meats, and I'm a little concerned about E. coli."

"If you were infected by E. coli, you would definitely have symptoms by now. All your vitals are fine, but I need blood samples to run some tests."

"What are you looking for?"

"An elevated white blood cell count," she said. "I want to see if there's been a . . ." She seemed uncomfortable. "You're either fighting off the infection or your system is adapting."

"I'm becoming a vampire?"

Her undead expression was stony. "There's no such thing as vampires. We have an autosomal recessive disorder due to an enzyme deficiency." Dr. Harding moved a rolling cart with phlebotomy equipment close to the exam table.

She then pulled on latex gloves, yanked a rubber hose around my upper arm, and banged on the inside of my elbow. "This takes a moment," she said. "My nurse usually does blood draws. Open and close your fist."

When she was done stabbing me, there were two dark amethyst vials of my own blood on the tray. I had never seen a color so tantalizing.

Then I looked at Dr. Harding. Her eyes were gleaming as she stared at the vials. She could call it any fancy medical term she wanted, but she was a vampire for sure.

I asked, "So what *do* you actually know about people who become infected? What happens to them?"

Dr. Harding was brusque. "We know very few medical facts. Yours is an extremely rare situation."

"What about the folklore?"

Her delicate nostrils flared slightly as if she was smelling something bad. "Nonsense and superstition."

"Why is there a recurring theme of drinking blood?" I asked, thinking of the vials.

Dr. Harding was putting the cart back against the wall. "UVA from the sun's direct light fragments our DNA. Our family's ancestors possibly experienced a biological desire to replace the damaged DNA and this was exhibited in a craving for blood."

Having only the faintest knowledge of human biology, I said, "That would explain why a member of your family might have a craving, which is genetic, but not anyone else."

"Yes," she said. "Unless . . ."

I felt a minor cramp in my lower abdomen. "Damn," I said. "What day is this?"

Dr. Harding glanced up from the vials of blood and told me.

"Oh, no wonder. Do you have any feminine hygiene products here?" Nancy and I thought the term "feminine hygiene" was hysterical. We said it more than was absolutely necessary.

"You mean you're having your menstrual cycle? That's odd."

If she thought having a period was odd, then perhaps she wasn't the sharpest scalpel dissecting the cadaver. "Yes, every twenty-eight days, like fine precision clockwork."

"Hmm, it's just that, well, some people are more fertile than others."

"And because I'm a Latina, you assumed I must be pregnant?" I snapped. "A tampon? A pad, please?"

Her eyes flashed angrily for a moment, and then she took a cardboard box out of an enamel cabinet. "The restroom is down the hall. I'll try to have the lab work done ASAP. In the meanwhile, get rest, drink plenty of red fluids, and take iron supplements. I'll give a bottle to Mrs. Grant. Also, most of us are photosensitive, so wear sunscreen and use sunglasses."

I gathered up my clothes. "Thanks," I said. "Doctor, do you think I'll ever be normal again?"

"I suppose that would depend upon your definition of 'normal.' "

Dr. Harding seemed unnecessarily bitchy for someone in the healing profession. "By the way," I said, "how are you connected to the family?"

Her smile was glacial. "I am Oswald's fiancée."

nine

excuse me for living

I was not at a loss for words; I just couldn't choose which ones to use. They ranged from "I am very sorry, I didn't know he was engaged," to "You should keep your boyfriend on a shorter leash, the bastard infected me!" The truth was I felt skanky compared to this somber, willowy, multilingual woman who dedicated her life to saving others.

With a morose shuffle and clomp, I returned to the lobby. Edna was tapping her foot with such impatience that she was practically doing a sedentary jig. She stood, turned sharply on her heel, and led the way out of the building.

Once we were in the car, Edna sighed heavily and said, "What on earth are you sulking about, young lady?"

"You mean besides being stalked by madmen and infected

with a possibly incurable condition that's been reviled in popular lore for centuries?"

"Yes, besides that."

"Well," I said, regretting that I sounded shrill, "you might have mentioned that Dr. Harding is engaged to Oswald."

"That has nothing to do with anything. Unless you have your sights set on him, in which case you are more, more . . ." Oddly enough, Edna seemed restricted by politeness.

"More idiotic? More desperate? More pathetic? More of a slut than you imagined?" I offered all these suggestions. "I do not have my 'sights set' on your precious Oswald. The man doesn't even own a decent suit. Also, he's deceitful. And, for your information, he had his sights set on *me.* He's a cheating, lying, no-account vampire who lured me to his room."

Edna's scathing look practically ignited my dreadful clothing ensemble. "You sound like a bad country song," she said. "Vampires are a myth." She was a total bitch, but I still wanted like mad to perfect her repertoire of gestures and expressions.

Any illusions I might have had about shopping were shattered when Edna drove to a huge chain discount store. I was one of the better-dressed customers.

"Get only necessities," she ordered as she steered me to the women's clothes section. "Here, this looks like you." She yanked out a peach polyester T-shirt with "Classy Lady" written on the front in glitter and rhinestones.

"Thanks, Edna, but that's more you." I picked out a pair of basic blue jeans and a pair of black pants.

"Aren't those too big?" Edna asked.

"I plan to build back up to my flirt weight," I answered,

immediately regretting giving her the impression that I was a fleshy tart. Edna was probably calculating how much of her food I would be consuming to achieve my trampy goal.

Edna grudgingly indicated a clearance rack with some pretty cotton sweater sets. I got one in black, one in burgundy, and one in cream, colors that suit my usually olive skin. I was happy to find blouses and matching skirts.

We went on to the "Ladies' Intimates" area. Edna waited by the socks while I selected cheap bras in boring beige, the only things I could find in my regular size. I tried to convince myself that their utilitarianism was extravagantly sexy in a WWII sort of way. This was the bra that our brave boys dreamed about at night while shivering on the front. I grabbed two packs of cotton panties that had pretty floral patterns and several pairs of socks. In the shoe department, I settled on a pair of sneakers, pink rubber flip-flops, and a cute pair of black strappy shoes.

Checking the prices of my items, I calculated that I was spending less for all these clothes than Edna had spent for her accessories. Which reminded me to pick out a belt and a straw bag. We went to the personal products aisles and I tossed all the daily necessities into the shopping cart.

As I rolled the cart to the makeup section, Edna said, "You're staying at the house, not trolling for sailors."

"That's hilarious, Edna. I'm totally about to start laughing." I chose products based on their names, like Pinkation Vacation, Gold A-Go-Go, and Smudgy Smoke.

At the checkout line, we waited behind a woman who was buying large quantities of toilet paper, Velveeta, and generic bourbon. As the woman rolled away with her cart, Edna muttered, "I'm glad I'm not invited to that party."

I doubt that Edna ever got invited to any parties, and my plan was to get away from her as soon as possible. "Edna," I asked, "Sam said a resolution of the conflict with CACA was 'imminent.' How soon is that? How soon can I leave?"

"As soon as it's safe." She said it without conviction, as if my life back in the City would never be safe. The air-conditioning was on too high in the store, and I shivered.

On the drive back, while nursing the large cherry Slurpee Edna had grudgingly bought me, I pondered my status as a serious and sincere woman in a modern, vampire-infested society. Pros: I was alive. The weather was delightful. I would have an opportunity to write. My friends were still my friends. Cons: I was infected with a weird virus. My rent was late. Sebastian had mysterious and hideous plans for me. Oswald had toyed with me and I meant nothing to him. The vampires might not be telling me the whole truth about themselves and their situation.

I forgot all that when I saw the first stars coming out in the sky and the pale crescent moon over the hills. "Edna," I said, "this place is really beautiful."

"Yes, yes, so you've said. Now that you're better, we expect you to contribute around the house, just like everyone else."

Instead of waiting for her to tell me I had to scrub the floors, I said, "I can garden. And I can cook a little." My cooking consisted of putting things into tortillas.

"I suppose that will have to do."

When we arrived at the house no dogs greeted our

approach because they were slobbering around a big grill on the back patio, where Sam and Gabriel were cooking something that smelled delicious. Sam, holding gleaming barbecue prongs and a cleaver, said, "Winnie called and told us the good news that your condition looks promising."

What exactly had the doctor told them? By "my condition," did he mean that I was bleeding now, able to feed the monstrous appetites they claimed not to have? "I have to put things away," I said, going into the house before they could detect blood on me.

I locked the door of my room and dressed in jeans, a sweater, and sneakers. I felt like a Hitchcock character, if Hitchcock had had a thing for lively raven-haired girls instead of aloof ice queens like Dr. Harding. Through the open window, the family's voices were low, conspiratorial murmurs. I edged to the side of the window and listened.

I heard Sam say something about the "plan proceeding well," and then Gabriel laughed and said, "I love it when they're gullible." What if there was no plan to overcome CACA? What if I was the gullible one?

At the bottom of the shopping bags were the iron and multivitamin supplements that Edna claimed came from Dr. Harding. The foil seals *looked* as if they were intact. But how did I know for sure? I flushed them down the toilet.

Again, I edged to the window to listen. Sam's voice was a low rumble, but Gabriel's lighter tones were clear: "Fatten her up a bit and she's quite yummy." Ordinarily, I would have taken this as a compliment, but now it had more sinister implications.

There was a knock on my door and Edna's imperious voice: "Young lady, do you intend to keep us waiting all night long?"

Standing next to the door but not opening it, I replied, "I'm not hungry. Go ahead without me."

I waited to hear her leave. After a few seconds she said, "Personally, I don't care if you starve to death, but Dr. Harding said you are supposed to eat."

What a cheap trick to lure me out of safety! "That's okay. I'll forage for something later." When Edna finally left, I lodged a chair under the door handle. It didn't give me much security. I wished I hadn't smelled the food on the grill. My stomach spasmed with hunger.

Fatigue came over me and I fell asleep. I awoke a few minutes past midnight, famished and disoriented. I felt a sudden urge to leave this place, but I had no idea how to escape. Layering sweaters against the cool night air, I tried to remember how far away the town was.

Luckily, I had learned a lot of survival information from my literature classes at F.U. For example, in Herman Melville's terrifying story "Benito Cereno," a naive sea captain discovers all too late that the supposedly cowering Babo is really the diabolical leader of a cannibalistic crew. It's an important cautionary tale: Never automatically assume that your new pals aren't cannibals.

Unfortunately my literature classes had not taught me that fabulous men were probably already engaged to arctic blondes.

I placed a change of clothing into one of the plastic shopping bags and made sure I had Mercedes's money. The house was silent as I slid the chair from beneath the doorknob. I waited a few more minutes before slipping into the kitchen.

I quietly opened the refrigerator and surveyed the remnants of this evening's feeding frenzy. The fiends must have finished the barbecue, because the only things left were grilled Portobello mushrooms, tofu, and red pepper on skewers. These went into my bag, Tupperware containers and all.

I stood at the back door for painfully long seconds, trying to see into the dark night, hoping that my captors thought I was knocked out by fake multivitamins. I was torn by the urge to bolt out the door and by the worry that any rushed movement would draw them down upon me like, well, like the fiendishly undead.

The door was unlocked. Stepping outside, I took care to walk softly, keeping to the dark shadows at the edge of the drive. I was so focused on not snapping any twigs that I almost got to the front gate before I realized that it might be monitored by cameras. I veered left, along the property line that ran parallel to the road, hoping to find a way to get over or through the fence.

When I was far enough from the house to risk the sound of the Tupperware lid snapping, I opened a plastic container and began eating the mushrooms. They were delicious, with lots of ginger. If I wasn't worried about escaping, this would have been a really lovely night stroll. How nice it must be to have a country home, to eat al fresco, to leave one's doors unlocked, to see the myriad stars in the clear night sky, to awake to a rooster's crow, to hear the thundering footsteps of a pack of creatures behind you in hot pursuit!

I only had to look back once to see the wolves racing to me before I began to run, my plastic bag slapping against my legs. I took a sharp turn, in an effort to outwit their herding techniques and walnut-sized brains.

I threw my plastic bag down, hoping that the scent of kabobs would distract them. Crashing through shrubbery, I saw the light from the neighbor's white cottage shining like a beacon. I scaled the fence around the house by jamming my feet on the horizontal rails and fell into a thorny bush on the other side. The wolves yelped in frustration and I yelped in pain as I tried to extricate myself from the brambles.

I breathed hard and tried to calm myself. I had escaped the beasts. I turned toward the modest white cottage, the sort of *casita* humble yet honest country folk would own.

The wolves were struggling to scramble through the fence when, to my great relief, the front door opened. I ran toward it, so happy I could have cried, and directly into the dark silhouette of a man who said, "Milagro, what the hell are you doing?"

Oswald gazed down at me and he looked decidedly puzzled.

ten

whereupon our heroine confronts the cad

Seeing him up close, in a navy sweatshirt and jeans, the bastard looked more handsome than I remembered. His wide brow was unlined by difficulties, his creamy skin free of anxiety-induced acne, and his body was unreasonably healthy and lean. Only his hair looked troubled, the locks tousled in a the-world-is-too-much-with-us, let's-go-back-to-bed sort of way.

I heard a scuffling by the fence and knew one of the red-eyed monsters had gotten through. I lifted my hand to grab Oswald's arm. Sure, he had wronged me, but it still seemed unfortunate that his muscled flesh would be ripped to shreds.

Perhaps Oswald thought I was going to strike him, because he moved away and said, "Hey, Daisy."

I turned to face the creature straight on, ready to fight until the bitter end. I was confronted by a shaggy dog.

"Oswald," I said. "'What the hell are you doing?' is hardly an appropriate greeting when it's your fault that I'm here!" I blinked away tears and dropped my shaking hand to my side.

"I meant what are you doing crawling over the fence and riling the animals." Oswald stared and I averted my face so he wouldn't see the hollows under my eyes. I was embarrassed that I looked so hideous and I'm sure he was wondering why in the heck he'd ever looked at me. I crossed my arms in front of my chest. Finally he said, "Would you like some oatmeal? You look like you need a meal. It will help you think more clearly."

"I don't want your pity."

"I'm not offering you any. I'm offering you oatmeal. Come on in." He had a rich, low voice that caressed words and made everything he said sound provocative.

I stayed where I was. "Edna said you lived in a shack."

"My grandmother thinks this *is* a shack."

I took a few tentative steps forward. There was a large, airy all-purpose room with a miscellany of unmatched furniture. Anatomical posters of domestic animals were tacked on one wall. Thick textbooks covered an olive metal desk. Oswald gestured toward it and said, "That is my command post." Through doorways I could see a bedroom and a bathroom.

"What do you command?" I asked.

"I'm helping Gabriel track down CACA's membership right now. Since I was under house arrest."

"Is that why you weren't at the barbecue tonight?"

Oswald shrugged. "I eat enough vegetables."

"What's wrong with vegetables?"

"Nothing. I just eat enough of them. Do you have a problem with that?"

"Oswald, I have a lot of problems right now, but your relationship with vegetables is not one of them." Somehow that didn't come out as scathingly as I intended.

"Do you want oatmeal or not?" He walked toward the open kitchen. The family must have had a cooking fetish, because all of the appliances were expensive new models designed to look like vintage pieces. In a dish rack beside the sink was a lonely tableau of a single plate, a wineglass, and a mug.

Oswald filled a pot with water and added a dash of salt. Obviously, he was unfamiliar with the adage that a watched pot never boils. Maybe it wasn't in the vampire lexicon. Maybe they said something like, "An observed blood vessel doesn't burst." While he stared at the pot, I had ample opportunity to stare at him and remember that dizzying time at the Hotel Croft.

Occasionally, he stole a glance at me, his gray eyes framed by dark lashes. The glances were definitely stolen, because he looked guilty as hell.

"I'm so relieved that you're all right," he said at last.

"Am I really all right, Oswald? After all, I am staying in a house full of vampires. They could attack me at any given moment."

"You are in greater danger from malnourishment than from any mythical creatures. Perhaps you are letting your imagination run wild."

If I hadn't just mistaken the dogs for the hounds of hell, I would have had a clever retort. "What about an apology?"

Oswald's jaw tightened, and I wondered if he had tried to blame me for this mess.

"Damn you to hell, Oswald, you didn't even tell me you were engaged. I was examined by your fiancée today at the clinic. Do you want to know how humiliating that was?"

Oswald grabbed a tin of Irish oatmeal and measured some into the water. "I should have told you about Winnie. She's a wonderful woman, remarkable and dedicated."

He didn't have to say, "And you're not." "If she's so wonderful and remarkable and dedicated, why did you take me to your hotel?"

Oswald let his gray eyes rest on me for a moment and I stopped breathing, again feeling that connection to him. He reached out to brush a strand of hair from my face, and my skin grew hot at the touch of his fingers. "Milagro," he said in a deeper voice.

I can't say what I would have done, but then there was a hiss and sizzle and we both jumped away from each other. It was only the oatmeal boiling over, but it was enough to change the atmosphere. In a suddenly crisp tone Oswald said, "I saw you talking to Beckett-Witherspoon and I was intrigued, curious. I thought you could provide information about him."

"Oswald, your so-called curiosity almost cost me my life! Now I'm a damn vampire like you and your crazy family."

"That's preposterous. There's no such thing as vampires. You are not a vampire. You're just a girl with an infection."

"Just a girl with an infection!" I shouted. "That's all I am? I'm just a girl to give rug-burn to on the carpet and who cares if

I get sick and almost die and you come back here to your dedicated and remarkable fiancée and everyone laughs about it?"

"No, no, that's not what I meant!" he said. "I never wanted any harm to come to you."

"Oswald, you never wanted any harm to come to me and you never wanted any good to come to me, because you didn't even think of me that way. I was just a *thing* to you, a momentary and forgettable diversion."

Maybe I really wanted him to say how extraordinary the connection had been, how strong it was still. Maybe I wanted him to tell me that I was beautiful and irresistible and he was overcome by desire because of something true and real and his yearning for me was even stronger than my yearning for him. Instead he repeated, "I should have told you I was engaged. Honestly, I'd like to make things better for you. Tell me how I can do that."

"I am sure I will think of something, Oswald, and when I ask, you better remember that you owe me. You owe me bigtime." I tried to stomp out of the cottage, but the dog got in my way. "Daisy, let's go."

I trudged back to the house feeling worse than before. Beyond the fence, the other dogs ran up to join Daisy and me on our walk of shame. Okay, *my* walk of shame. Maybe Oswald's physical relationship with Dr. Winifred Harding, based on his deep admiration of her, was even more compelling than what I had experienced with him at the hotel. Perhaps choosing boyfriends based on trivial desire resulted in relationships with a short shelf life.

I didn't feel that I was an especially frivolous individual. But maybe really shallow people could not comprehend their own lack of depth. Perhaps we only saw the shining surface of our personalities, whereas others saw the 3 FT. DEEP, NO DIVING sign clearly posted.

One of the dogs, a black and tan model, proudly dragged my plastic bag to me. "Good dog," I said. The container of kabobs was unmolested, so I opened it and chewed thoughtfully. At least as thoughtfully as a shallow person could chew.

Ahead, the house looked warm and comfortable. I was upset, but I did feel better now that I had eaten. Low blood sugar made normal people do insane things. Once, when Nancy was on a severe Geneva Spa Youth and Limberness diet, she had bought a beige wide-wale corduroy dress just because it was on sale.

I would find the best in my situation and try to be serious in my writing and as a human being. I would reject relationships based on mere sexual attraction and therefore I would not appeal to men who sought only a ha-ha roll in the hay.

Edna was in the kitchen drinking a cup of tea. I blocked the other dogs from coming inside, but Daisy slipped in. I shut the door.

Without looking up, Edna said, "Young lady, it is far too late to be gallivanting about. Go to bed."

I hesitated. "Can Daisy come in my room?"

Edna turned to look at the dog, who waggled her rump like a hooker at a convention of missionaries. "Hmph."

As I was walking back to the maid's room, Edna called, "Lie down with dogs, wake up with fleas." I had the feeling she wasn't talking about Daisy.

I fell into the deep, self-satisfied sleep of others like me, jailhouse converts and crackheads and kleptomaniacs, who truly believe that tomorrow they will be reformed.

eleven

new and improved

The alarm went off with an annoying beep-beep-beep. Daisy was gone. I could have sworn that I'd locked the door before I went to bed. It bothered me that someone had come in while I slept, even if it was just to let the dog out.

At least I had my own bathroom with those nice little octagonal tiles which made me think fondly of old bars and gyms. After showering and dressing, I troweled on makeup to hide my sallow complexion. Ignoring the fact that my WWII bra crumpled in where there was no bonny flesh to fill it out, I looked better than I had the day before.

I reminded myself to try to think before speaking. I mourned for all the blithe bon mots that would never be uttered. Now I would never even need to learn what "mot" actually meant. I suspected it meant "zinger."

Edna had donned another of her *Town & Country* outfits and was drinking a cup of joe. One place was set with a bowl of dry cereal, a glass of the blood orange juice, and a mug. I smiled politely and said, "Good morning, Edna."

She raised her eyebrows, then said, "Good morning, young lady. You look mildly less ghastly today."

Being serious doesn't mean that you have to tolerate abuse. "Gee, thanks. I'll cherish your compliment forever," I said as I poured a cup of coffee.

"We can't have you dilly-dallying about because I can tell you'll cause nothing but trouble. What are your plans for today?"

I suspected that Edna did not consider writing a serious enterprise. Looking out the window, I saw the neglected climbing rose. "I can prune that rose and also take a look at your garden."

"A familiarity with dirt does not make one a gardener."

"Edna, I know so much about gardening it would knock your color-coordinated socks off. Which is to say that I have had extensive experience and training as a gardener."

This was true, even though my father believed my gardening approach was radical because I was anti-lawn. Lawns were Jerry D's specialty. Flawless emerald carpets maintained by hard work, irrigation, and massive infusions of chemicals had made his fortune, such as it was. His company's motto was "Let Jerry D-light you with a perfect new lawn!" Before he sold his last business and moved, he had several crews working full-time on suburban landscapes, from homes to corporate campuses. I could go to a development I had never seen before and identify Jerry D's work just by the edging and border shrubs.

I'd barely finished my coffee when Edna said, "If you are finally ready, I'll show you the gardening shed."

We went to the mudroom and did the sunscreen routine. This time I grabbed a cute straw hat before she could give me something worse. We walked around the house and Edna pointed to the fence that screened the car park. "There's a shed back there with garden tools."

I found a miscellany of tools that would suffice and returned to Edna. It was early spring and everything should have been healthy with new growth. Instead the plants looked as if they were begging to be euthanized.

"The horses eat everything," Edna said. "What they don't eat, the dogs trample. The animals run this place."

"Good fences make good gardens. Do you think it's okay if I make some changes?"

"Do whatever you want, young lady. I'm sure my grandson won't mind."

"You mean Sam, right?"

"I am not so mentally feeble that I cannot tell my grandsons apart, if that is what you're implying."

"You know, talking to you is as satisfying as smashing my fingers with a hammer."

"Hmph," she said, but I was convinced that this was Sam's ranch. Edna just couldn't bear to answer yes to any of my questions. Besides, it wasn't as if Oswald was living in the house or even had a job.

The rose was overgrown with dead canes in a tangle with the weak new ones. Two unhappy blossoms had opened. "Oh, it's Climbing *Sombreuil,* one of my favorites." I turned to Edna and added, "When she's healthy, she's exceedingly beautiful. You have no idea."

"I'm sure I do," Edna responded cryptically.

There really wasn't anything else that was salvageable. "Any ideas of what you'd like here, Edna?"

She shrugged. "How should I know? This is all too rustic for me." I must have looked puzzled because she explained, "I've always lived in cities. The boys insisted that I come and stay here."

Suddenly I could see Edna in a metropolis, wearing a perfect little black dress, a martooni in one hand, the other flung up as she laughed, those exotic eyes narrowed seductively. I wished she would tell me more, but I knew she'd just insult me if I asked. "I guess both of us are stuck here then, Edna."

She looked at the pastures, trees, and the incredible blue sky above. "I suppose there are worse places."

"A trailer park by the freeway?" I offered.

"I was thinking more of Istanbul in a heat wave," she said.

I got the distinct impression that she spoke from personal experience. "I can start working on the garden, but I won't accomplish anything if I don't have a fence to keep out the animals."

"Then go to the barn or the turnout and find Ernie. He can build one for you if he has the time." She turned and walked back inside the house.

Who was Ernie and what was a turnout? As I walked down

the lane to the barn, I spotted the dogs barking and tumbling with one another in the field. When they saw me, they veered in my direction. All the dogs but Daisy abandoned me at the barn. One ran off to harass stylish black-and-white-speckled chickens pecking the ground beneath an oak tree.

The barn's doors opened to a shadowy and cavernous interior. Thinking that Ernie was some shriveled, toothless Old World serf of the vampire clan, I steeled my nerves as I entered. There was a fecund scent, definitely animal, but not offensive. There was a row of doors on either side of the barn. Some of the doors were closed and some had the upper half open.

I looked into a stall and got spooked when a chicken suddenly squawked and flapped. "Hello?" I called out. "Hello?"

At the next stall, a horse swung its head over a half-door and glared at me. I stepped out of range of its dangerous teeth and said, "I don't suppose you're Ernie."

The T-shirt–clad torso of a meaty young man arose from behind the half-door. His hair was as slick and black as my own, but his skin was a much richer brown. "Yeah, I'm Ernie."

Pushing the horse to one side, he leaned over the door. He gave me a slow once-over and I didn't have to see the rest of his compact body to know that he was solid with muscle. He had sharply angular Mexican Indian features and an easy smile under a mustache that was remarkably suggestive. A porn mustache, Nancy called them. I could tell that he was trying to figure out *what* I was.

Because that's how it worked. You saw other Latinos and tried to determine if they were from here or not, if they were old country or assimilated, if they preferred Spanish or English. And what you really wanted to find out was: can we relax with each other, count on each other, understand each other?

I learned a lot about Ernie from the first thing he said to me. "You must be Milagro 'cause you look like a miracle to me." He had a slight modulation in his speech and spoke at a leisurely pace.

I'd heard the line before, but I grinned. "That's what they tell me."

He wiped his hand on his shirt and reached over to shake hands with me. "*Mucho gusto.*"

"*Encantada.*" He had nice, strong hands. Is it so wrong to appreciate men in all their wondrous variety?

I told him that Edna suggested I ask him about putting up a fence for the garden.

"Sure. How long you gonna be here?"

I wondered how much Ernie knew about the family. I supposed it was bad form to ask the ranch hand if he knew his employers were vampires. "*¿Quien sabe?*" I said with a shrug. "A few weeks *mas o menos.*"

"Yeah, okay. I'm waiting for Oz to look at this horse, and then I'll come up to the house and do some figuring."

"Oz? You mean Oswald?"

"Yeah, he's good with the animals. This girl here, Stella, got an infection. See?" He bent out of view and I had to lean over the half-door to see him point to her swollen front leg. "With Oz around, we usually don't have to call the vet."

"Oh, he told me he wanted to be a vet."

"He's crazy," said Ernie, laughing. "He *is* good with animals, though." Ernie told me about the ranch, how only a few acres were used for alfalfa and how the crows ate most of the grapes in the vineyard. "We got about forty-five acres this side of the creek and another fifty on the other side into the hills that's only good for riding. This place is mostly just to be."

As I was leaving, I remembered to ask, "Ernie, what's a turnout?"

"That's what they call the corrals."

Near the barn, I spotted a large rectangular structure. When I swung open a wide door, I was astonished to discover an indoor pool. I guess vampires would need a protected recreation area. I dangled my hand into the water, which was far too cold for swimming even if I had been feeling well.

The ranch was set in a large valley and narrow ribbons of fog were draped on the hills around us. A few corrals held the usual collection of Old McDonald's farm critters. I followed a path around the fields that led to a briskly flowing stream. Redbud trees cloaked in pink blossoms and pines grew along the water's edge. On the other side of the creek, the land sloped up into a wood.

On the way back to the house, I detoured by Oswald's cottage. A black granite slab sculpture centered in the orderly garden didn't exactly scream "honest, simple countryfolk." I was peering through the lush plants, trying to see through the cottage windows, when I heard an amused voice say, "Looking for me?"

I turned in a guilty panic to see Oswald grinning at me. He had nice white teeth, but you'd expect that from a vampire, and dimples, which you wouldn't expect. It was probably a genetic trait to throw prey off guard. "Certainly not," I blustered. "I was merely examining your vegetation. Your soil must be very fertile to generate such growth."

"Yes, my soil *is* very good. In fact, it's volcanic."

He was staring directly into my eyes and I had the uneasy feeling that he knew exactly what smutty thoughts (involving eruptions, explosions, and all that) were percolating in my mind. I merely nodded my head, mumbled "Lucky you," and walked away as calmly as possible.

Ernie was pacing off the area around the kitchen garden. "The boss said to go ahead with this. Thought Edna would enjoy it this summer."

There was no reason for me to be happy about building a fence on someone else's property, but I was anyway and told Sam so when he came out of the house. "We'll need plants, too, and seeds. And I need to know what you would like here."

"I am sure your decisions about the garden will be acceptable to all of us," Sam said in his soothing voice.

"I hope you won't be disappointed," I said.

"I'm sure we won't. Also, the family and I would very much appreciate your including our grandmother in your project."

How suddenly a sunny day can turn stormy! "I thought she wasn't interested in gardening."

"My grandmother has never had the opportunity to garden, but I'm sure an endeavor like this could be satisfying to all parties."

I thought she might be more entertained by target practice on bunnies, but I didn't say so.

He continued, “There are several nurseries in the county. You two can shop together. I will pay for all the plants, of course.”

The clouds cleared away and the sun shone on me again. “I would be pleased to teach Edna how to garden,” I murmured. “Also, Sam, I need to be able to write here . . .”

“I haven’t forgotten our agreement. I believe that trust is essential to a positive and stable relationship,” he said. His brown eyes were as sincere as a dog’s.

He was so very right: it was *trust,* not *lust* that was essential to a positive and stable relationship. “Sam, you and I are so alike on these important points.”

He ducked his head modestly.

I asked Sam if he’d heard from Dr. Harding about my lab results. I felt as if I was improving, but I was still having periods of exhaustion and weakness.

He perked right up. “Winnie said something went wrong with one of the tests, so she’s running it again. I promised to call her today and see if she’s learned anything.”

“You know,” I said, “I want her to know that I feel awful about the accident with Oswald.”

“I’ll express your sincere regret to her.”

I wanted to find out more about the layout of the house, so I asked Sam for a tour. As he showed me around, I found out that his own business was handling family investments. “That’s what you do with a JD/MBA,” he said. “It’s not very exciting, but I like to think I’m contributing.” In addition to the rooms I’d already seen, Sam showed me a large, comfortable family room, a washroom, and a delightful little reading room with built-in bookcases and a deep violet velvet loveseat that I would look fabulous on.

The upstairs bedrooms had an impersonal, hotel look, except for the luxurious master suite, which had striking modern art on every wall. "Grandmama is using this room while she stays," Sam said. He'd even given up his bedroom for the old bloodsucker. Glancing in, I saw exposed beams—she probably hung upside down from them at night.

I slipped into Sam's office to call my answering machine and check my messages. I had a momentary fantasy that my parents would have called to say hello. Instead I heard Sebastian's angry voice saying, "Milagro, I strongly advise you to return as soon as possible. It is in your best interest to do as I say. The world is a dangerous place and I wouldn't want anything regrettable to happen to you." He wasn't foolish enough to leave his name or an outright threat, but the tone of his message was enough to frighten me.

Everyone but Oswald showed up for lunch. I made sure to sit next to Gabriel and was happy when he started playing footsie with me under the table. Our meal followed a red theme, which I later learned was out of consideration for me. We started with purple-red borscht, which was delicious, then moved to thinly sliced rare roast beef.

"So, Mil," said Gabriel, "I'm off after lunch."

"You're leaving?" I asked with dismay.

"Back to fight the forces of evil and save the world from CACA," he replied cheerfully.

"Don't gloat, Gabriel," said his grandmother. "Some of us must remain here in this cultural wasteland."

Well, there's nothing like a happy houseguest. Sam cleared his throat and said evenly, "Grandmama, I know you will really enjoy your own little garden. Think of the vegetables you can grow!"

Slices of rare beef had left a pool of dark juices on my plate. When the others weren't looking, I used a piece of bread to soak them up. I quickly shoved the soggy mess into my mouth, savoring the taste of the rich, salty blood.

"Samuel," Edna said, "vegetables have their place, but I am not one yet, nor do I plan to spend my remaining years tending to them."

I felt an urge to help Sam out. "I want to create a garden so you will always have cut flowers for arrangements and soirées."

Edna looked up at the ceiling. "Why grow flowers if you can buy them?"

"Why cook if you can eat fast food?" I answered.

Gabriel stood and said, "Okay, I'm out of here before you ladies start drawing your knives."

We all said our good-byes to Gabriel. As he hugged me close, I whispered, "Be careful, Gabriel."

He whispered back, "I'm the security dude, babe. I've got mad skills."

He made me laugh, but I believed him. I felt guilty for suspecting he meant anything culinary when he'd talked about fattening me up. I would miss him.

We were eating our dessert, succulent Bing cherries, when Oswald entered carrying a dark case.

"This is for you, Milagro," he said. He set the case on the table and opened it to reveal a small gray typewriter. "It's a beaut and works perfectly." Silver letters on the contraption spelled out "Olivetti."

"Surely you jest. I can't be expected to write on that relic."

Edna seemed amused, Sam's expression was unreadable, and Oswald looked disappointed.

"Yes, Oswald," Edna said. "Who could be expected to write anything on that contraption? I'm sure that no reputable work of fiction has ever been written on anything quite so archaic."

Oh, she was evil through and through. Just to spite her, I said, "I'm sorry, Oswald. It's just that I've never used one before. It's fine. In fact, it's great."

Oswald smiled crookedly and I forgot to hate him for about five seconds.

"Good. I didn't want to get you anything ordinary, and this machine is special. It belonged to a wonderful writer."

"Really?" I asked. Sam and Edna seemed uninterested in the typewriter's provenance. In fact, Edna was busy staring out the window.

"Yes, Dena Franklin. She wrote short stories, very clever. She was one of the great beauties of her time." There was a mischievous glint in Oswald's eyes.

"The name seems familiar," I said, but maybe I was thinking of Ben Franklin or Franklin Roosevelt.

"I'm sure the young lady is not interested in a forgotten scribbler," said Edna. "That will be all, Oswald."

I wish I could have dismissed him so easily.

twelve

a (ratless) room of one's own

That evening I found Edna in the kitchen, stirring a witches' brew in a blue cauldron.

"Nice of you to join the living, young lady," Edna snapped.

I swear that Edna was baiting me, but I resisted. I looked into the cauldron, expecting to see eye of newt and wart of hog and instead finding a lamb and red wine stew. It smelled delish. Edna assigned me menial tasks, like slicing bread, filling a pitcher with ice water, and washing lettuce. Then she said, "Set the table for four."

"Will Oswald be coming here tonight?"

"Oswald prefers to be in his shack this evening. I've invited Winnie to come stay with us."

I was sure Edna had invited the precious vampire princess

just to put me in my place. "That's very generous of you," I said neutrally.

"Try to behave yourself—consider what you've put her through."

This was rich, when Oswald was the one responsible for this whole mess. "Perhaps you'd be more comfortable if I ate in the kitchen."

"You really are too much, young lady," Edna snapped. "Just be quiet and do as you're told."

Winnie arrived soon after. Sam greeted her with a cousinly embrace before he hauled her bags upstairs. I edged into the foyer and said, "Hi."

Winnie examined me with her eyes. "Your condition seems to have improved. Are you taking your iron supplements?"

Since Edna was out of earshot in the kitchen, I said, "I must have misplaced them."

"You could pick up a generic supplement in town," Winnie said as she led the way to the living room. Sam had put an ice bucket and glasses on a side table. "Campari?" Winnie asked.

"Sure, thanks." Campari tastes awful, but it looked so fabulous that I liked to drink it anyway.

"You won't mind if it's mostly soda. You need to stay hydrated."

"Dr. Harding—"

"Call me Winnie."

"Winnie, when I came to see you, I had no idea . . ."

"I understand," she said.

I looked for jealousy in her eyes or even anger, but all I saw was weariness. Probably world-weariness. Her European education had taught her how to enjoy bitter aperitifs and accept the straying ways of men. I didn't think I would ever be so cosmopolitan and didn't know if I wanted to be.

"Nothing actually happened, you know," I said. "He cut his mouth falling and . . ."

"And you just happened to have your mouth attached to his at the time." Her smile was bitter like the Campari and I suddenly warmed toward her.

"That does sound bad, doesn't it? But . . ."

"Milagro—"

"Call me Mil."

"Mil, I know that this was anomalous behavior on Oswald's part and I would like to think it was not typical of you either. He has assured me that it will not happen again."

"Absolutely! There's not a chance . . ."

We heard Sam coming down the stairs, and we stopped talking and sipped our red drinks in the natural conspiracy of women through time immemorial.

We ate by candlelight and the conversation became lively. Even Edna acted almost human. No one mentioned Oswald. Winnie told us how her neighbor, a gentleman who went by the name of Pepper, had knocked on her door after an accident in his meth lab. "I treated Pepper's burns and he wanted to pay me with a gun because 'There's some real scumbags round here,'" she said with a dry laugh.

Sam said, "Winnie, you should have left that dangerous neighborhood and come here sooner."

"So Edna's been telling me, but I'm here now." She smiled serenely at him. "Even if the situation is a little complicated."

I froze, thinking that she meant me, when Edna held up her hands palms outward and said, "Must we talk about CACA at the table? Their recent acts show that they no longer have any boundaries."

"Okay," I said, "I can understand about not going to the police about my kidnapping, but can't you expose them to the media?"

"Expose them and we expose ourselves," Edna said. "Besides, they own most of the media."

"Sam told me that CACA may want to patent your DNA," I said. "But why couldn't you just come out and do that yourselves?"

Winnie gave Sam a warm glance and said, "I suspect Sam is right, as usual." Turning to me, she added, "We would like nothing more than to come out to the medical and scientific communities and conduct research that might benefit mankind. But we've learned that most people are governed by emotion rather than reason. If we announced ourselves . . ."

"CACA would feed all the old fears and superstitions," said Sam. "They would certainly use their power to try to deprive us of our rights as citizens by claiming we're a threat to national security. Then they'd see to it that no one could benefit from any medical research unless CACA profited from it."

"Are you sure you're not being paranoid?" I asked.

"No," said Sam. "It's happened before. In the old country, our family was routinely hunted down and slaughtered. History wrote off the atrocities as territorial disputes."

"But that was long ago, when people were ignorant."

"It's happened more recently here, too," Sam said. "The

organization that formed CACA has instigated the hysteria time and time again." He asked me if I'd ever heard of an especially heinous serial murderer who'd slaughtered several families fifty years ago.

"Yes, he was a madman."

"He was paranoid schizophrenic to be precise," said Winnie.

"Our adversaries found him after he'd been released from an asylum, convinced him that the victims were demons, and let him loose," said Sam. "Afterward nobody noticed that the families' properties, sitting on a critical tract of land, were taken over by an agent for the Witherspoon family."

"They hate you that much?" I asked in amazement.

"They don't see us as quite human," Winnie said sadly. "If we're not human, then they feel justified in taking everything from us, even our lives."

"We won't talk of it further," Edna said with a flip of her hand. She began to speak of a goat farm she wanted to visit. Sam and Winnie politely joined in the intriguing chèvre discussion and I said "Really?" a lot in an attempt to be a gracious dinner companion. But all the while I was ruminating on the ruthless and powerful Beckett-Witherspoon family.

Why hadn't I paid more attention to Sebastian's delusions of superiority? How could he believe that I'd only cared for his money and his status? What if he was right? What if I had been drawn to him because of what he represented, not who he was? I didn't want to think it was true. I didn't want to be my mother Regina's daughter.

After dinner, Sam gallantly offered to walk Winnie to the cottage to visit Oswald.

Left alone, I felt lonely. The books in the maid's room were a hodgepodge of bestsellers, nature guides, and popular classics. I picked up an old favorite, *Jane Eyre.*

My mother Regina didn't object to my friends so long as they lived quietly within the covers of books. Jane had been my companion from childhood. Opening the pages at random, I found young Jane suffering from cold and hunger at her terrible boarding school. I wished that I could give her a warm bowl of oatmeal.

thirteen

the arduous demands of country life

I awoke to someone sharply rapping on my bedroom door and heard Edna bark, "Enough lollygagging, young lady! Time to get up." The clock said seven-fifteen.

I crawled out of bed, grabbing a robe on the way, and opened the door. "For future reference, at what awful hour does lollygagging begin?"

"Seven a.m. You've had a full fifteen minutes of it. Help me get breakfast." She left before I could counter that according to my sources, primarily P. G. Wodehouse novels, guests at country houses lounged indolently before arising to enjoy a bath drawn by servants. I quickly showered and dressed in a skirt and blouse, regretting that my clothing still hung loosely on me.

Edna judged me sufficiently competent to make toast. Sam

and Winnie came downstairs grinning and effusing wildly about toast. Imagine how they'd respond to waffles.

After breakfast, Winnie said she wanted to check my vitals. She put her stethoscope to my heart and told me to breathe deeply and exhale slowly. She took my pulse, blood pressure, and temperature. When Winnie went into her doctor mode, she seemed far more adult.

"You are a somber girl," I told her.

She laughed, surprised. "Do you think so?" She was putting her medical equipment into her bag.

"Are you worried about my condition?"

"A little." Her eyes searched my face as if she was trying to make a decision. "I'm betting you'll be fine and I'm hoping that you'll overcome the infection. We call it an infection, but it doesn't act like a virus or retrovirus or bacteria. We have no idea of outcomes because experimenting on other humans could never be ethically condoned."

Perhaps I'd be able to ask informed questions if I'd taken a human bio class instead of "The High-heel Shoe in Post-WWI Literature: End of Innocence." "Anything else on your mind?" I said, trying to encourage her to tell me more.

Her pale eyebrows knit toward each other. "If the infection remains in your system, you'll be an outsider, always having to be careful with others, knowing you'll never fit in."

"Doc, I'm already there."

"You joke, but what about marriage? If we intermarry, it's a huge risk to have children with our partners. The infant mortality rate is about twenty-five percent. Of course, those are old numbers from the nineteenth century. We learned not to try."

"At least you have each other," I said.

"Yes, at least we have that," she said with a small smile. "But our fertility rates are extremely low."

I realized that I had misinterpreted her comment about fertility when she'd examined me at the clinic."

"Actully," she said, sighing heavily for such a slight girl, "Oswald and I were both screened and matched for fertility. No, don't look at me like that! It's our own dating service and children are important to both of us." She ran her fingers through her hair and said, "Don't forget to buy those supplements and get lots of rest."

I wanted fresh air, so I put on sunscreen and a hat and went outside. I returned from a walk to find Sam watching Ernie and Oswald mark off the postholes for the fence. Sam was neatly dressed in khakis and a polo shirt, while Oswald and Ernie wore plaid work shirts and jeans. Sam was the first to notice me and he said, "Hi, Mil."

"Fellers," I replied.

Ernie shook his bottom in my general direction, which I thought was pretty dang funny. Oswald looked up at me, but his expression was that of a man who already has a perfect fiancée.

I kicked the soil underfoot. It was compacted, but still damp from the winter's rains and would be easy to work. "This is such a beautiful place," I said.

"Yes," said Oswald, as if I had been talking to him. "I'd like to do some landscaping, but I get busy. The animals seem to take up all my spare time."

"Yeah," said Ernie. "Doc here did a great job with Stella. I thought she might need antibiotics, but he made a poultice and the swelling's gone down." How sad for Oswald that even Ernie humored his veterinarian fantasies.

Sam said, "My grandmother's in the family room if you'd like to discuss your ideas for the garden."

"Sure," I said as enthusiastically as if I'd just found out I was being given a pop quiz in astrophysics.

Edna was drinking coffee and watching a television show set in a courtroom.

"Edna," I said, "I thought you'd want to help plan out the garden."

"Young lady, you fail to grasp my utter lack of interest in the subject."

"Only dreadful people don't like gardens," I said, thinking of my mother Regina, who thought soil was dirty.

Edna deigned to let me sit beside her and sketch a plan. She even volunteered, "I've always liked lilacs."

We spent an hour devising a plant list, and every now and then Edna would let out a bit of tantalizing information, such as, "I went to a midnight ball that was decorated completely in white and black flowers. White tuberoses and hyacinths, black tulips and pansies."

I chattered about the garden in hopes that she would tell me more, but she finally said, "If you don't stop talking, I'm going to slit my wrists."

"Don't encourage me, Edna," I said. "Do you have any landscape books around? Just so I can show you pictures?" I asked.

"Will this hell never end? Do I look like someone who knows about books? Where are books usually kept?"

Pleased that I now had an excuse to snoop, I sashayed into the study. Luckily, no one was there. I skimmed quickly through the titles on the shelves. There was a lot of nonfiction, especially true-life adventures, with a mix of respectable biographies and autobiographies.

On the bottom shelf, there were books about wine country gardens. I lugged three oversized volumes to the desk and settled in the cushy leather chair. I opened the books, composed my face into a scholarly expression, and slowly eased out the middle desk drawer. Pens, paper clips, a packet of Juicy Fruit gum, and business cards from local merchants. I took a piece of gum and chewed it with loud snaps, like a bad girl in a gangster movie.

The drawer on the right held files. Remodeling bids, receipts, and indecipherable spreadsheets. I pulled the drawer out further and there at the very back were folders titled "CACA" and "De Los Santos, Milagro."

Flipping through the CACA folder, I saw photos of Sebastian and other clean-cut all-American men. The jargon-laden documents seemed to be internal strategy pieces and referred to "desired outcomes." There was an itinerary of Sebastian's literary tour as well as an organizational chart. Sebastian was on the fourth tier. His father was in the third tier and his grandfather was in the second. The top tiers were blank.

A sheet listed CACA's political activities, which included fear-mongering legislation that would financially benefit their consortium. In college, Sebastian had been disdainful of materialism as a guiding principle.

I opened the file with my name. It contained my F.U. transcript and photos of me from various public sources. There was my shabby employment history and dismal financial report. The file even contained a copy of the newsletter I had written for the nutritional supplements company.

The worst thing in the folder was a photo of Sebastian and me. It had been taken at an English department party and published in their quarterly. I had been midway through my junior year; Sebastian had been a senior. We'd been inseparable since we'd met the year before. In the photo, we were leaning against each other, his arm over my shoulders as we sat on a ledge, his head resting against mine, his mouth open in laughter that I could still hear. I was smiling as if I held the world on a string.

In an instant, I reverted to the girl who had been dazzled by Sebastian, a beautiful boy who rendered powerless all the criticism from my mother Regina—that I was too clumsy, too noisy, too peculiar, too garish, too inexcusably alive. When Sebastian would listen attentively to my musings or surprise me with a book of poetry or look at me with those clear azure eyes, I knew that I was special.

Seeing Sebastian at Kathleen's had been easier than seeing this photo. I thought I'd reinvented myself as one cool tomato, hobbing where he was nobbing, full of clever zingers and urbane insouciance. But my feelings still hurt from *then,* from the marvelous boy abandoning me for reasons he would not explain.

How often had I written to him, called him, tried to find out why he had cut me off so completely? I had lived in a dark netherworld for months, waiting for Sebastian, as for Orpheus, to lead me out into the light again.

I hated the vampires for digging up dirt on me, for finding details about my life (many inaccurate) that made me out to be a deluded pea-brained slut who groveled after Sebastian and wrote purple prose in praise of herbal remedies. I was not the sum of these insignificant and distorted parts.

"Milagro."

Sam stood in the doorway. I forgot my plan to pretend that I was reading the landscaping books. "How dare you!" I cried.

"You have no business in those drawers," he said nervously.

"I don't want any business in your drawers!" That came out all wrong, so I tried to fix it by saying, "And you have no business in my drawers! I mean, you have no business prying into my life!" Now everything I said was going to come out with an exclamation mark—I was that furious. "How dare you!"

Sam came closer. "There is no need to shout. We can discuss this civilly."

"Yes, yes, there is a reason to shout! You are the most unconscionable . . ." I had a lot of other multisyllabic words to hurl at him, but I started choking up. "You have the effrontery to, to, to . . ." To my embarrassment, I started to cry.

"Mil," Sam said, and approached me like an insane asylum attendant edging toward a particularly unstable patient. "Mil." He put his hand on my shoulder. I jumped up and shook him off.

"You had no right!" I was shuddering with fury and shame.

"I do not invade personal privacy unless there is a pressing need. We only did it because our lives are at stake. It seemed unlikely that Beckett-Witherspoon had used you to get access to us, but we had to take every precaution. You did talk to him at the party and you did go to the hotel with Oswald—"

"Oswald picked *me* up! Oswald lied to me!" I was back in exclamation-markville, wiping tears from my face and sniffling. The Juicy Fruit was bitter, bitter in my mouth.

"Mil, you're an attractive woman. I'm sure you know ways of encouraging susceptible men to make the first move."

"Oh, so I stage a fight with Sebastian in order to gain Oswald's attention? Why the hell would I want Oswald's attention in the first place? Your cousin is a nut and a loser!"

"You don't mean that, Mil," Sam said calmly.

"Yes, I do. I sincerely pity Winnie for what will undoubtedly be a horrible extended vampire lifetime of marriage to him and his cheating heart and slacker ways. Just because he is a liar, that's no reason to assume that I am some CACA stooge!"

He spoke mournfully, as if the truth hurt him personally. "Mil, Mil, you *did* withhold information, specifically about your relationship with Beckett-Witherspoon."

"I have no relationship with him," I said, but I knew how it must have looked to them.

"But you did once," someone said in the doorway. It was Oswald.

I saw from his expression that he'd heard me call him names. "Yes, I was his friend once. That was a long time ago."

"Friend?" Oswald asked. "Or something more?" He wore a ridiculous T-shirt from some town called Ypsilanti, Michigan, that said "Baiter late than never" and had a chorus line of dancing fish.

"Friend. I thought he was my *friend.* I was wrong. Sometimes I'm wrong about people. For example, I was wrong thinking you were harmless. And you have never even apologized to me for what you've done!"

"I wish it—" Oswald began.

Sam quickly cut him off with "Oswald, let me handle this. Please go."

Oswald looked as if he was going to argue, but then he turned and left.

I didn't realize I was shaking until Sam put his arms around me. "Mil, it was something we had to do. As you know from personal experience, Beckett-Witherspoon is capable of anything."

The more I tried to stop crying, the worse I sobbed, all the while fully aware that I was lowering myself in Sam's eyes. Since when did I need the approval of the undead? I pulled away from him and rushed from the study.

As I ran through the kitchen, I saw Edna at the table eating a sandwich and reading a book. Without glancing up, she said, "Your lunch is in the fridge when you want it."

I made an unsuccessful effort to speak in a normal voice. "Thank you, Edna." I then went to my room and locked the door. I wasn't lying. Sebastian had been my friend.

fourteen

a million tears

Of course, I'd wanted more: I'd been in love with Sebastian.

By the time we met, I'd dabbled in relationships, never satisfied with one or another. I can say with some certainty that my beaus had felt the same way about me. Sebastian's girlfriend was a refined brunette named Tessie Kensington, who dressed in casual, subtly expensive clothes. She was pretty, but not too pretty, as if excessive prettiness was gauche. She hadn't seemed to mind Sebastian's friendship with me because she was absolutely confident that she was worthy of his utter devotion.

As our relationship evolved and deepened, I convinced myself that friendship was enough. Sebastian liked teaching me and I liked being taught. He showed me the world that he knew and it was one filled with art and culture and beauty.

I remembered everything about our last day together. Sebastian had been house-sitting for a professor and invited me to join him for dinner. I asked him if Tessie would be coming, too. Sebastian reached for my hand, squeezed it, and said quietly, "I've been wanting to tell you—we broke up. It was for the best."

We went shopping and bought fresh crab, vegetables, bread, raspberries, and chocolate. While we waited in line, he ran back to the wine shelves and picked up a bottle of champagne. "For my favorite girl," he'd said with a dazzling, joyful smile that made my heart stop.

The professor's house was one of those perfect places with floor-to-ceiling bookcases, old rugs, and antiques. We cooked and drank, had dinner and drank, and talked and laughed. We were sitting close to each other in front of the fireplace, listening to music, when Sebastian kissed me for the first time.

We made love on the sofa and then went to the bedroom. All through the night, we explored each other and talked and laughed until our bodies were worn and our voices hoarse. He said he loved me. I told him I loved him and always would. He was beautiful, brilliant, and mine.

It was the happiest night of my life.

The next morning, Sebastian took me back to campus, kissed me, and told me he would see me the next evening. He would take me out to celebrate Shakespeare's birthday. He held me tightly and his last words were, "I already miss you so much, Milagro."

And he never spoke to me again. Until the night at Kathleen's. I'd heard later that he and Tessie had reunited, but they broke up again soon after his graduation.

In the years that passed, I had been with men I cared for and men who were far more experienced and men who seemed genuinely delighted to be with me and a few men who swore their love. My experiences with these men had been nothing compared to what I had shared with Sebastian—until that bewildering, dizzying encounter with Oswald.

This proved that desire would only lead me to worse men. Not that I could get much worse than a corporate supremacist maniac and a cheating, slacker vampire.

I cried until I bored myself. Sometime around three, I snuck out to the refrigerator. There was a tuna sandwich with a side of carrot salad on a plate. I took the plate and a bottle of cranberry juice to my room.

I couldn't even think of facing these quasi-people again when Edna barged through the door.

"I'm going into town. Winnie said you 'misplaced' your iron supplements. Come along and you can get some more."

"I don't feel like going."

"Young lady, your feelings are hurt, but Sam is a good, decent man who was looking out for his family. So let's get on with our lives." This argument for rational behavior wasn't working, so she added, "If you behave, I'll buy you a mascara."

I only went because the mascara I'd bought before was too clumpy. On the way to the car, I noticed that Ernie had put in all the fence posts. Edna didn't speak until we got out on the road to town. "Young lady, in my experience I have found that sulking is a particularly unrewarding activity."

"Edna, why do you always call me 'young lady' instead of using my name?"

We were at a sharp curve in the road, so it was lucky Edna didn't do any eyeball gymnastics. "I call you 'young lady' in the hope that you will be motivated to act like a young lady at some point."

We were entering the town. It was as cute as a bug. Small stores lined one main street. I saw signs for a feed shop, a post office, and a few breakfast joints.

"Well," I asked, "what would you do if you found out that someone had dug up your life history without your permission?"

Edna turned into the parking lot of a medium-sized market. "I would be delighted that anyone was interested enough to investigate my life."

"Okay, but what if much of the information was incomplete or distorted?"

"So long as it was intriguing, young lady. After all, what history is not inaccurate?"

We went into the store and I pushed a cart around while Edna loaded it with food. The store was modern and attractive, with tiers of brilliant fruit and vegetables. There was a mix of products catering to both winery owners and their workers. Edna picked up some pricey cheese and good red wine and I lingered near a display of tortillas and Mexican spices.

"Go ahead and get whatever you want," she said. "I expect you to do more than wash vegetables at some point."

"I'll try."

"Didn't your mother teach you to cook?"

"My mother Regina considers eating to be a moral weakness. She subsists on black coffee, Diet 7-Up, rice cakes, and iceberg lettuce dressed with lemon juice."

"That's preposterous."

"Oh, we are on the same page, Edna." It was my theory that culture was carried through cuisine and that my mother Regina had deprived me of part of my heritage because she had not cooked for me. It was my father's mother who had fed me chilled slices of watermelon with a tang of lime juice and salt, *chocolate* flavored with almonds and cinnamon, *frijoles* savory with *chorizo* . . . Her food had been love and history and artful compositions of color, taste, and texture.

My mother Regina would have been happy if everyone ate freeze-dried space meals.

True to her word, Edna took me to the drugstore, where I picked out iron supplements, a tube of mascara and a bottle of pink nail polish. This should have cheered me up, but on the way back to the ranch I felt peculiar.

Edna didn't seem to mind the silence—then she caught sight of me. "What is it?" she asked in alarm.

"Edna, I feel peculiar."

fifteen

do the hokey-pokey and turn yourself around

I thought I felt peculiar in a sensitive, philosophical way, but I was entirely wrong. Edna hauled the car to the side of the road just in time for me to try to release my inner peculiarity. My stomach heaved, but nothing came up. My once-trustworthy carcass was attempting to turn itself inside out, like a double-sided coat.

Long story short: the sensation that I was burning, blurred vision, and a race back home. Edna pounded the horn as she sped down the drive and Sam came running out. He carried me into the house, which made me feel annoyingly helpless. I said, "I thought I was supposed to be better."

"At least she can still talk," said Edna.

"It's a gift," I answered.

"Samuel, look at her face."

"My God!" he said in shock. "How did this happen?"

Sam carried me to my room and put me on the bed. I was dripping in sweat and I kept trying to pull my clothes off, but my fingers had ceased to function. "I'm hot, so hot . . ."

"She was crying. Maybe the tears washed off her sunscreen," Edna said to Sam. "Young lady, did you remember to put on sunscreen before you went out?"

I shook my head and it felt as if my brain was melting and might spill out of my ears. "Shouldn't I be in a hospital?" I asked before I passed out.

Then I dreamed. I dreamed that Oswald was in the room with me and he had Winnie's medical bag. The water was running into the bathtub and he went to the doorway and shouted, "I need more ice!"

Sam dashed in with trays of ice and took them to the tub. He asked Oswald, "What do you want me to do now?"

"Just let me take care of her and I'll call you if I need anything." Oswald closed the door behind Sam and came to me.

He must be playing vet again. "I may ruminate, but I am not a ruminating animal," I said. I was a witty dreamer.

"How do you feel?" Oswald said.

My dream was so vivid that the touch of his hand burned my wrist as he checked my pulse. His eyes were a gentle dove color and I told him so.

He smiled and said, "We need to get your fever down." He began undressing me. In the natural perversity of dreams, his actions were not sexy at all, but beautifully efficient. Even so, I shivered under his hands. He carried me to the bathroom.

The tub was almost full and ice cubes floated on the surface. He slid me into the chilly water and it felt as refreshing as a breeze. I sunk in further, enjoying the sensation. Oswald yanked me up just as my head went under. He grabbed a washcloth, dipped it into the icy water, and draped it across my forehead.

"Milagro, I need you to stay above the surface of the water, okay? Can you do that for me?"

"Oswald, I am not unreasonable. I am a serious and sincere young woman." From my angle below I could see all his eyelashes and the copper tones in his hair. "Your hair is pretty."

"Thank you and please listen to me. You have a temperature of one hundred and eight and I need you to stay awake."

He rushed out of the bathroom and I tried to remember what I had promised him while sliding deep into the water. When he returned with the medical bag, I sat up to admire ice cubes bobbing around my breasts. Oswald filled a glass with water, then opened a plastic bottle and shook out two pills. "Mil, acetaminophen will help bring your fever down."

"You give me fever, Oswald."

He fed me the pills and held the glass to my mouth so that I could drink. Taking a tube from the bag, he said, "This antibiotic ointment will help stop infection. It doesn't sting." After kneeling beside the tub, he very gently stroked the ointment onto my face.

"Oswald . . ." I reached for his hand and placed it on top of my breast. "Oswald, is my heart still beating?"

"Yes, Milagro, your heart is still beating."

"Does your heart beat?" I stretched out my hand to his

chest, but there was no reassuring pulse. "Ah, poor Oswald, you are undead and your heart does not beat!"

He moved my hand to the left side of his chest. I could feel the rhythm beneath my palm. I smiled at him. "You're not heartless."

"No, Mil," he said softly, "I try not to be even if I don't always behave the way I should."

"Don't I mean anything to you?" I asked, but before he could answer, a horrible knifelike pain went through me. I cried out and pulled my knees up, trying to endure it.

"What is it?" Oswald asked anxiously.

The jabbing came again, harder and longer, and I couldn't even speak.

"Milagro, can you describe how it hurts, where it hurts?"

It felt like a sharp knife slashing my organs. It felt like death approaching. "It feels like I need you," I gasped, my eyes pleading with him to help me. He knew what I meant.

Oswald shook his head and said, "It's a craving, Mil, it isn't real."

I grabbed his hand and rubbed it against my teeth. Then I turned it to see the blue veins of his wrist. "Please, please." I curled up in agony, heedless of the water splashing out of the tub. "Please."

I saw the panic in his eyes. Finally, he reached into the medical bag and took out something sharp and shiny, a scalpel. When he cut his index finger a bright scarlet line of blood appeared. I took his finger into my mouth and sucked hungrily. The stabbing pain subsided and I was suddenly aware of being cold. I shivered and goose pimples rose on my flesh.

Oswald placed his hand on my forehead. "Thank God," he said, "thank God." He lifted me out of the tub and wrapped me in a towel.

I leaned into him and he slid his arms around me. I had never felt safer or more loved. "Oswald, let's always stay this way."

"Why do you do this to me?" he groaned as he held me tight. "I need you to fight this, Milagro." He pressed his soft lips to my forehead. "We can get over this."

Then the dream ended. They always end too soon.

sixteen

freak-of-nature girl

It was Winnie who had cared for me. I knew this because I awoke in the wee hours to find her sleeping in the armchair, a blanket tucked around her, her medical bag by her side. I got out of bed quietly, feeling better than I had in weeks, and wrapped a robe over my T-shirt.

Winnie's face was soft and childlike in sleep. Her eyes moved under their delicate bluish lids and I wondered if she was dreaming of inappropriate acts with inappropriate people.

I'd been hoping for the solitude to mull over my intriguing dream, but I wasn't going to get it. In the kitchen, Edna and Sam were slumped at the table, still wearing their clothes from yesterday.

"Young lady, we thought you were . . . ," Edna began, and then paused.

Winnie shuffled into the kitchen looking exhausted, the blanket over her shoulders. "We were *very* concerned."

Feeling as well as I did now, I found it difficult to believe I'd really been so ill. "Thanks for your concern, but I'm really okay." I opened the fridge and spotted a glass bowl of vegetables and rice. As I took it out, the bowl slipped, crashing to the floor and shattering.

Sam said, "Milagro, be careful!" just as I took a step away. At first I didn't feel the shard slice my foot and it took a moment for me to say "Oh, hell."

The vampires began talking and moving at once to help. Standing on my one good foot, I reached down and pulled the shard from my other foot. A crimson crescent welled with blood. We all stared in amazement as the wound quickly closed and the skin seemed to knit over the cut. "Damn," I said. "Damn, what the hell was that?"

Sam moved me to a chair and he and Edna quickly began cleaning the mess. Winnie smiled at me. "Milagro, how many times have you been sick in your life?"

"I don't really get sick. I get headaches sometimes."

"I ran the tests three times and kept getting the same results. Normal white blood cell count might go up to eleven. Someone fighting off pneumonia might go up to twenty."

"What was mine?" I asked.

"Your white cell blood count was one hundred and ten. I've never seen anything like it."

Edna sighed. "I knew this girl was an odd one. I'm going to

bed. I suggest everyone else try to get a little rest now that we know Milagro is over the worst." As she passed me, she briefly put her hand on my shoulder.

"What about the way my foot healed?" I asked.

"I'm so glad for you," Winnie said. "We heal like that, too. So far we haven't been able to isolate one gene that accelerates the healing process. We think it might be multiple factors that act in concordance."

"But I don't share the same gene pool as you," I said.

Winnie rubbed her brow and said, "I'm sorry, I can't explain it. We only know what we know."

Sam looked at Winnie's weary face and said, "I think we should take Grandmama's advice and get a little rest," and then he led Winnie out of the kitchen.

I didn't know whether to feel happy or sad that I was a freak, overjoyed or dismayed that I could heal myself without a physician, delighted or mournful that my interlude with Oswald had only been a dream. I desperately needed something to occupy my mind and this was the right time to begin writing again.

My novel was about a bright, sexy young Latina who unwittingly takes a job with a lobbyist for a corporation that is stealing land from impoverished Central Americans. There was a hunky activist and also troops of zombies representing the powerless peons.

I opened the typewriter case and after some experimentation I figured out how to roll a piece of paper evenly in the machine. I had to hit the keys hard to peck out my first page, with the title *Who Do That Voodoo.* Rewriting on a typewriter was difficult. There's only so much x-ing out a girl can do on a page before it looks like something redacted by the FBI. I decided to act like a shark and move forward only.

The window in front of my desk had a view of a walnut tree and the vineyard beyond. As I worked I saw the limitless sky going from black to cobalt to azure. Wasn't there a story that began, "They did not know the color of the sky"? I knew the color of the sky. It was the clear blue of Sebastian's mad, mad eyes.

At dawn I took a break and ventured into the cozy parlor. I was drawn to a shelf with glass doors to protect the books. Inside were five slender books, collections of short stories by Dena Franklin, the previous owner of my typewriter.

I took one volume and opened the frontispiece. It was a first edition. The table of contents listed the following titles: "A Girl and Her Banker," "Waiting for the Boat to Paris," "Crying over Spilt Gin," "Dinner Party for a Fool," "My City Costume," and "Kindly Indulge My Whim."

After arranging myself attractively on the purple velvet loveseat, I read the first two stories. The writer's delicious, barbed style seemed familiar. The stories were set in big cities and the women wore chic hats and had affairs, while the men gambled, drank excessively, and unexpectedly fell in love with their wives to the dismay of their mistresses.

I flipped to the back of the dust jacket, but there was no information about Franklin. She must have had the sort of life I'd sadly attempted to lead when I was in the City. Only with my life, you would have to replace the debonair ambassador with a scruffy acting student, the designer gowns with garage-sale sundresses, and the penthouse digs with a rat-infested basement.

My stomach growled and I realized that I was starving. In the kitchen, I made a pot o' java and mixed up a pan o' corn bread. I had just finished setting the table when Edna came downstairs as fresh and revived as if she had slept the whole night in a velvet-lined coffin.

"Well, I stand astonished," she said.

"Why not sit astonished?"

Sam and Winnie soon joined us and we ate together like one happy family of the walking undead.

"Sam, do you know where Sebastian's been lately?" I asked.

"He's still in the City and probably expecting that you'll return sooner or later. Would he look for you at your parents'?"

I shrugged. "That's the last place I'd go if I needed help and he knows it." Sebastian knew that the milk of human kindness ne'er flowed from my mother's breasts because she believed it would make them sag.

"Your friends?"

Of my F.U. friends, I only stayed in regular contact with Nancy and she was sworn to secrecy. I realized that I would have to find a way to get to her bridesmaids' tea or fear her wrath forevermore.

Sam rubbed his watchband in a nervous manner.

I said, "Sam, what aren't you telling me now?"

He grimaced. "Gabriel called this morning. CACA broke into your apartment last night. They carted away boxes."

"Wait a minute!" I said, feeling violated and angry. "Breaking and entering is absolutely something the police could have stopped! Gabriel could have called anonymously."

"Mil, all Sebastian has to do is say that he's an old friend and you've asked him to collect some things for you," Sam said all too reasonably. He paused as if debating something.

"What else?" I asked warily.

"One of them spray-painted some graffiti above your bed," he said. " 'Burn in flames, dark-skinned succubus.' "

I let loose a stream of profanities and added, "Wouldn't that be a clue to the cops that these were not my friends?"

"This is negligible compared to many of the things CACA has done across national and international lines, such as union busting, racketeering, bribery . . . Perhaps they thought you had Oswald's address or family information."

My warm corn-bread happiness vanished. "So Sebastian and his neofascist militia are free to ransack my apartment?"

Edna gave me a look out of the corner of her eye. "Really, young lady, you make everything so dramatic."

"Really, Edna, how would you put it?"

"Why should I need to put it in any particular way? I am not the one claiming to be a writer."

For some reason, Sam and Winnie thought this was hilarious. I was furious at Sebastian and annoyed that the vampires didn't seem to think the burglary was awful, so I went to walk it off.

As the dogs ambled around me, I tried to think seriously about my situation. My skin crawled at the idea of Sebastian going through all of my things, fingering my underwear, reading my letters, scoffing at my humble possessions. No doubt he would think me a complete fool for keeping mementos from our time together.

The sun was shining over the glorious mountains that bordered the valley. I saw a white crane standing at the edge of the creek where it pooled into a small pond. The dogs rushed forward, barking wildly, and the bird flew gracefully away.

I was startled by someone shouting, "Bad dogs, bad dogs!" Then I saw Oswald was sitting on a boulder. He stood and said, "The dogs know they're not supposed to bother the egrets."

"I thought it was a crane," I said nervously.

"Cranes are taller," he explained. "This was an egret. They like to fish here."

"Oh, I didn't know they came this far inland."

"Yes, they do." He paused and finally said quietly, "How are you feeling?"

"I'm fine. Evidently I now possess the ability to heal instantly." It sounded more amazing when I said it aloud.

"I just saw Winnie on her way out to work. She told me."

"Don't you think that's bizarre?"

"You're a surprising girl."

His clear gaze unnerved me, and I said, "Well, I better go back."

I thought he would stay where he was, but he fell into step with me. I kept my eyes straight ahead. He occasionally bent over to pet the dogs or throw a stick for them.

When he spoke, his voice was too loud. "You look healthier."

I kept telling myself to act normal. "I feel better."

"High fevers sometimes make people delusional."

"I wasn't at all delusional," I said apprehensively, afraid that

I had said something about Oswald in my sleep that Winnie had overheard.

"You weren't?"

"Not to my recollection. And I will be forever grateful to Winnie for taking care of me and staying by my side all night and making sure I came out of it."

His smile rose up on one side. "Winnie took care of you?"

"Yes, the whole time. She is a very dedicated person," I said pointedly, reminding him of the quality he so admired.

We were silent for uncomfortable minutes before he asked, "Do you like birds?"

What kind of question was this? "I appreciate their role in the ecosystem," said I. "Cranes and egrets are quite lovely. I like little sparrows and robins, of course. I am conflicted about carrion eaters. Hummingbirds are always a delight."

"And what about chickens?"

"Very tasty when roasted."

"Not as a meal. How do you feel about chickens as animals?"

"I have not yet formed an opinion of the chicken."

"I'm so glad to hear that you are not closed-minded about them," he said, and glanced at me, his gray eyes gleaming with good humor.

"I am willing to hear any reasonable argument in defense of or against those of the chickenish species," I rambled on.

Oswald laughed and I felt such relief that we were on safer ground that I laughed, too. He said, "Most people these days seem to confuse 'fowl' with 'foul.' "

"Alas, one of the perils of the homonym."

Oswald picked up an old tennis ball in the grass and with a fluid movement hurled it into the distance.

Searching for another safe topic, I ventured, "So how are your veterinary studies going, Oswald?"

He was delighted by the turn of conversation and grinned widely. "I'm thinking about applying to school next year."

"Well, good luck. Do you have all your prerequisites?"

"I suppose," he said nonchalantly. "Perhaps you could write a letter of recommendation for me. I would really appreciate it."

"I'm sure you could find a better reference," I said. "But I could say how in touch you are with all that is beastly."

"That's good. Say that I have an innate appreciation of animal instincts. I can sense what animals are feeling even if they lack the ability to express their desires." His facile mouth turned up at the corners.

Bad thoughts flitted through my bad brain, and I felt the need to put the conversation on safer ground. "Oswald, you promised that you'd help me in any way you could."

"Mmm?" he said. It was a cautious "mmm."

"My friend is having a bridesmaids' tea. It's in the City." I told him the time and date and said, "You're going to loan me your car."

"I don't think so," Oswald began. "Gabriel's said that CACA is still—"

"Oh, don't even start with me, Oswald Grant. One, I'm going. Two, Gabriel's not going to know. Three, you're going to cover for me."

"Is there a four?" Oswald asked grimly.

"Yes. Four, you promised."

He looked unconvinced. "What if I tell Gabriel and the family?"

"Do you plan to hold me against my will?" I asked, and I immediately regretted my choice of words.

"If you're determined to go, I'll take you. I'll even come up with an excuse for where we're going," he said. "Someone's got to make sure you don't get into trouble."

"Well, that's reassuring," I said sarcastically. "After all, you've never caused me any trouble." I held back my smile of satisfaction that I would be seeing Nancy-pants soon.

We ran into Edna, who was returning from the barn with a basket full of fresh eggs. "Oswald," said Edna, "whatever are you going on about?"

"Good morning, Grandmama. I was just telling Mil that I'd like to go to veterinary school."

"That's the most preposterous thing I've ever heard." Edna waved her hand at him and went into the house.

Oswald leaned toward me and said quietly, "You see, no one supports my intellectual pursuits." His eyes strayed downward to my breasts. Intellectual pursuits, my less-opulent-than-usual ass. "Well, I've got things to do, people to see," he said, and then jogged off toward the cottage, the dogs scampering joyfully around him.

I wrote several pages that day, taking short breaks to imagine ways that I would enact my vengeance upon Sebastian Beckett-Witherspoon. Some French guy said vengeance was a dish best served cold, but when the opportunity arose, I would make my retaliation as hot and painful as a *habañero* on a raw cut.

seventeen

sense and insensibility

When Ernie finished building the fence, Edna and I went shopping for plants. I'd mapped out a route to a few excellent nurseries in the area. I was waiting by the car when she came out of the house wearing a snazzy white eyelet shirt with pale blue slacks and darling white slip-ons. "Edna, I miss my own clothes."

"You don't mention your parents, but you miss your clothes."

"The clothes treated me better."

"I *saw* some of your clothes and I beg to differ," she said snidely.

Instead of succumbing to an urge to say something snippy, I asked, "Do you think we can do a little clothes shopping after we buy plants?"

All Edna said was, "Come along. Snap to it."

I realized it was one of those "sn" days: everything would be snappy, snippy, snotty, snooty, snazzy, snide, et cetera. Considering the options before me, I resolved to be snoopy.

We took the big truck. Edna handled it easily over the grades and turns. "Edna, where did you grow up?"

"Are you quizzing me?"

"It's just a generic question for two gals on a road trip."

"Oh, goody. Next you'll propose holding up a gas station and dancing on a bar top."

"No need to be snarky, Edna," I said, although I'd always enjoyed dancing on bar tops. I leaned back against the seat. Really, a girl can never see too much of chartreuse countryside, purple fields of lupine, and hills yellow with wild mustard. We passed large ostentatious vineyard estates, modest ranch houses, and dilapidated shacks.

"Edna, you see those trees with pink blossoms? They're the native western redbud."

"Did your father teach you about gardening?"

I was surprised that she knew about my father until I remembered that they had read my unauthorized bio. "No, he is big on lawns and perfectly trimmed everything. He likes boxwood, junipers, and low-maintenance ground covers."

"Your mother, then?"

My laugh sounded harsh even to my own ears. "My mother Regina would never sully her hands in soil! No, one of the guys on my father's crew used to be a garden designer in Nicaragua." I told her about Cesar, the middle-aged man who had been wild for dramatic foliage. He had shown me how to examine root growth, look for disease, and appreciate both the ordinary and the extraordinary. "I was his protégée," I said. "Have you ever been someone's protégée?"

"Einstein had great hopes for me."

"Albert Einstein!"

"You should see the look on your face," Edna chortled as she parked the car.

I said, "Har, har, har, very hilarious." I yanked my sun hat further down on my head and we got out of the car. I didn't have time to feel foolish because we were at a wonderful family-run nursery that specialized in rose varieties over a hundred years old. The roses growing on the fence were pruned to perfection.

We walked through the aisles and a short, plain woman came out of the store and said, "Can I help you?"

"Whoever is pruning your roses is a master," I said.

"That's me," she said.

We had a fascinating discussion about different pruning techniques while Edna walked around reading plant descriptions scrawled on laminated cards.

Edna liked some of the creamy roses and I said, "White roses are perfect for an evening garden. They almost glow in the dark." We chose some tea-noisette and hybrid musk roses. My heart soared when I spotted a very healthy *Rosa englanteria* in a two-gallon pot. "Edna, this is Shakespeare's wild rose! 'I know a bank where the wild thyme blows / With sweet musk roses, and with eglantine.' You've got to have it."

"Fine, I'll take it. Now choose something for yourself."

I looked around carefully. In honor of the vampires, I decided upon sanguinea, a China rose with bloodred flowers.

At the next nursery, the sturdy middle-aged owner talked effusively to Edna about fruit trees. He insisted on giving her a discount on a persimmon and three espaliered pears that would go against the fence. I grabbed some pretty deciduous shrubs.

The owner even volunteered to arrange the plants in the back of our truck to accommodate the young trees. As we watched him I said, "Edna, I have totally lost sense of our original planting scheme."

"Do you want lunch or not?"

It was well past noon and I was hungry. "I want lunch and we've totally lost sense of our original planting scheme."

"Who cares? There's a pretty good little Mexican joint nearby."

"We forgot to get lilacs."

"We can get lilacs next time," she said, and I almost clapped my hands in delight.

She drove to a small diner with a faded sign outside that said JOE'S GRILL. We walked through the screen door into a dark, cool restaurant with six tables covered with bright oilcloth. My mouth watered at the scent of *frijoles* and *carnitas.* A calendar from a tortilla factory displayed a brawny Aztec warrior carrying a buxom maiden up a pyramid. I'd be kicking and screaming if any zealot wanted to cut my heart out, no matter how gorgeous he was.

"The chicken with *mole* is always good," Edna said.

"Sounds fab."

The waitress brought us a basket of warm tortilla chips and Edna ordered *mole* and Bohemias for us both. I caught her staring at me and said, "Yes?"

"You're a generally cheerful girl, aren't you?"

I munched on a chip and thought about her question. "My grandmother used to say that I woke up happy."

"You liked her better than your mother?"

I smiled and said in a light tone, "*She* liked me better than my mother Regina liked me." I was halfway through my beer, so I was more forthcoming than usual on this subject. "My mother Regina tried everything to avoid getting pregnant. And when she did, she starved herself until her doctor had to put her on an IV. She went downhill skiing in her third trimester. She 'forgot' me at the mall when I was three months old."

Maybe it was because Edna had finished most of her beer, but she was fighting to maintain an even expression. Then a chuckle came out. By the time I said "She bought an above-ground pool and let me play in it unsupervised. She told me I was old enough to cross the street by myself when I was three. She fed me meats past their sell-by dates!" we were both howling.

"How horrible!" Edna finally managed to say.

"Well, they don't taste that bad if you use lots of catsup." I told her that my grandmother finally threatened to go to the police if I had any more "accidents."

"My grandmother, my *abuelita,* pretty much raised me from the time I was an infant until I was almost ten. I went to my parents on weekends."

Our food had arrived and Edna ordered a second round of beer. "What happened then?"

"My grandmother died in a car accident and my mother Regina cut off connections with the rest of the family." I shrugged. It had been a shock to go from my *abuelita*'s cozy, crowded home to my parents' antiseptic, white-on-white, lifeless house.

"Why do you call her that? 'My mother Regina'?"

"Because then I can treat her like a character, not a person."

"And your father?"

"Oh, he worships the ground she walks on." When I had cried for my grandmother, my mother Regina would lock me in my room, on the far side of the house, away from her and my father. "My friend Nancy thinks that my mother Regina is a sociopath." I fought against the tears welling in my eyes.

"Young lady, there's no shame in mourning the loss of love," Edna said, and patted my hand.

"Ah, but there is shame in letting our food get cold," I said, determined not to let my mother Regina ruin a good meal.

After lunch we bought perennials, herbs, annuals, seeds, pruners, leather gloves, and sturdy trowels. I would be properly garbed for garden work, but there was the rest of my life to consider. "Edna, I apologize, but I need some new clothes and I don't have any money."

"You don't need new clothes. No one ever sees you and you're certainly dressed better than when you came here."

"I had an absolutely marvelous wardrobe and I *do* need clothes."

"Why? I thought you wanted to write. What sort of clothes are required for sitting at a typewriter?"

I couldn't tell her that I needed a stylish puce outfit for Nancy's party, so I thought of another approach. "I bet Dena Franklin wore terrifically glamorous ensembles when she wrote. How am I supposed to be inspired when I feel so hideously drab?"

Stunningly, Edna conceded. She drove to the prosperous little town on the other side of the mountain. As she searched for a parking space, I peered in the boutique windows. Most had a "sexy is too vulgar for us" aesthetic that I could not begin to embrace. Edna parked, got out of the car, and directed me down the street.

"Here we are," she said, and stopped in front of a shop called Ye Olde Rose and Grape Consignment Charitee Shoppe. Perhaps she thought I would be interested in a whalebone corset. She saw my disappointment and snapped, "You really try my patience."

To Edna's credit, there were no buskins, bustles, or other historical garments in the shoppe. I had looked up "puce" in the dictionary. The color, brilliant purplish red, was more appealing than the origin of the word, which meant flea-colored. I scanned the racks for puce items, but the only thing I could find was a skimpy dark plum knit dress that was a size too small and showed all the deficiencies of my WWII-era bra. I decided that fitting in with the theme was more important than my vanity, so I took the dress.

I discovered a slinky sleeveless dress in hot pink, a pair of tight capri pants in turquoise silk with a snug-fitting matching shell, a black chiffon skirt that floated nicely around my bottom, and a white cashmere sweater embroidered with beads. I also selected cute beige heeled sandals with tiny seashells on the straps, simple black loafers, and, joy of joys, leopard-print sandals with narrow heels.

After we left, I said, "Thanks, Edna. Now where do we go for underwear?"

"You already have perfectly functional underwear."

"I do not. My bras are all rumply. Look," I said, and thrust out my chest to demonstrate. "It is very humiliating seeing people staring at my chest and thinking that I don't know how to buy a bra that fits." As I said this a teenage boy walked by and snickered. "See what I mean?"

"I'm sure that's not what they're thinking when they look at your chest."

"Edna," I said, and quoted Dena Franklin, "kindly indulge my whim."

She gazed at me with those feline eyes and I thought it was a complete waste that she wasn't off seducing and abandoning elderly ministers of state. "You are a ridiculous girl. Why can't you just say that you want pretty lingerie?"

I pondered various answers and decided on the truth. "It sounds so frivolous."

"Young lady, frivolity has its place. A lady should have nice undergarments to please herself."

"Fine. I'd like some nice undergarments to please myself."

She led me to a small shop filled with bleak natural-fiber garments in the front and exquisite European lingerie in the back. The clerks greeted her so obsequiously that I wondered what Edna's underwear drawer looked like. My *patrona* handed me a wad of cash and went to the corner café to wait for me.

I couldn't decide if a deep and sincere lady would wear demure white lacy undergarments or worldly black or red silk.

I thought the most sensible route was to buy some of each kind, so I did.

While meandering toward the café, I passed shops for imported kitchen goods, shoes, and wines. A store called Oaxaca caught my attention and I detoured into it. The tiny shop had swell crafts from Mexico: matte black pottery, silver jewelry, paintings of the Virgin de Guadalupe, and crepe paper flowers.

A skinny chick behind the counter in elaborate Frida Kahlo garb said, "*Hola.*" Her dark brown hair was braided into a crown on her head, two caterpillar brows sat above huge dark eyes, and her lipstick was bright red. I was dying to run back to the ranch and pencil in my eyebrows.

"*Hola,*" I replied. "Great stuff."

"Thanks. I take a few trips a year to buy it," she said pleasantly with no inflection. She was an assimilated Latina like me.

"Cool job," I said enviously. "Is your family from Oaxaca?"

"Yeah, and Taxco. That's where I buy most of my jewelry."

I found a miniature shelf filled with tiny replicas of kitchen items. I thought Edna might like it and took it to the counter. The shop owner wrapped it in a turquoise bag, and I happily sauntered out of the shop.

Just as I stepped onto the sidewalk an eerily familiar voice cried, "Milagro!"

I turned to see Kathleen Baker staring at me. She and a cohort were laden with packages. I stepped back into the store and said to the owner, "Is there a back exit? There's someone I don't want to see."

In a moment I was crouching behind the counter under a brightly colored oilcloth.

"What the hell!" Kathleen said as she entered the store.

"What is it?" her friend asked.

"The oddest thing," Kathleen said. "I could have sworn I just saw this girl who used to be my reading consultant."

I heard footsteps approaching the counter. "Miss, did a young woman come in here just a second ago?"

"Sorry, *señora,*" said the store owner.

"You've got to stop mixing Vicodin with vodka," Kathleen's friend said. "That doctor upset you. There's no such thing as being 'addicted' to plastic surgery. It's simply good manners to look good."

Kathleen ignored her friend's comment and said, "This girl, Milagro, took off who knows where, and Sebastian Beckett-Witherspoon is dying to find her."

My heart stopped at his name.

The bread heiress prattled on. "I don't know why. She always looked a little slutty, if you want to know the truth. Am I the only one who thinks real breasts are gauche?"

"Oh, no, they're awful, so tacky and jiggly," said her friend. "But maybe Sebastian has a taste for that sort of thing." They chortled away at my expense.

"I doubt it. He's been seeing a remarkable young woman, Tessie Kensington. Very refined, excellent family."

So Sebastian was back with Tessie. How very predictable.

My knees and back ached by the time they selected and paid for several *luminarias,* one *retablo,* and three silver bracelets.

When they were finally gone, I shook out my legs and stretched. "Thanks for covering for me."

"*De nada,*" the shop owner said, and looked me over. "Don't pay attention to those nasty *viejas.* You look wonderful."

"Thanks, *mujer,*" I said gratefully. "For everything."

I peered out the door and then made a dash for the café.

"Where have you been?" Edna said, but she didn't wait for an answer as she headed for the car.

If I told her that I'd been spotted by one of Sebastian's friends, the vampires would never let me leave the ranch again. Besides, what was the likelihood of being spotted again by someone who knew me? I told Edna that I'd been browsing in a bookstore, but I surreptitiously kept glancing back to see if Kathleen's blue Mercedes was following us.

I didn't relax until we returned to the ranch and I saw two sweaty, dirty men sitting on boulders in the garden. Ernie and Oswald had edged the planting beds with rocks carted from the creek.

"Hope you don't mind," said Ernie. "We went ahead and got these rocks. I thought you might like the gray ones."

Most of the stones were a foot in width and a dark slate color. "They're perfect," I said. "Thank you."

"Very nice, Ernie," said Edna. "Oswald, don't you have something better to do with your time than help Ernie?"

No matter what Oswald did, he riled his grandmother.

Oswald hung his head. "Guess I could get to some paperwork," he said, but I saw him wink at Ernie.

What on earth was he doing in that cottage? He couldn't actually be studying veterinary medicine, could he? I watched him as he strolled off. He wore a T-shirt that said "Use an accordion, go to Cotati. It's the law." The fabric hung loosely from his muscular shoulders to his nice, firm—and then I stopped myself. I was transferring my ridiculous dream of a dashing and capable Oswald to the reality of an aimless and nitwitty Oswald.

I realized that Edna and Ernie were watching me. I assumed a neutral expression. "Ernie, can you help me unload the truck?"

When we were sliding the trees out, I said casually, "Edna doesn't seem to approve of Oswald."

Ernie looked at me as if I was clueless. "He's her favorite."

"But she's always criticizing him."

"Oh, that's her way, like she is with you. You don't take it serious, do you?"

I wasn't going to admit that I'd begun to like her barbs and the opportunity to respond. "Nope."

"Oswald don't either. They disagree on some things but there's lots of love there." He leaned against the truck and brushed back his black hair. "They're complicated people, *mi amor.*"

eighteen

the wind beneath my (chicken) wings

I knew where I wanted the persimmon and the pears in the garden, but I had to decide about everything else. Creamy roses would clamber over the fence and gates. I designed an herb knot with sage, oregano, lavender, and thyme. After placing the plants, I began to dig them in. My brow grew damp and I could feel the grittiness of the soil on my face.

When I was finished planting, I looked up to see Oswald standing nearby and watching me. He held a chicken that was making a charming "brrr-brrr" sound.

"You're angled," he said.

At first I thought he was making some crude observation about my body. But he was looking at the persimmon tree. He was right; I'd planted it crooked.

He put down the chicken, a stylish black-and-white deco model with a red thingy on its head. The chicken immediately set about pecking the ground.

"I'll fix it," I said, and picked up the shovel just as he reached for it.

"I'll help you," he said.

The backs of our hands brushed. Even through my gloves, I felt a surge that made me give up the shovel and step back.

"Some things are better done with a partner," he said calmly.

I'm sure it was an innocent comment about shared labor. "Many hands make light work," I babbled. "Be careful of the roots."

He wielded the shovel dexterously. "You know, some people think I have good motor skills. Especially small motor skills."

Was he trying to impress me or trying to flirt? I centered the tree trunk in the ground and he stood so close that his breath was warm on my cheek. I couldn't help glancing into his eyes, silver as trout flashing through water in this light. Something about Oswald made me feel crazy and I looked away. "You have never apologized. Now that I know how nice Winnie is, it's even worse."

He shoveled the dirt back around the roots. Once, his shoulder touched mine and another time his leg slipped against my thigh. I made sure not to flinch from his touch even though the sensation was as disturbing as sticking my hand into a fire while jumping into an icy pool.

"You can let go," he said. The tree was straight now. "Don't be so sure you know everything about my relationship with Winnie."

"Let me guess. It's one of those continental, urbane vampire liaisons where you are permitted to have lovers so long as you spend Sunday dinner with the family." I watched a glistening drop of perspiration slide down his throat and into his shirt.

"We're not vampires," he said, "and when I get married, I want a wife who will be as faithful to me as I am to her."

"Oh, don't even presume to talk to me about faithfulness."

"Milagro, I wish the circumstances were different and I've been trying to change them," he said earnestly. "But I need cooperation. I can't do it on my own." He turned and left me standing there.

Agh, why did I suddenly feel as if I'd been the one behaving badly? "You forgot your chicken," I yelled.

Oswald didn't stop walking, but shouted back, "It's for you. It's your garden chicken. Her name is Petunia."

When is a chicken just a chicken and when is a chicken an apology? Like many great thinkers before me, I was unable to answer this important metaphysical question.

I wrote like a maniac until I realized that the afternoon was almost over. I had to get ready for Nancy's party and Oswald was nowhere to be seen. I dressed in the dark plum knit dress and the black strappy shoes. The dress fit even more snugly than I remembered, so I put on a sweater to cover myself until I got to the Croft. I made a few skinny braids and pulled them back with the rest of my hair into a ponytail.

I examined the demurely made-up face in the mirror and

remembered how I'd tried to fit in at Kathleen's party. Oh, hell, some people were just not meant to be demure. After letting my hair down, I added more eyeshadow and mascara and lipstick. I felt better immediately. I so wanted to see Nancy again, and I felt that marvelous anticipation of going out on the town again, of the City at night.

There was a rap at my bedroom door. I opened it to see Oswald looking remarkably stylish in a charcoal-gray suit and lavender shirt. His chestnut hair was still damp from a shower and brushed straight off his forehead. "You ready to go?" he asked.

"About time," I whispered. "What are we telling them?"

He walked out to the kitchen and I followed close behind. Edna was reading a cookbook at the table. She looked at us suspiciously.

"Grandmama, I'm taking Milagro to a lecture."

"A lecture," she repeated, deadpan.

"On cactus. One of the wineries is having a talk by an Australian horticulturalist."

"Hmm, is that right?" Edna did not look entirely convinced that Oswald was telling the truth.

"Yes, Edna," I said sincerely. "Not cacti especially, but hardy succulents that can survive freezes. I'm also interested in the yucca and epiphytes. You can come with us if you like, or I can take notes for you."

Edna's smile was cruel. "Oh, take notes, please," she said. "I'll look them over tomorrow."

"There's a wine and cheese thing afterward," said Oswald. "So don't hold dinner for us."

"Fine," said Edna, and just stared at us.

I stared right back before turning to Oswald with a smile. "Almost forgot a notepad," I said. "I'll meet you outside."

I went to the study and grabbed a notepad and pen from the desk. I also snuck a gardening book on xeriscapes in my purse.

Oswald looked pleased with himself when I got into the car.

"Cactus?" I asked.

"You're kind of a prickly personality," he offered. "Besides, I didn't want to make the lecture too tempting for my grandmother. She might have joined us."

Once on the highway, I took the garden book out of my purse and flipped through to a section on succulents.

Oswald kept his eyes on the road and said, "You're going to get a headache if you try to read and write."

"If I want medical advice, I'll ask Winnie."

I did get a headache, but I'd also written several pages of flagrantly tedious notes. After placing the notepad and book at my feet, I said, "That should bore the heck out of Edna."

Oswald smiled. "You should be grateful that she didn't tell Sam. He wouldn't have let you go."

"He couldn't stop me."

"He would have argued persuasively and you would have buckled." Oswald shifted from his normal voice to Sam's more modulated tone and characteristic hesitation. "Mil-a-gro, it is in-cum-bent upon our famil-y to ensure your well-be-ing."

I couldn't help laughing. "Don't be unkind to Sam."

"I'm not being unkind. I admire Sam. He'd be right anyway. Sam is always right." Oswald then pulled over to the side of the road and parked. He turned toward me and I panicked, thinking that he was going to make a pass at me. I looked everywhere but at his face, waiting for the inevitable and thinking that I'd been a fool to give him another opportunity to treat me like a disposable amusement.

"Milagro, are you absolutely sure that you need to go to this party? Your friends may well tell Beckett-Witherspoon."

"I promised," I said.

Ho, now he'd suggest we stop at some motel or tell me that his car seats reclined!

"Okay," he said with a sigh. "I just thought I'd give you a chance to change your mind." He started the engine again and off we went to the Hotel Croft.

Oswald found a parking space near the hotel. I got out of the car and started to walk to the Croft, when he took hold of my shoulder. "A few ground rules," he said as gloomily as if he was telling me I had inoperable ugliness. "We use the side entrance because we don't need the staff to notice us. You go straight to the party, and you'll meet me in the bar in exactly an hour. Any problems, you meet me by the car. Got it?"

"An hour? An hour's not enough time to have fun. Three hours." We bickered and settled on one hour and forty-seven minutes.

He steered me to the side entrance of the hotel and said, "Be careful, Milagro. And have fun."

"That is my intention." I took off my sweater and handed it to him. "Take care of this for me, would you?"

Oswald stared at me from head to foot, but mostly lingered on those regions that were neither my head nor my feet. He asked, "That's what you're wearing?"

"It's puce. The theme of the party is puce. What's wrong with it?"

"It's not what's wrong with it that's the problem," Oswald said as he took my sweater.

I looked critically at Oswald's outfit. "Why were you wearing that old suit at Kathleen's party?" I asked.

"Sometimes I like to wear my grandfather's old clothes."

"Well, sometimes I like to wear puce," I lied, and then headed for the elevators. Once out of Oswald's sight, I couldn't help grinning with delight at seeing my pal again.

Nancy had given me a room number on the third floor. I assumed it was for a small suite where her other friends and I would exchange clever banter and swill champagne while Nancy flitted around the room. What I did not expect was a reception room with a huge crowd of tipsy, mostly blond young women dressed in pink and shouting over a five-piece combo playing popular love songs.

I plunged into the crowd and saw a few vaguely familiar F.U. faces and a lot of strangers. I recognized one of Nancy's sorority pals and was about to say hello when she thrust an empty glass toward me. "Get me a refill," she ordered.

"What?"

She peered through a wave of honey-colored hair and laughed. "Oh, it's you. I thought you were a cocktail waitress in that dress." The girls nearby, in delicate blush ensembles, snickered. "Didn't Nancy tell you to wear puce?"

I could feel the heat rise in my face. "This *is* puce. Where's Nancy?"

The girl pointed across the room and I forged into the

crowd. I found her standing shoeless on top of a chair, singing "Get Me to the Church on Time." Nancy looked like a grown-up version of the cutest kid in kindergarten. She had sandy curls, rosy cheeks, a saucy turned-up nose, twinkly blue eyes, and a petite body. She was wearing a filmy little pink slip dress held up with tiny straps.

I took her hand and pulled her off the chair.

"Silly Milly!" she cried, and gave me a hug. "I thought you didn't love me anymore."

"Nancy, you know that I love you madly. I thought this was a bridesmaids' party, and why is everyone wearing pink?"

She either flashed the peace sign at a waiter or signaled to him to bring two glasses of bubbly. "My mother always says it's just as easy to entertain ninety as nine and I told you it was puce. The whole thing is puce."

"I looked it up in the dictionary, Nance. Puce means purple-red and flea-colored."

We both said, "Eewh," and the waiter brought us drinks. We toasted to her engagement and she said, "So how's that cute guy coming along? Oh, I mean your writing."

"My writing is swell. I'm so totally in the zone it's like I'm *channeling* the zombie dialogue. The guy didn't work out," I said grimly. "Nance, why do you think I always end up with the beach reads, instead of a work of literature—guywise."

"That's easy. Literature got you through those years with your mother Regina. But now you need balance, and that's what the beach reads have been for. It's all Chang and Lee."

"Chang and Lee were Siamese twins. You mean yin and yang. So do you think I'm destined for a life of beach reads?"

"Mil, why do *I* have to do all the hard critical thinking? It makes my head hurt. You just need to find a guy who's fun *and* serious, too. Like that guy in that book you like."

"Which guy in which book?"

"All of them," she answered. "Speaking of guys, you'll never guess what's up with Sebastian."

"Don't tell me he's still calling you!"

"Not me, but Todd's been talking to him. Did you know B-W and Tessie are a thing again? Do you like her ring better than mine?" Nancy waggled her left hand at me and I was momentarily blinded by some huge glittery thing attached to her finger.

"How would I know?"

Nancy shrugged a bare shoulder. "She's coming over here. Just sneak a glance at her hand."

I turned and saw Tessie making her way through a conga line of dancers and heading straight in my direction. I knew Tessie was pretty because everyone else said so. She had small features and monochromatic coloring: brown hair, hazel eyes, lightly tanned skin. She had never been my friend, but she'd tolerated me as Sebastian's little pal. Funny, she didn't look so tolerant anymore.

"Nancy, I've got to run. Fabulous soirée." I kissed her cheek and moved through the crowd toward the door. I heard someone calling, "Wait, wait!" but I kept going.

nineteen

the tingling sensation means it's working

Unfortunately a girl dressed in puce is easy to spot in a sea of pink. Once out the door, I raced down the hall. I found a stairwell and hurried down, but Tessie proved to be surprisingly swift in her tasteful sling-back shoes. I finally managed to ditch her by darting into the basement, hiding in the parking garage, and then taking the elevator back to the lobby. I paused to catch my breath before I went into the bar.

Oswald was a picture of elegance, relaxing in a leather chair, listening to the pianist. At a nearby table, women in business suits cast hungry looks in Oswald's direction.

As I drew near, Oswald said, "Has it been an hour and forty-seven minutes already?"

I slipped into the chair across from his and took a sip of his

Scotch. "I've decided that it's better to be safe than sorry. A stitch in time saves nine. Get going while the going's good."

He was instantly alert. "What happened?"

Editing always improved a story, so I said, "I spotted a girl who dates Sebastian and left immediately."

"Did she see—oh, why the hell am I even asking?" Oswald took out his wallet and put money on the table. "Let's go." He handed me my sweater and then grabbed my hand and pulled me after him. The businesswomen glared at me with envy; obviously Oswald couldn't wait to get me to his room.

"Side exit," he said brusquely.

"I'm sure she didn't see me and won't say anything even if she did somehow find out . . ." I was saying as I trotted along with Oswald. We turned into a hall that led to the side exit. Sebastian and Tessie were facing each other and I heard her say, "Sebastian, you'd better be telling me the truth."

I would have loved to listen further. Even more, I would have loved to take off my shoe and beat Sebastian to a pulp. I think Oswald sensed my forward momentum because I was suddenly yanked sideways into a closet. I was tightly wedged between Oswald and a linen hamper. Oswald eased the door shut and we stood face-to-face in the pine cleanser–scented darkness.

Tessie's muffled voice became clearer as she and Sebastian came down the hall. Their footsteps stopped directly in front of the closet. My heart raced and I expected Sebastian to fling open the door. Instead I heard Tessie say, "Where is she? Where did you hide that slut?"

Oswald and I were so close that his chin rested on my head and I felt the rise and fall of his chest.

"Tessie, I swear to you that I haven't seen her and I don't want to see her. Besides, I didn't even know it was Nancy's party. You just told me it was a pink tea."

"Puce," Tess said with a sniff.

"Puce is a purple-red color," Sebastian corrected.

"It's just too coincidental. And how do I ever trust you again after what happened in college?" There was a sob in her voice. "I can't believe I was so stupid that I didn't realize what you were doing at first when you wanted me to wear that black wig and trashy lingerie. You were having sex with me, but fantasizing about Milagro De Los Santos!"

Oswald's body shuddered and I realized he was stifling a laugh. In order to assist his stifling, I kicked his shin.

"Tessie, let's not get sidetracked by the past," Sebastian said soothingly. "Let's be logical. You might have expected her to show up at Nancy's party. They are friends."

Tessie's crying subsided. "Maybe you're right, Sebastian. It's just that when I saw her, all that old stuff came up again. Tell me that you love me."

"I love you, Tessie. You are my favorite girl," Sebastian said, and the phrase was like a knife in my heart. "Why don't you freshen up and go back to the party? I'll come get you in a few hours."

"Okay."

Footsteps padded off and I thought the coast was clear. I was reaching for the doorknob when Oswald pushed my arm down to my side. Then I heard Sebastian's voice again.

"Peters, I've got a situation here at the Croft. De Los Santos has been spotted again. I want a team here within fifteen minutes and this time don't let that bitch get away." Then there was silence.

This was the perfect opportunity to jump out and clobber Sebastian. I felt around in the darkness, searching for something heavy and hard. My hand fumbled over a stack of toilet-paper rolls before discovering a broom handle. Before I could act, though, Oswald wound one arm tightly around me and covered my mouth with his hand.

Instinctively, I bit down, feeling the flesh between my teeth and hearing his sharp intake of breath. His body was pressed against me, and we both knew that if I bit harder, I would break the skin, taste his blood again. He nuzzled my ear and whispered softly, "Please, Milagro," and I didn't know if he meant please do or please don't or please don't stop.

My chance to commit felonious assault on Sebastian was slipping away because I was overwhelmed by the contact with Oswald, the feel of his flesh between my teeth, his body warm against mine, and my depraved desire to taste his blood once again. I thought, just one more second and one more and one more and I will push this vampire away and then attack Sebastian Beckett-Witherspoon, but the seconds kept passing.

Oswald finally released me. I shoved him as forcefully as I could in the confined space. "Don't ever grab at me again, Oswald," I hissed.

He slowly opened the closet door and peered out. "I had to keep you quiet. You were about to kill Beckett-Witherspoon."

"What if I was?"

"This is not the place or time, Milagro. Please let's get you out of here and somewhere safe."

I would never be safe as long as Oswald was nearby, but it was better to leave before Sebastian's troops arrived. Storming past Oswald, I went down the hall and out of the Croft into the chilly night. I pulled my sweater on and buttoned it up to my chin. I felt dirty. Not only had I starred in Sebastian's sick fantasies, but I was so pathetic that I still desired a man who was both engaged and uninterested in me.

We got safely to the car. Oswald drove quickly and I stared out the window. Once we were into the woods, he said, "I don't know what we should tell the family about tonight."

"Do you need to tell them anything?"

"I suppose they don't need to know that I snuck you into the City, that Sebastian almost caught us . . ." He paused. "And certainly not how he dressed his girlfriend like you for sex games." Oswald glanced my way and a smile turned up the corner of his mouth.

"We will never speak of this again," I said, and slumped in my seat.

twenty

shaken and bestirred

The next day, I threw myself into my writing. Focusing on the skin maladies of zombies was far easier than dealing with my emotional turmoil. In my excitement about Nancy's party, I had forgotten the downside of social events: snotty rich girls who treated you badly, depraved ex-boyfriends, and fabulous men who were frustratingly unavailable.

I hadn't realized it was late until Edna knocked on my door and announced, "Time to help with dinner, young lady."

I put away my few pages and followed her into the kitchen. "Edna, I've always associated country life with drinking martinis in the evening."

"You've read too much Cheever."

"I thought you said you didn't know anything about books."

"Ha!" Edna cried. "I said I didn't *look* like someone who knew about books. But I suppose we could have a cocktail." She turned to Sam, who'd walked into the kitchen. "Samuel?"

"Count me in. I'll meet you out front."

Edna had an extensive variety of good booze, unusual liqueurs, mixers, garnishes, and recipe books. I thought that she might understand the allure of a drink in a coconut.

Red still attracted me, so I decided to make strawberry daiquiris. Edna stopped me when I was about to dump rum from the bottle into the blender and made me measure it in a jigger.

Winnie returned from the clinic just as we were setting out drinks and snacks on the terrace. The sun glowed low over the mountains. We were quiet for some time, listening to the birds calling, leaves rustling in the breeze.

There should be an expression for this pleasant mood. Other languages had phrases to describe elusive feelings, like *esprit d'escalier.* We seemed to be sharing a relaxed and companionable mood, and I was sure it would sound better in Spanish, like *espíritu de los cocteles.*

I thought of Ernie and asked, "Do you ever invite Ernie for drinks?"

"Ernie prefers it when we go to the barn and drink beer with him," Sam said.

"In the barn?"

"Yes, he's got a one-bedroom apartment there. The first door on the left. He also owns a few properties in town."

The vampires talked of the news, current events, and whatnot. Winnie had a radiance that I attributed to her being in love and being loved. Meanwhile, I was badly dressed, penniless, and alone—and my former boyfriend wanted to drive a stake through my heart. I vowed not to think of Sebastian and to enjoy the peaceful sunset, but then Gabriel's truck came trundling down the drive.

After all the vamps had greeted Gabriel, he gave me a warm hug. I was enjoying his lies about how marvelous I looked when I saw Oswald strolling across the field toward us.

We poured more drinks as the sun slid behind the mountains beyond and the sky turned a pure sapphire. Oswald sat between Winnie and me, and he took her hand. I turned away to look at Gabriel, who was standing in front of me, leaning back against a pillar. "Milagro, thought you'd want to know that Beckett-Witherspoon's driver, Peters, has almost fully recovered."

"Perhaps he will learn from this incident," I mused. "Perhaps he will see the error of his ways and not insult and kidnap innocent girls."

The vampires exchanged skeptical looks with one another.

My *espíritu de los cocteles* was ruined entirely when Gabriel told me that my landlord had had all my things hauled away by Goodwill. Had my bosoms meant so very little to him? Perhaps their only power lay in their proximity. So far from the City, they had no influence.

"From thrift store you came and unto thrift store you shall return," I said sorrowfully. My things were meager, but they were still mine: salvaged chairs, fake jewelry, chipped coffee mugs, and used books. Most could be replaced, but I couldn't replace the photos I'd loved most, those of my *abuelita*.

Winnie reached across Oswald and put her hand on mine. Her gesture pushed us all together a bit and I could feel Oswald's body tense. She said softly, "I'm so sorry, Milagro."

Edna stood up and said, "Come help me with dinner," even though I hadn't finished my drink. When I was cutting the basil and inhaling the pungent herby scent, she said, "Maybe it is a good time for you to start over, young lady."

"It's harder to start without anything to start with."

"On the contrary, it's easier to begin when you're not dragging around the past," she said. "Don't burn the rice."

During dinner, I thought about starting with a clean slate, and I remembered one of the short stories I'd just read. A young woman loses both her bank account and wardrobe when her transvestite boyfriend takes off with an heiress. Instead of succumbing to self-pity, the young woman seduces and marries the heiress's father and has him disinherit the wayward couple. Thinking about the character's pluck and ingenuity cheered me.

"Edna, I am very much liking these stories by Dena Franklin," I said. "What's her connection to this family?"

"She was someone we knew," Edna said in her marvelously informative way.

"And?"

"And she wrote fiction. It's rather silly stuff, don't you think?"

"No, not unless you think Henry James is silly. She deals with the same issues of European and American cultures clashing, of new riches and old money, of class, of trust, and betrayal."

"But James was very serious, right?" said Sam.

"Sure, but he's hilarious, too. Franklin's style is light, but that's what she's trying to achieve, like a great flan, you know." They all looked at me as if I was an idiot, so I elaborated. "I mean, flan tastes delicate and silky, but it's got tons of eggs and cream—it's substantial."

"Yum, flan," said Gabriel.

Edna lamented that my opinion was the result of a substandard education. I did not rise to the bait and ask for her academic credentials. I was sure she'd claim that she had been a Rhodes Scholar or transcribed the Bible from the original Aramaic or invented gravity or something.

Oswald stroked his forefinger in a distracting way along his neck, down to his collarbone, and said, "I think Franklin is a delightful writer. You read her stories and can imagine her perfectly. It's as if you know her."

It was odd how he echoed my feelings. "There is something about her writing that seems so . . . I don't know, *identifiable.* Whatever happened to her?" I asked.

"Marriage, children, no time, the usual," Edna said. She then began talking about the vineyard and the possibilities of actually making wine. I didn't listen. I was thinking about marriage and children and writing.

Oswald's presence changed our dynamics more than Gabriel's visit. Instead of being a group, he and Winnie were a couple, and we were extras. After dinner, he sat with his arm around his fiancée's shoulders as we watched *The Philadelphia Story.* Kate Hepburn was a wealthy young divorcée about to marry a dullard, while suave Cary Grant glowered in the background and cynical Jimmy Stewart began to fall for her. A sassy but poor reporter-girl was completely ignored by everyone. Isn't that the way it always is?

After Edna went to bed, Oswald looked at Winnie and said, "Shall we?"

I knew they were engaged, but it still sounded like a lewd proposition. I would rather not think of them together that way.

Winnie frowned and said, "I've got a terrible headache."

Oswald's expression of irritation was brief. "Good night, then," he said tersely, and left.

Sam touched Winnie's shoulder and said, "Go to bed and I'll bring you chamomile tea." He really was the most considerate of men.

I was feeling left out from all the guy attention when Gabriel grabbed my hand and said, "Let me tuck you in."

He sat on my bed and told me about a new boy he'd met while I brushed my teeth, washed up, and changed into my sleep tee. "Not that I have a spare moment to do anything about a pretty boy," he said with exasperation. "It's all work, work, work with me, you know."

Before I got into bed, I vented all my frustration at what was happening. "Gabriel, what exactly is the plan to conquer CACA? Isn't there any way I can help?"

Gabriel scrunched his face one way and then the other. Finally he said, "What's your handwriting like?"

I shrugged. "Boring. I write exactly the way I was taught in grade school. But I'm very good at copying other styles, if you have samples." My best part-time jobs at F.U. had been in the fund-raising office, where I created poignant and inspired "personal" letters from department chairs to major donors. My supervisor had wept openly when I left.

"Well, isn't that interesting?" he said brightly. "Let me check with Sam and we just might have a project for you."

He turned out the lights and said, "Sweet dreams, baby."

Wishing doesn't make it true: I dreamed of rivers and fountains and pools of thick crimson liquid.

twenty-one

the lady is a vamp(ire)

The next morning, Winnie came to the kitchen looking fresh and elegant in an apricot silk blouse and a navy skirt. "Would you like a cup?" she asked as she went to the coffee.

"Thanks. How's your headache?"

She smiled. "All gone."

"How is it," I asked, "that some people are so perfectly groomed, and others are always a bit of a disaster?"

Winnie considered my question and said, "Maybe some people are very careful and others are more impetuous."

"We both know which camp I fall into."

To my surprise, Winnie said, "Sometimes I worry that I am too careful. I think one would be happiest with a balanced approach to life, a happy middle ground."

"Why don't we try for that?" I asked.

Cheered by the idea that Winnie and I were beginning to be friends, I spent a blissful hour tending to the garden before Gabriel asked me to come to the study.

An open briefcase sat on the desk, filled with files. "Hi, Mil," said Sam. "Gabriel says you've offered to help us."

"I'd love to do whatever I can," I said.

Sam directed his sincere brown gaze to me. "Milagro, you are under no pressure or obligation to participate in any activity. If you have any qualms, please tell Gabriel. There is no need to discuss any details of this matter with me." He left the study and closed the door behind him.

Gabriel said, "You know how lawyers are. They don't want to know you've done anything illegal so they can maintain deniability."

"Whatever," I said.

Gabriel removed a folder from the briefcase. "Okay, here are copies of documents that CACA has been gathering. These jerks want to present these lies about predatory vampires, human blood consumption, and slaughter as historical evidence against us. Have I said how much I hate these guys today?"

"How much do you hate these guys?" I asked as I took the folder and flipped through copies of letters in old-fashioned script.

"Way more than a lot," Gabriel answered. "So the deal is that we want to switch the originals with our own forged versions and they gotta look authentic on first and even second examination."

"They need to be perfect?"

"Close, but not perfect. An expert's got to be able to tell

they're fakes. If things escalate to the point where CACA's bringing the documents to the public, forgeries will totally discredit them."

Gabriel provided me with supplies and videos on the history of penmanship, forgery techniques, and forensic handwriting analysis. I discovered that I loved forgery and was quite good at it. Gabriel was thrilled with my fraudulent documents.

I was not the only one with a new activity. Oswald started leaving the ranch in the mornings and often didn't return until well after dinner. He would wear grown-up clothes and looked surprisingly stylish in jackets, slacks, and ties. I wondered what in the heck he was doing, but I wasn't going to ask and give the impression that I gave a fig about him.

I felt almost normal so long as I remembered not to ignore my hunger pangs. Tragically, I couldn't regain my more extravagant curves. I tried to fatten up by eating rich, sugary products, but they held no appeal for me. At least not compared to the hunks of meat, glistening in their own ruby juices, that called to me from the refrigerated bins at the market.

Some evenings we watched movies and others we played cards or read. While I missed my life of cheap amusements, I enjoyed Gabriel's company, Edna's cooking lessons, and the respectful friendship that was developing between me and Sam. I was seeking the happy middle ground. Oddly, this was not much comfort when I awoke alone in my bed, longing for a man's warm body next to mine.

It was then that my undisciplined mind wandered to Oswald. I resisted lingering on the image of his smooth body holding me close, his hands on my bare flesh . . . Instead I envisioned a life with someone serious and the mature joy that could be shared listening to classical music and playing chess. Someone like Sam, perhaps.

As Winnie and I became more amiable, my admiration for her grew. The only time I ever saw her self-conscious was when she slipped into my room to borrow some feminine hygiene products.

"Thanks," she said. "It's just that . . ." She paused. "It's just that I don't have a regular cycle and it's a surprise."

"As long as you're around me, you're going to be like clockwork." I relayed the heartwarming tale of my supposedly infertile roommate who lived with me for four months, got pregnant, and was now happily married with two children.

Winnie said patiently, "Anecdotal evidence can be persuasive, but it is irrelevant to my situation."

Fine, I thought, go ahead and bake a little Oswald bun in the oven and then try to find a wedding dress to cover that. Don't say I didn't warn you.

Still, I appreciated her formal manner. In fact, I came to respect all the vampires and what I considered their refined ways.

One night when I was particularly restless, I got out of bed, dressed, and decided to walk off my discontent. I felt as though I'd missed something, like when you're going on a trip and you've checked your suitcase several times, but you know you've forgotten something. *Espíritu de un mal viaje.* But it was also a nameless longing, a yearning for a fabulous man of one's own. *Espíritu de* spinster. And, of course, a feeling that I would never be taken seriously even if I was talented. *Espíritu de Charo.*

Daisy dashed ahead of me toward the barn. "Daisy, Daisy," I called in a low voice as I followed her into the barn. I peered into the darkness and heard her scratch and whine. Then a stall door opened midway down the barn beyond Ernie's apartment. Oswald appeared, looked down at Daisy, and said, "You are a nuisance." Daisy wiggled by him, there was laughter from inside, and then the door closed.

What in the hell was Oswald doing having a party in the middle of the night in the barn? I crept into the gloaming, expecting the swishing of bats, unearthly howls, the cacklings of a madman.

Once by the door, I felt a shiver run down my spine, but not of fear. It was some primitive, savage reaction that I had no control over. Suddenly bold, I flung open the door expecting to see an awful vision of carnage. I don't know who was more surprised, the vampires lounging in old-fashioned armchairs or me, shouting, "Aha!"

The stall had been converted into a cozy sitting room. Ernie and Oswald stood beside a sideboard set up with a few slender green bottles, a variety of mineral waters, and glasses. I said, "You're having a wine tasting and didn't invite . . . ," but I stopped because there was a scent I recognized. I was horrified. I was disgusted. And, worse, I was excited.

"This isn't what you think," said Sam nervously.

"Oh, puhleeze," Gabriel said. "Give the girl some credit."

Ernie looked at me and shrugged. "Hey, it's just a job to me."

"A job?" said Oswald, offended. "You're an artist, Ernie, and don't ever forget that."

I walked to the sideboard. Edna shrugged and said, "Oh, go ahead, Ernie, give her a glass if she wants one."

"Which one?" he asked, indicating the green bottles of dark liquid.

Winnie spoke tentatively. "Maybe she would like the one with the hint of lavender."

Ernie poured a small portion of crimson liquid into a wineglass, and then filled the glass with Evian, saying, "Noncarbonated water works better with this one." The blood colored the water dark rose. "I don't drink this stuff, so I just have to take their word for it."

"You'll enjoy it more if you let your hand warm the glass," Sam started to say, but I'd already begun to drink. I shuddered with delight at the taste and the sensation of the liquid flowing into my mouth and down my throat. I held the glass upside down, trying to get the last drop. I thought that this must be the way morphine feels, so potent that a tiny amount can infuse the body, starting from one point and blooming until every nerve ending tingles.

I dropped into a chair and savored the moment, even though a small, sane voice inside my head was screaming that I was a monster. I felt a little dizzy, but I didn't know if it was the blood or the self-loathing. "It's not human, is it?" I whispered while thinking, too late, too late!

Sam came to me and took my hands; I was so sensitive that his touch set off a throb of desire. He must have felt it, too, because he quickly released me. "Of course not. That was lamb. We raise animals specifically—"

"We don't hurt our animals," Oswald said evenly. "We take only minimal amounts, far less proportionately than you'd give if you were donating blood. Our animals are treated humanely and kept in the best health possible."

Sam looked at me anxiously. "We enjoy a glass or two now and then, in moderate amounts. We observe the strictest quality control . . ."

"Samuel, she doesn't care," said Edna. "She just wants another glass." She turned to me. "And if you're going to swill it again, young lady, we'll just give you the swill."

"Oh," said Gabriel, "don't even talk about the turtle. It tasted like algae."

"Gabriel," Winnie said delicately, "Ernie only made that because you suggested it."

Ernie picked up another bottle. "This is the angora rabbit. Crisp and grassy with a clean mouth feel, so they say."

"Rabbit?" I repeated inanely as I watched Ernie pour blood and water into the glass.

"Yes," said Oswald. "It's nice for a beginner. Not too strong." He was right. It did taste lighter and more, well, quaffable. It was the type of drink you might serve at brunch.

Which reminded me to say to Oswald, "I thought you said you ate a lot of vegetables. You didn't mention blood."

Oswald's gray eyes were dark and mysterious in the dim light. He put his finger to the side of his mouth. "You've got a spot there."

I ran my forefinger over my lips and found the wayward drop, and I sucked hungrily at my finger until I realized that all the men were staring at me. "How long were you going to keep this from me?" I looked from one to another. "Winnie, why didn't you tell me about this?"

She was polite enough to look discomfited. "I didn't know

how you'd react. Remember I asked you if you'd been eating anything odd? You said no."

"Uh, I think I said something about steak tartare," I muttered, trying to dress up my culinary crimes.

"We didn't consider it to be pertinent information since you had not disclosed your own inclination," Sam said. "We wanted to avoid causing you any undue emotional distress."

I liked how he was always so polite even when he was caught chugging livestock blood in the middle of the night.

It's funny how you can be disgusted by something but disappointed it's over. My heart fell when Ernie put the corks back in the bottles and said, "I'm beat. Let's call it a night."

"Lovely selection, Ernesto," said Edna, standing and patting his shoulder. "Oswald's right. You're an artist." She then gazed at me. "Young lady, stop looking like someone stole your jelly donut. You may join us from now on."

We left Ernie, Gabriel, and Oswald in the barn to put things away. Our feet crunched on the gravel path back to the house, but I felt as if I was floating, encased in a bubble of general warm fuzziness. Sam took Edna's arm to guide her through the darkness, and I fell in step beside Winnie. "I don't understand how Ernie got involved in this."

"It's our custom to have a trusted non–family member harvest and blend the product."

"Why do you take that risk? Why don't you do it yourselves?"

"Can't you guess?"

"Because a family member would drink the whole thing and wouldn't care about the earthy notes or the hint of raspberry."

"Yes, exactly. Hard to believe but in the old days, someone

would just cut the throat of a chicken, drain the blood into a bucket, and pass it around. Can you imagine?"

I didn't say, well, ain't we civilized. "So that's what bothered the Old World neighbors?"

"That's the least of it," Winnie said. "The essence is that our family's village broke off an alliance with their village. At the time, both groups were continuing some pagan practices while others were fighting over Eastern and Western religion. It's ancient history."

Edna and Winnie went upstairs, but Sam lingered in the kitchen with me. "I want to be sure you feel all right about this," he said, and placed his hand solicitously on my shoulder.

I again felt a frisson from his contact. "I don't suppose it's any worse than eating meat." I thought I could hear our hearts beating, the blood flowing in our veins, our lungs inhaling and exhaling. Then footsteps sounded in the dining room. We jumped apart just as Winnie came into the kitchen.

"Oh," she said, looking at us. "I was just getting some juice."

"That sounds great," Sam said too enthusiastically. "Would you like juice, Mil?"

A glass of OJ was not going to satisfy any of my cravings. "Thanks, no."

Winnie got the glasses, poured juice, and handed one to him.

"Thanks," he mumbled.

"Are you coming up to bed now?" she said to him in a soft voice.

The evening had distorted my perceptions; her innocent comment sounded suggestive. Sam nodded and followed her. Our "good night's" echoed in the empty rooms.

twenty-two

little fictions

The next morning I showered and wore my new red silk bra and panties under the black skirt and the burgundy sweater. I was trying to think of myself as sexy and sophisticated instead of being horrified that I was a blood-quaffing freak. I sashayed out of my room and walked smack-dab into Oswald.

He was so close that I could smell his minty-fresh toothpaste breath. He wore a soft suede blazer and coffee-colored slacks. I thought that he must spend his entire meager paycheck on clothes.

"Good, you're up," he said. "Do you think you could help at the clinic today?"

"I don't know anything about animals," I said, hoping to escape this request. His shirt was open at the neck and I imagined I could see the pulse at the base of his throat.

"You don't need to know anything about animals," he said, and a smile crept on his face. "The receptionist has a personal emergency and all you have to do is answer the phones and try to make the clients relax. I'd really appreciate it."

He looked so earnest and handsome that I forgot he was Oswald for a second and I did what I usually do when an earnest, handsome guy asks me for something: I said yes. "I suppose I can toss them kibble if they get cranky?"

"That'll do the trick," Oswald said, and I could see he was relieved. "We can have breakfast there."

As we left, we ran into Sam, and Oswald told him, "Milagro is helping me out at the clinic today. Don't do anything I wouldn't do."

Sam smiled nervously at this hackneyed attempt at banter.

We took the midsize sedan that I had first assumed was Edna's and the radio came on to National Public Radio. Oswald said, "You choose," and I fiddled with the tuner until I found a funk oldies song. Too late I heard the blatantly sexual lyrics and chorus of moans, so I just left it where it was.

Clearing my throat, I said awkwardly, "I'm sure your experience at the clinic will help you get into vet school."

"Milagro, your confidence warms the cockles of my heart."

We drove over the mountain and I asked a question that had long been on my mind. "Oswald, do you always speak suggestively or is it just me?"

He flashed a bright smile. "It's just you."

For the rest of the ride, we sat in silence while the radio spewed seductive songs about doing the horizontal hokey-pokey. We drove through the quaint town where I'd seen

Kathleen, passing a large animal hospital, to an unmarked modern building off the main street. Oswald drove behind the building into a reserved parking space.

"Doesn't the clinic have a sign?" I asked.

"The clients like their privacy." He led me into the lobby of the building, then unlocked a door and held it open for me. It wasn't until I was passing through that I saw the discreet copper nameplate, "Oswald K. Grant, MD."

I stopped short and he bumped into me. I pointed at the nameplate and said, "Oswald, what the hell does this mean?"

Oswald was laughing as he said, "M.D., me doctor."

"You jackass! Why have you been telling me you want to be a vet?"

"You were so devoted to the idea, I couldn't bear to disappoint you."

I would have yelled at him further, but a pleasant-looking older woman with a fluff of dyed blond hair and silver glasses came through the lobby door. "Good morning, Dr. Grant."

"Morning, Mrs. Walintiny." Oswald took my elbow and pulled me into his offices. He flipped on the lights and punched in the code on a security system revealing a simple but elegant waiting room. "This is Milagro. She's going to work the front desk today. Susie's out on a family matter."

"Nice to meet you, Milagro," she said. "Thanks for helping."

"Nice to meet you, too, Mrs . . ." I faltered on her last name.

"Walintiny," she said, and winked. She lifted a paper bag and said to Oswald, "I brought your favorite muffins."

"You're a queen among women," he answered. "I'll put on the coffee. Would you mind showing Milagro the phones?"

When he went down the hall, Mrs. Walintiny stared openly at me, head to foot. "No work done on you, right? I can tell every time. Great boobies by the way."

"Thanks. Some people think the real ones are trashy."

She chuckled. "They're just jealous. I wish I had my real one back." She puffed out her chest to show me her tidy bazooms. "Had one removed 'cause of breast cancer. Couldn't ask for better replacement than the one the doc gave me, but I still miss old floppy."

"Oh," I said as realization dawned. "Oswald's a plastic surgeon?"

"One of the best. 'Course, I may be biased."

She showed me how the phones and intercom worked and what the schedule was. "It'll be pretty easy today," she said. "Just consultations, but they get real nervous, so it's nice to listen to them and help them relax."

Oswald returned with a mug of coffee and a carrot-zucchini muffin on a platter. I gave him a look of pure viciousness and he said, "Milagro is a very sympathetic girl. She'll be fine."

And, apart from accidentally hanging up on a few people, I was. Mrs. Walintiny checked on me frequently, chatting about this and that, asking if I knew Dr. Harding. "She's a lovely person," I said. "Very dedicated and admirable."

"A real catch," said Mrs. Walintiny. "Especially with that nose Oswald gave her. It makes her whole face."

It figured. I imagined myself standing in front of Oswald in old-lady panties while he marked up all the imperfect parts of my body with a red pen. "I suppose he could find something wrong with anybody's body," I said.

"No, sweetie, she was the one who insisted. Oswald likes variety, but lots of people just aren't happy with themselves. Not everyone can be like you."

When she saw my confusion, she explained, "They're trying to get on the outside what you got oozing out from the inside." Putting her hands on her chubby hips, she said, "Honey, you're walking sex."

"I think I'd rather be taken seriously," I said.

Mrs. Walintiny laughed so hard, tears rolled down her face. She eventually managed to say, "Learn to use it, sweetie, and enjoy it while it lasts."

I expected the clients to be like my mother Regina and Kathleen Baker, but they were a mixed bunch. A widower told me that he wanted to get the bags under his eyes removed so he could start dating again. A teen wanted to fix an ear damaged in an accident, and a woman came in determined to improve the chin she'd always hated. An executive type joked that she'd risen to the top of her field and she needed her breasts to go with her.

The Oswald I saw today was not the flirty oddball from Kathleen's party or the aimless slacker at the ranch. He spent an hour on the phone trying to find someone to assist an indigent patient; he sat on the floor with a toddler who had a cleft palate; and he treated Mrs. Walintiny and me to burgers.

With some patients he teased to make them relax, and with others he was all professionalism. In fact, he reminded me of Sam, and now I understood why Winnie wanted to marry him.

The joke was on me: I had never even been in Oswald's league.

twenty-three

tequila mockingbird

I took my typewriter outside to write. I could enjoy the garden while Daisy lazed at my feet and Petunia pecked, scratched, and chirped in a way that I found endlessly amusing.

Edna would occasionally stop by the table and offer helpful advice, like "I hope you proofread," and "You've spilled ice tea on your blouse."

Gabriel left that evening to fly to Washington on business. He collected my forgeries and said, "I'm bringing you back something rare and wonderful, Mil, something you'll appreciate."

"I'm going to miss you, honey buns."

"Sometimes I worry about you, Milagro. But then I think

that you're more resourceful than anybody realizes." He gave me a strong hug and a big kiss, then made me laugh by dancing out of the room, singing "I Will Survive."

Ernie had rescued a fawn whose mother had been hit by a truck. I'd found this event touching until I found out *why* he had taken in the animal. That night, as I drank Bambi's blood, I caught Ernie gazing at me and I thought there was disappointment in his eyes. It was gone in a second, hidden behind his good ol' boy grin.

Winnie and I were the last ones to leave the barn and she said to me, "It's balmy enough for a swim."

"Great idea." We found a few one-piece suits in the changing room by the pool. Mine was blue with pink starfish and hers was yellow with daisies and ruching.

There was a console of buttons on one wall. Winnie pushed the one labeled "roof" and the panels above us slid open, revealing the sky spangled with stars. Then Winnie selected a movie sound track to play on the sound system. Her choice of sappy strings and melodramatic yodeling made her seem almost like a regular girl.

She dived right into the pool, but I did a lot of toe dipping before finally jumping in. After a few minutes of thrashing, I discovered that the water felt splendid. While Winnie swam precise laps up and down the pool, I practiced underwater handstands and somersaults.

I grabbed an inner tube and kicked lazily, enjoying the evening breeze, twinkly sky, and residual warmth of fresh blood in my body. Winnie finished her laps and reached for an inflatable mat.

She said, “You know, Milagro, I’m glad you’re here.”

I was as pleased as punch. “Thanks, Winnie. I’m glad I’ve gotten to know you and Edna and Sam.”

The only sound was our legs splashing in the water. “He is a really nice man,” she said evenly.

“Sam, nice? Nice isn’t a tenth of it. Sam is handsome and smart and responsible and he always says exactly the right thing.” It wasn’t until I’d spoken that I realized the extent of my respect for him. “How do some people know how to say the right thing all the time? It boggles the mind. I am boggled.”

Winnie laughed. “It *is* boggling. Okay, he is a lot more than nice and he always says the right thing.”

“You’re like him that way.”

She swirled in the water and then asked casually, “What do you think of Oswald?”

“He’s nice,” I said carefully, and when she laughed I added, “You two seem so different.”

“That’s true,” she agreed. “But in the most important way, we’re perfectly compatible.”

She must mean that they have incredible sex. I felt insanely jealous because I was trying so hard to be sincere and serious. Winnie didn’t have to try. She was naturally serious and sincere and she also got to boink her sophisticated brains out. With Oswald.

When I spoke, my voice was warm to reflect the real fondness I had for the pale sylph nearby. “Winnie, when is the wedding?”

When she named a date only a month away, I was as

shocked as a toddler playing with a fork and an electrical outlet. "But there has been no planning! No one said anything to me." Had our *espíritu de los cocteles* been only a meaningless, gin-fueled illusion?

"We've gone back and forth on it," she said. "Oswald wanted to wait until things are settled here, but who knows when that will be? I want to have children . . ." She gave a resigned sigh. "My mother's been making all the preparations. We're going to be married in Prague."

I didn't know why I was so upset. "And where will you live after you're married?"

"Here, of course."

"Winnie, don't you think that Oswald's place is too small?"

"Oh, we'll only be in the cottage until this blows over. That was one of the reasons we thought of waiting. When Edna and Sam leave, we'll move into the house."

Perhaps this was just Sam's country house. "You mean Sam doesn't live here all the time?"

Winnie stopped kicking and turned to look at me. "He usually doesn't live here at all." She told me that he had his own town house in the City.

"So this ranch . . . ," I trailed off.

"It's Oswald's."

It was clear that I knew nothing at all.

Sam was waiting for us outside the house, a flashlight in his hand. "The moon is full tonight," he said with a plaintive tone that I'd never heard from him before. He caught my expression and laughed. "No, you don't have to worry about werewolves. There's no such thing."

Winnie began, "But there are documented cases of—"

"No more medical discourse for tonight, dear doctor. I only wanted to ask if you ladies wanted to join me on a walk."

Upset that I'd been so wrong about so many things, I said I was going to bed. I hoped the dedicated physician and the somber lawyer would stray from their usually serious conversations and find a topic that amused them both.

The next day I was simmering with so much frustration that I couldn't enjoy the new growth in the garden, the shrubs leafing out and buds appearing on the annuals. When Edna came outside, I whined, "Edna, no one tells me anything around here."

"I have no idea what you're talking about."

"I mean no one told me that Oswald was really a doctor and no one told me this was his place and no one told me you drink blood and no one told me that Winnie and Oswald are getting married next month. What else don't I know?"

"Young lady," she said with a sigh, "I simply don't have time to tell you all the things you don't know." And with that she walked away.

I didn't stop working until Winnie came home from the clinic. Her pale lilac suit made her eyes sparkle. She was so cheerful and happy that I thought she must have cured some putrefying disease.

When we entered the kitchen, Edna was doing something unseemly to a chicken. I said, "Hey, Edna, I believe what you're doing to that chicken is illegal in forty-eight states."

Her left eyebrow rose slowly like an opera curtain and the right corner of her lips turned down infinitesimally as she put one shoulder back. Genius. "Young lady, do not antagonize a woman with a boning knife." She turned to Winnie. "Your cousin Cornelia called a little while ago."

"Cornelia! What's she doing?" Winnie asked excitedly.

"Why don't you ask her yourself when she gets here? She and Ian are on their way." Edna jabbed at the chicken. "Ian's staying in town, but since you have an extra bed in your room, I thought Cornelia could bunk with you."

"Who are Cornelia and Ian?" I asked.

"Oh, they're my very glamorous second cousins," Winnie said with delight. "You'll see."

I'd about had my share of glamorous people recently, but I brushed out my hair and dabbed on lip gloss anyway before I went to help Edna in the kitchen. She took green bottles, dewy with condensation, from the refrigerator.

"Champagne?" I asked.

"Prosecco, an Italian sparkling wine. This one is dry, but has a nice fruitiness."

Fruity, cookie, nutty, words such as these beckon to me like sirens, enticing me to cast myself upon the rocks.

Edna saw me open my mouth and said, "Not a word, young lady. Pour it in flutes. Add a raspberry to each if you feel so inclined."

Oswald, dressed in a soft ecru shirt and olive slacks, came into the kitchen. He noticed the Prosecco and said to his grandmother, "Is this from the crate that the wine shop sent you?"

"Maybe," said Edna with a small smile.

"You and your admirers," Oswald said with a grin. "Smells terrific. A special meal for the beautiful Cornelia?"

I suddenly felt like day-old guacamole.

Winnie, dancing and humming like a child, helped to carry our drinks out to the terrace and I carried a platter of appetizers.

"What has gotten into you, Winsome?" I asked.

She smiled zanily. "It's just such a beautiful day! Don't you think it's a beautiful day?"

"I agree one hundred percent."

"And I'm not going to let anyone ruin it for me."

I held up a skewered prawn to her mouth and she took a bite. "Anyone who would ruin your fun would be a monster."

Or, to be more precise, a couple of vampires.

The gleaming ebony Mercedes arrived so silently the dogs didn't notice. It stopped in front of the terrace and a painfully thin woman stepped out of the driver's side. She was dressed head to foot in black: black boots, black skirt, black sweater, black sunglasses, and a black jacket. Her dyed black hair was cut in a perfect Louise Brooks bob. Her red lipstick was stark against her ivory skin. She practically took the fizz out of my Prosecco.

Then the passenger door opened and a sturdy but dashing man got out. The fluid lines of his beautiful suit made him appear taller than his average height, but it was his face that caught my attention. His features were lush, decadent, sensual. His mouth was wide, with full, curved lips, and his large eyes were hooded and shadowed. He had black curly hair and was as swarthy as his sister was pale.

"Ah, the beautiful Cornelia!" Oswald shouted as he walked to her. He lifted her effortlessly off the ground and twirled her around. Her boots were so pointy, he could have hurled her like a javelin and done some damage. Her sophisticated, low laugh rippled through the air.

I stood back as the vamps exchanged greetings with kisses all round. When Cornelia came to Winnie, she held out her praying mantis arms and crooned, "Dearest."

I wanted to scream, "No, Winnie, don't! They mate, then kill!" but I thought that would be impolite, so I sat still and awaited my introduction. Ian, too, stood back and watched.

"Cornelia," said Edna, "you never age."

The younger woman did have an eerily preserved look to her pallid face. She removed her sunglasses to reveal eyes rimmed in so much kohl and mascara that it would have embarrassed a transvestite. "Dearest Edna, always a delight." The women exchanged air kisses.

"What a wonderful surprise!" Winnie said.

"Yes," said Cornelia, "Ian and I were on the coast and we thought, why not give little Winifred a treat?" Her accent was indefinable, not American, not English, not from any specific European country.

"I'm so happy to see you," Winnie said. "You are always so chic!"

Cornelia held out her arms, displaying herself. "It is what I do, no?"

Oswald slipped his hand around Cornelia's tiny waist. "As svelte as ever," he said. "Most of my patients would die to look like you."

I was pretty sure this look could be easily achieved by dying and waiting three months.

"Oswald, don't," Ian said. "Flattery just spoils her." He

turned to me. "Hello, I'm Ian Ducharme," he said in a warm, liquid voice. He took my hands in his dry, firm ones and held them for several seconds too long. He wasn't a handsome man, but he made handsome seem irrelevant. He looked as if he was in his thirties, but something about him seemed ancient and powerful.

"This is Milagro De Los Santos," Sam said. "Our friend."

"Say hello, young lady," Edna ordered.

"Hello," I said.

Cornelia turned to me and said, "Why, she's adorable!" The full force of her attention made me feel like being adorable had been my life's dream.

"Delectable," Ian said. His eyes were full of dangerous meaning.

Cornelia plucked Sam's drink from his hand, tossed it back, and gave him a sultry look. "Edna, when did Sam become so utterly devastating?" Sam blushed at the attention.

"He's always been a good-looking fellow, Cornelia. You were just too busy to notice."

Cornelia examined Sam again and I knew what she meant. Dealing with CACA had brought out very interesting qualities in Sam. The oblivious mathematician had been replaced by a brooding and complex Sam. Cornelia smiled and said, "I'll take especial care to notice from now on."

Edna turned to Ian. "Have you really decided not to stay with us?"

"Alas, I am a creature of the night, *ma chère.* I would disrupt your household."

"I'm sure you're right," she responded.

The conversation flowed as quickly as the wine. Cocktails became dinner as we moved from the terrace to the dining room. Cornelia told wonderful stories about their travels and mentioned their château, villas, city apartments, and even a boathouse. She spoke of the famous and infamous with the same amused air that she mentioned shopkeepers and locals. Oswald seemed to know a great many of her friends, too, and I wondered how long he had traveled in her circle.

Ian listened attentively to his sister, but also turned to Winnie beside him, drawing her out about her move to the country and plans for the future. Occasionally I caught him watching me, a smile playing on his lips.

Someone must have told the brother and sister about my situation, because they weren't surprised when Sam began talking about CACA. "Gabriel's contact in the organization is about to deliver. If all goes right, we can get them to back off very soon."

"That's wonderful, Sam!" Winnie exclaimed.

"Sam, I never know what you mean when you say 'soon,' " I said. "And what is it exactly that you're doing to CACA?" I didn't expect him to provide any real answers. The vampires generally ignored my questions, but I felt obligated to keep asking anyway.

"Must you badger Sam at dinner, young lady?" Edna sniffed.

"By very soon, I mean within weeks," Sam said.

Ian reached across the table and refilled my wineglass. *"Young Lady,"* he said, and everyone laughed. "I hope you are not planning to rush away."

That's exactly what I was planning on doing, getting away

from Oswald and the rest of the vampires as soon as possible, even though the prospect filled me with unwarranted regret. "I will be leaving as soon as Sebastian Beckett-Witherspoon has been stopped."

Cornelia looked at me and said, "Sam tells me that you know him. Is he as handsome as his photos?"

"More," I said truthfully. "All golden and light. However, he is morally bankrupt."

"You say that like it's a bad thing," Cornelia said with a laugh. "Not that I find blond men especially handsome. I prefer men with dark hair, dark eyes." She smiled at Sam. "So much more intriguing."

After dinner, I trailed behind as the vampires walked to the barn. Ernie had put his newest creations on the sideboard of the tasting room. There was a delicate calf recently weaned and Tibetan lamb flavored by a diet of thyme and sage. We each got a few drops of blood from squirrels that had been fed on hazelnuts.

Cornelia regaled the family with a story about a rubber dynasty heir who had followed her from one luxury resort to another, proclaiming his love.

Ian said, "My sister neglects to mention that insanity runs in his family."

"True," said Cornelia, "but he had exquisite taste in jewelry." She reached under her collar and lifted up an ornate gold and topaz necklace. "The foolish fellow gave me all his family heirlooms in exchange for a few dates."

"Cornelia," said Edna coolly, "you could have bought those trinkets yourself."

"Ah, but that is too easy. It isn't the cost that makes something dear, Edna. It is the torment that accompanies a gift." Cornelia laughed as innocently as a schoolgirl.

As the blood cocktail slid down my throat, I felt a current run through me. It tasted the way a lagoon looks, rich with life, dark with mystery, textured and layered. I felt as if I was evolving into something more than what I had been and this mood was still upon me as we walked back to the house.

Sam and I were at a distance from the others, and I felt an urge to confide in him. "Sam, do you think there is some secret to finding a partner who is both intellectually and physically satisfying?"

"What serious question, Young Lady," Sam said. "I don't know that it's a secret so much as recognizing an opportunity. How many people bypass their soul mate?"

"Like Winnie and Oswald," I said. "I used to think they were mismatched, but they're both doctors and she told me last night that they have an incredible physical relationship."

He looked shocked at my unladylike gossip.

"I shouldn't have said that," I added quickly. "It was wrong of me to share a private conversation."

Before Sam could answer, Ian slipped beside me, putting his arm though mine. "Let's enjoy the night," he said, and he began steering me away toward the fields.

"Ian," Edna called out. "Be careful with that Young Lady."

"I won't do anything to harm her," he answered.

"I'm not worried about her. I'm worried about you," she said. Ian laughed, but I didn't find her comment especially hilarious.

The other voices faded in the distance as we walked on. "Should I be frightened to be alone with you?" he asked playfully.

"Yes, terrified," I responded, even though he made me as nervous as a June bug at a chicken dance.

"Excellent."

When we were far out in the field, he stopped to turn to me. His eyes glimmered in the dark and I could see the shine of his white teeth. "Do you endanger my mind, body, or soul?"

"You have a soul, Ian?"

"That is a matter of some debate," he answered. "How did you ever convince this cautious family to let you stay with them, to share their secrets?"

"I lived."

"So you did."

His eyes coursed over my body and it was all I could do not to rip my clothes off then and there. I wasn't thinking about intellectual satisfaction, and I didn't even know if I liked Ian, but he radiated sex, sex, sex and brought out all the desires I had been repressing.

"I hope we shall become well acquainted," he said. "It is a novelty to me to meet someone who survived transmission."

"It is a novelty for me to associate with a vampire," I said carelessly. "I'm sorry, not a vampire, but . . ."

Ian laughed warmly. "Please don't apologize. My sister and I know what we are and are not ashamed. We are not so modern as Edna's brood, not so concerned to fit into a narrow mold that cannot contain us."

"So you admit that you are vampires?"

"That is a given. The question is, Milagro, what are you?"

Before I could come up with an answer, he said, "Shall we?" and began leading me back toward the house. At the back door to the kitchen, he stopped. "Until tomorrow, Young Lady." He leaned toward me and I expected a *besito* on each cheek in the European fashion, but instead he brushed the hair away from my neck, and his sensuous mouth was at my throat in a hot, long kiss.

He smelled of sandalwood and blood, and his cheek was rough against my skin. Stepping back, he said, "I shall think of you tonight." And then he was gone.

His touch ignited my reckless, beach-read instincts. After hours of wakefulness, I came to the conclusion that a sincere and serious young woman could learn much from the company of a mature and worldly man.

twenty-four

the road to hell is paved with fabulous men

Late the next morning, when Oswald and Winnie were already at work and Sam was locked up in the study, Cornelia found me toiling in the garden. She was wearing a slinky black sweater and trouser set and a wide-brimmed straw hat. She drank something that might have been a Bloody Mary. "What does a girl do for fun around here?"

I took a wild guess that Cornelia would not consider hand-weeding fun. "I've been staying around the house for the most part, but I'm open to suggestion."

"Let's call Ian." In less than an hour, I had changed into a skirt, blouse, and my seashell-trimmed sandals and was seated in the front seat of the Mercedes with Ian. Edna wasn't interested in sightseeing, but Cornelia had pried Sam away from his work. Sitting beside Cornelia in the backseat, Sam looked like a kid cutting school for the first time.

Ian drove swiftly and smoothly along a narrow country road heading into the hills. Sam cleared his throat and said, "We are going twice the speed limit, Ian."

"Oh, we always go fast," Cornelia observed. "It's never a problem."

"You never get pulled over?" I asked.

"Certainly we do," said Ian, "but I just give the officers a *mordida* and everything is resolved."

"*Mordida*?" Sam asked.

"It means bite," I said, "a bribe." At least I hoped Ian meant a bribe.

He turned into a drive with a sign out front that warned PRIVATE PROPERTY. CLOSED TO THE PUBLIC. NO TRESPASSERS. More signs repeated the message farther down the drive.

"Here we are," Ian said as he pulled in front of a winery set among fields of lavender and surrounded by vineyards. "I've arranged for a tour and lunch."

A weathered man in overalls came to greet us and, contrary to the hostile signs, treated us like we were his new best friends. He guided us into the dark, cool building that stored the casks. The air was ripe with fermentation, and I could hear the squeak of mice in the shadows and see the glinting eyes of cats hunting them. Ian pulled me behind a row of barrels and asked, "Do you take pleasure in the darkness, Milagro?"

"It depends on what's hiding in it."

"How do you know anything's hiding in it?" He took a lock of my hair and twisted it around his finger.

"Let me amend my comment. It depends on who is hiding in it."

Ian chuckled, and then we rejoined our friends. We went outside and through a fragrant lavender field. Ian and Sam strolled beside the vintner. Cornelia walked with me and spoke enthusiastically about the beauty of the day and place. "I'd wondered why Winnie was so pleased to be in the provinces." Cornelia looked around happily and her eyes settled on Sam, who was asking the vintner a question about harvesting. "Now I understand. I could come to like living here."

"Are you sure you wouldn't find it dull beyond belief?"

"Given time, anything can become dull, little one," she said. "Parties, clothes, beaus, anything . . . that's why I am so grateful to my dear brother. He never gets tired of life."

We had lunch and several bottles of wine under a pergola covered with white wisteria. I was embellishing the glamour of my life in the City to Cornelia when I felt Ian shift closer to me. "Of course, one deplores the Norway rats, and—*watchale,* Ian, please remove your hand from my thigh."

He was completely unembarrassed. "Must I?"

Sam swayed against Cornelia, who rested her head on his shoulder. "If Young Lady says you must, then you must," Sam said with a loopy grin.

"It's a very nice thigh," said Ian. "Smooth and tender. Allow a lonely bachelor this small pleasure."

"When you put it that way," I said, "it's just rude to say no."

Ian was the only one of us who wasn't affected by the alcohol. The ride home was a blur of silliness and laughter. We stumbled out of the car in front of Winnie and Oswald, who were sitting on the terrace.

Sam dropped into a chair and Cornelia sat on his lap and put her arms around his neck. "It's so good to be around family," she said.

Sam stroked her hair as Winnie and Oswald watched in shock. "Sam," said Oswald, "are you drunk?"

"This is not an admission of the accusation in question," Sam said, speaking so slowly that each syllable was independent of the next. "But alcohol is a legal substance, and as an adult representing myself, I have the right to . . . to whatever." He gave a bleary look to Oswald and Winnie. "I have a right to see a beautiful thing and want to have it for my own."

Cornelia snuggled close to his chest. "That's lovely, darling."

Edna dragged me off to the kitchen and made me help with dinner. "Young Lady, try not to slice your finger off."

"What difference does it make, Edna? It'll heal back up."

"Be careful anyway."

Perhaps because they had worked all day, Oswald and Winnie were quiet at dinner, but the rest of us had a grand time. Sam basked in Cornelia's attention, and Ian's flirting made me feel like a real human girl again. I saw Oswald watching him and I thought, ha, Oswald, just because you're not interested does not mean that I am completely undesirable.

Ian claimed he had another engagement that night, but before he left he grabbed me in the hallway and pulled me into the little parlor. "What are you doing?" I asked, laughing. The room was dark and his arms were around me.

"Saying good night," he murmured.

"Good night, then."

"I yearn to taste you," he said. His teeth nipped lightly at my neck and I felt a thrill run through me.

"Keep yearning," I answered, and pulled away from him.

I could hear him breathing in the dark. I knew he could hear me, too. "I'll wait," he finally said. "I can wait until you're ready."

He left silently. I didn't know if I'd ever be ready for whatever Ian had in mind. But it excited me.

The next day, Cornelia got up late again. She came to my room while I was stuck at a critical point in my zombie story: should the young doctor fall in love with a zombie or would that be over the top?

"Edna says there's a spa in town," said Cornelia. "Let's go."

As a *chica* on a budget, I said regretfully, "I can't. *No tengo dinero.*"

"My treat," she said.

It had taken some time, but at F.U. I had learned to graciously accept the generosity of others. After life with my mother Regina, I'd been surprised to realize that some people actually enjoyed giving gifts. And so I said, "Fab!" and we were off for a massage, a facial, and, for me, a trim and styling of my hair.

"You look marvelous," Cornelia said as we walked out.

"It is better to look marvelous than to feel marvelous," I said.

"Absolutely. But when you're one of us, you can look marvelous *and* feel marvelous." She adjusted the brim of her sun hat. "I hope my brother has not been too forward with you. He's a very direct and passionate man."

I thought it was a little creepy for a sister to talk about her brother's passion, but I supposed it was her continental way. "Oh, who doesn't like to flirt?"

Cornelia stopped and lowered her sunglasses to look me directly in the eye. "Oh, no, Young Lady, don't take him too lightly. Ian's interest is not easily aroused. He was immediately attracted to you."

I didn't have the heart to tell her that when one was blessed with gaudy *chichis* and curvy *nalgas,* one immediately attracted a lot of men.

The man in question was occupying the carriage house of the only hotel in town, a huge white Victorian building. He was barefoot, wearing a beautiful pale blue linen shirt and navy trousers. "Ladies, you look exquisite. What shall we do today?"

"Shop?" offered Cornelia. "Swim, ride, slum, steal cars, go antiquing?"

There was a knock at the door and Ian called, "Enter!"

A girl dressed in black slacks and a white shirt opened the door. It was hard to tell how old she was under a mask of white and black Goth makeup, but she had a teenager's insolent slump. Her lank, dyed black hair hung past her shoulders. She wheeled in a room service cart with a bottle of champagne in a silver bucket and a bowl of strawberries.

"Ah, Tiffany," Ian said to the awkward girl. "You come like a dream to me."

She ducked her head to hide her smile. "Here's the champagne you wanted, Mr. Ducharme. You want me to do up the bed for you now or later?"

"Later will be perfect, my raven-haired angel."

She giggled nervously and practically ran out of the room.

"Really, Ian," said Cornelia. "You have that girl in a tizzy."

"The child is bored and I provide her with a little attention."

"How very philanthropic of you," I said, feeling foolish for being another bored child to this jaded creature.

"I am not interested in children," he said evenly. "Am I, Cornelia?"

"Not in ages, darling."

Ian uncorked the champagne and said, "What say we venture out to meet the local flora and fauna, primarily fauna?" He poured the bubbly into three glasses. "Cornelia, do you think Sam would like to join us?"

Cornelia took a glass from Ian. "How thoughtful you are, dear brother. I'm sure Sam would love it."

So I was already somewhat tipsy when I found myself walking behind three vampires into a biker bar in the township of Lower Sky. The day outside was bright, but inside it was dim and smoky, some of the smoke generated by legal substances and some by illegal. It was a workday, but the room was filled with rough-looking white guys who didn't seem to be on lunch break. There were a lot of prison-variety ballpoint pen–and–needle tattoos among the clientele.

Ian escorted me past guys who looked like they were deciding if they should kill him first and rape me later or the other way around. Cornelia and an uneasy Sam followed. "Here we are," Ian said at an empty booth.

A lump of rotten beef got up from his barstool and lumbered over while his friends guffawed. He hovered over our table and Ian said, "Yes, what is it?"

"This is my table, motherfucker."

Sam was already beginning to stand when Ian urged him to stay seated. "Are you the proprietor of this establishment?" Ian asked the biker.

"What the fuck?" growled the slab of meat. "I will kick your ass." Actually, the biker was drunk so it sounded like, "Ah well keg yer az."

Inebriated or sober, the biker looked deeply and seriously dangerous, but Ian smiled genially and said, "I doubt the ladies go in for that sort of thing, so why don't we talk outside?"

"Ian, no," I began.

Cornelia looked concerned and I thought she would stop her brother. "This is a problem," she said, scrunching her nose. "Do you want us to wait for you or go ahead and order?"

"Go ahead and order." Ian stood and handed her his wallet before saying to the biker, "Come along. I hate to ignore the ladies for long."

The rest of the bar patrons shouted curses of encouragement to their friend, who I gathered was named Artie, as the two men left the bar. Sam was studiously examining an obscene joke cocktail napkin while Cornelia was waving for the waitress. "Aren't we going to do anything?" I asked frantically.

"Young Lady, you must learn to enjoy yourself," said Cornelia as if her brother wasn't going to be slaughtered in the alley.

The meth-thin waitress, who wore a rhinestone necklace that spelled out "Sally," approached. Cornelia said, "Sally, my brother is feeling magnanimous today. How about drinks for the house for the rest of the afternoon?"

Sally snapped her gum and looked vaguely interested. "Well drinks or brand drinks?"

"Brand drinks of course," Cornelia said. "Whatever they want. And bring us a bottle of your best tequila." She took a credit card from Ian's wallet and handed it to Sally. "Make sure you give yourself a good tip."

Sally shouted out, "Drinks on the house courtesy of this lady here!" and there was a general hoot and holler and a lot of commotion as the bikers rushed to the bar, shouting orders for aged brandy and single-malt Scotch.

"Sam," I said. "Why are we sitting here? We've got to help Ian."

"Um," Sam said. "Cornelia, I think Mil is right. We should find Ian and go . . ."

Sally successfully balanced her tray and put down our drinks, lime wedges, and salt just as Ian slipped back into the booth, not a hair out of place. "Ah, tequila, excellent choice," he said.

I stared at Ian. "What happened?"

"Nothing interesting," he said. "Nothing as interesting as you." He dipped his finger in his shot glass, stroked the tequila across my wrist, and poured salt on it. I imagined that I could feel the blood pulsing there. Then Ian licked my wrist, tossed back a drink, and bit his square white teeth into the lime while keeping his eyes locked on mine.

It was not an obscene act, but it felt obscene.

I could tell by the amused expression of a nearby biker that he thought so, too. He strutted over to our booth and sat down beside Cornelia. Holding up his glass, he said, "Thanks for the round. Whadya do with Artie?"

"Artie? Your large friend? We had a brief chat and he realized he was being unreasonable. Why, there he is now."

We followed Ian's gaze to see Artie slowly entering the bar. He shuffled to a table and collapsed in a chair. He was ashen and the torn sleeve of his shirt revealed a long gash. You'd expect a cut that size to have dripped blood, but there was none on his shirt.

The biker at our table gave Ian an admiring look. "Glad you were able to come to an understanding. My name's Ernest Culpepper, by the way. Seeing as we're friends, you can call me Pepper."

The name struck a bell and, sure enough, Pepper turned out to be Winnie's old neighbor and a pretty nice guy, as meth dealers go. He was happy to hear that the doc was about to be married and even sprung for a round of drinks for our table.

The bar provided a wide variety of entertainment. Sam proved to be a deadly accurate pool player, especially after he switched from drinking tequila to mineral water. When he won a few hundred dollars, he was smart enough to lose it at darts. Then all the girls in the place, including Cornelia, Sally, and I, were inspired to dance on top of the bar to some country rock songs I'd never heard before. As much as I admired Winnie, I didn't think she would understand.

Pepper was inviting me for a ride on the back of his hog, suggesting that I remove my blouse and bra to better enjoy the fresh air, when Ian decided that it was time to leave. He hauled me over his shoulder as easily as he would fling a jacket and got a round of applause. When we left, Artie was still hunched over in the chair, his eyes glazed and unseeing.

Sam had come in his own car, so he left with Cornelia.

Ian took me back to the hotel as I knew he would. The Goth girl, Tiffany, was on the porch smoking a cigarette. She stared as we went to the carriage house.

I'd dated men in their thirties, but Ian's manner was far older than theirs, knowing and compelling. He took me in his arms and I was thinking that this was what I needed to stop fantasizing about unavailable men. I reached into his shirt, feeling his cool skin and smelling his spicy scent. He terrified me and a sick part of me liked that, liked the idea of facing someone powerful.

He unbuttoned my blouse and stroked my neck, his thumb resting on the pulse at the base of my throat. Our mouths met only briefly, mine open to his, enjoying the fullness of his lips, the slip and slide of his tongue. His hands were on my hips, pulling them close, and he moved his head down to my neck, giving me the most gentle *mordizquitos,* making me crazy for something more.

I yanked at his belt and he grabbed my hand. "No, not unless you let me taste you."

His dark eyes smoldered and I must have gone temporarily insane because I said, "Fine, whatever."

Ian picked up a wineglass and shattered it against a table. Taking a slender shard, he came to me. "I won't hurt you," he said softly, but I still shivered. He turned my hand palm side up and kissed it. Then I watched as he slid the glass fragment skillfully over my palm, slicing only the surface. A thin crimson line appeared and Ian put his mouth to it, sucking slowly and shuddering with pleasure.

When he pulled his mouth away, his eyes were shining and the cut had already healed. "Milagro," he groaned, and now he kissed me deeply and it felt so wicked, so wrong, and I let him take off my clothes and make love to me.

His clothes had hidden a robust body. His chest was deep and had a thatch of dark hair; his arms and thighs were thick with muscle. He used his strength skillfully, carefully, observing my reactions to his movements, turning me this way and that and asking, "Do you like this? Is this what you want?" While I was moaning with pleasure, I would be vaguely conscious that he had brought out the shard again to make another light incision on my breast, my hip, my neck, to taste my blood again.

When he was done, I felt satiated and guilty. My skin bore no marks.

Ian kissed my forehead. "I knew you would be extraordinary."

Every girl wants lavish compliments, but I tended to be skeptical of compliments that were too lavish. "Ian, you just like the way I taste."

"Yes, I do, because I can taste who you are."

"If you say I taste spicy, I'm walking out of here now."

"No, my dear," he said with a knowing smile. "You taste like life and death and life again."

What arrant nonsense. I suddenly thought about Edna.

"I'd like to go back now. Edna's probably wondering why I'm late to dinner."

Ian laughed. "Dinner was hours ago. But I will take you back if you wish."

Ian drove me to the ranch. He didn't come in, but turned to me and said, "I hope you realize how I feel about you."

Laughing nervously, I said, "We don't even know each other."

He looked as grave as death. "You don't know me, yet, but I know you. I've been waiting all my life for you."

Casual sex I understood, and I remembered too well what sex had been like with the beautiful boy I had loved, and I knew that Oswald had an irrational, intoxicating effect on me. But whatever this was confused me more than I cared to admit to myself.

twenty-five

one hundred years of sorditude

The next day was Saturday, so the whole family was around. I hid in my room, convinced that they would be able to tell that I was a shameless *puta.*

Edna caught me as I was trying to sneak into the small parlor. "Young Lady, I'm going shopping with Cornelia this afternoon, and it's about time you made a meal on your own. Write a grocery list of what you need."

Regardless of my internal agitation, Edna deserved an evening off. I dutifully gave her a list of ingredients for dinner and she went off to the store.

For cocktails, we could have mojitos. Mercedes and I had spent an afternoon experimenting with different recipes and mixing techniques when the rum drink became popular, and I had learned to mix a damn fine drink.

After Edna left, I realized that I had forgotten to put mint on the shopping list. I wondered if Oswald had any. I dashed across the field, went through the gate, and found a patch of mint and other herbs behind a thick screen of green bean vines. I was crouching there, picking out the healthiest leaves, when I heard the beat of hooves. Peeking through the vines, I saw Oswald and Cornelia on horseback. Once again, she was all in black, with shiny boots and a broad-brimmed hat.

I stayed hidden behind the greenery, assuming that they would ride off, but they dismounted and tied the horses to the fence. As they came through the gate, Cornelia said, "Really, Oswald, Winifred! Not quite your style."

"She is a good woman, Cornelia. We're well matched."

She stopped and faced him. "I don't see it. You know that I adore Winnie, but I cannot see you satisfied with a conventional priss when you could have so much more with your money and your looks."

Oswald's laugh was bitter. "She is not a priss, Corny. She's seen more in her career than most people see in a lifetime. I think I am doing very well for myself."

She made a face. "Oh, don't expect me to believe that! Not when I've known your previous conquests." She narrowed her eyes and said cheerfully. "Now, Milagro is a tasty little morsel. Ian is quite taken with her."

Oswald's smile was tight. "I wish you would tell him to leave her alone. She's a special girl and she needs . . . someone else."

"Really, Oswald, you are being very selfish. You never used to mind sharing your lovers. I was rather admiring how you ensconced her here under Winnie's nose. Or does Winnie enjoy her favors as well?"

"Milagro is not my lover," he said quickly, as if he was embarrassed to even be associated with me. "And she has no idea who Ian really is."

Cornelia smiled frostily. "My brother is a man of importance. It is an honor for him to show interest in her." She took Oswald's arm. "But, darling, let's not argue. After all, who knows, we could be seeing much more of each other soon."

"You can't mean Sam?"

Cornelia laughed merrily. "Isn't it a lark? I think he is such a dear man, so steady and kind. I am simply wild about his moral uprightness and integrity. Tell me you think it's a brilliant idea, Oswald."

He smiled but didn't answer her question. "Let's get that water you wanted and take the horses back."

When they went into the cottage, I crept out of the garden and loped to the house, my hands full of mint. My romantic life was none of Oswald's damn business.

I had plenty of time until dinner, so I wandered into the family room. Winnie, looking oddly ungainly and colorless, was staring blindly at a catalog on her lap. "Winnie, are you feeling okay?"

"I'm fine, I'm fine," she murmured. She was a girl who murmured naturally. "I'm fine. It's the wedding and everything. It's just a lot."

"If there's anything I can do, just ask."

She was a very different girl from the happy camper I'd seen dancing and singing a few days ago. The hollows under her eyes had a blue cast. "I have to pick patterns. I don't know what I want—except my mother. I wish my mother was here."

I plopped down beside her and took the catalog. The prices listed next to the pictures of china made my head spin. I picked up a pen and struck out an overdone floral pattern. "Too Home Shopping Network," I said. "Your turn."

She stared listlessly at the page. "Too modern," she said, crossing out a set with a geometric border.

"Too New Wave," I responded as I eliminated a swirly pink and gray pattern.

Winnie's next exclusion was a peach pattern. "Bland," she said.

"Winnie, you can do better than that. Tell me why you completely hate it."

She shrugged and said tentatively, "Too vomitous," and I laughed. After an hour, we'd selected an everyday pattern and a special occasion set, as well as silverware and crystal.

"Young Lady," she asked, "are you having fun with Cornelia and Ian?"

"They're very lively."

"Do you think Sam likes them, too?" she asked, and I realized that she had been left out of our fun.

"Sam?" I said, surprised. "I'm sure he does. Cornelia is quite fond of him, and it's about time poor Sam got some attention. You and Oswald are lucky to have each other—you can understand why he would want to be happy, too."

She nodded her head and her cornsilk hair swung forward. "You're right, of course." She held up another catalog. "Tomorrow can we work on linens and silver?"

"Of course." I decided to ask her something that had been on my mind. "Winsome, if things aren't resolved with CACA by your wedding, do you think Oswald will let me stay here on my own?" I asked.

Winnie pressed her lips together tightly, then said, "You can stay here with Sam. He's not going to the wedding."

I could see how upset she was and said, "Winnie, Sam doesn't have to babysit me! It's an important occasion—"

"It's not about you, Milagro. Sam thinks that someone needs to be here, to be the 'responsible' one." It was the first time I'd heard harshness in Winnie's voice.

The only thing I could do was hope that CACA would be vanquished in time for Sam to attend Winnie and Oswald's wedding.

Cooking kept me in the kitchen that evening and I was glad for it. Ian sauntered in while I was working, and his eyes lit up at the sight of the sharp knife in my hand. He stood behind me and I felt a wave of desire as his hands caressed my hips. In an uneven voice, I told him to kindly get the hell out.

I thought dinner was especially nice that night. We started with *ceviche* and mojitos, followed by Drunken Chicken in a *chorizo*-flavored sauce with capers, tequila, and orange juice. There was Spanish rice on the side, cooked in *caldo* (chicken broth), and even though it was a little soggy, it was tasty. Salad was romaine lettuce and avocado dressed in lime and oil.

Ian saw my nervousness and kept his distance, but I thought that Edna could tell that something had happened between us. I felt as guilty as the time my *abuelita* had caught me feeding her goldfish to the cat. Oswald avoided looking at me or talking to me, but I sensed his disapproval. Not that he had any right.

I'd baked a dense, double-layered chocolate cake. "Now for one of Mexico's greatest gifts to the world: chocolate," I announced in a too-bright voice, but I was envisioning an Aztec warrior carrying a maiden for a blood sacrifice.

"Well, Young Lady," said Edna. "I must say this is one of the best birthday dinners I've ever had."

Everyone turned to her in surprise. "Grandmama," said Sam, "I'm so sorry! I don't know how it slipped—"

"Oh, Edna!" cried Winnie. "I had no idea—"

"I forgot," said Oswald woefully. "How could I forget?"

"What good news, Edna," said Cornelia, and Ian said, "Congratulations!"

Edna hushed everyone. "At my age, sometimes it's best to forget a birthday. Having you all here is enough."

I dashed into my room and came back with the little turquoise bag that I'd gotten from the shop in town. "Happy birthday, Edna," I said, handing it to her.

She took the tissue wrapping off the tiny shelves and admired the miniature kitchen replicas. "*Muchas gracias,* Young Lady."

Oswald led us in singing "Happy Birthday," Edna blew out the candles on the table, and we clapped. It was as swell as the birthday parties I'd had when I was living with my grandmother. In fact, the only thing missing was a piñata to whack to smithereens. Too bad Sebastian wasn't around.

Ernie brought a few bottles of blood to the house that night. The evening became one big lovefest. Cornelia sat beside Sam, listening to him like he was revealing the secrets of the universe when he answered a question about tax shelters. Winnie drank more than usual, finally getting some color into her face, as Oswald sat beside her. I'd never seen her so affectionate toward Oswald; she held his hand, refilled his glass, ruffled his hair.

Oswald said, "Ian, tell me where you and Cornelia will be next month and maybe Winnie and I can arrange to visit with you on our honeymoon."

Ian glanced across the room at me. "I haven't confirmed any plans yet."

"Ian," said Cornelia, "I like it here. Let's lease a house for ourselves."

Sam brightened at the idea. "I would be happy to help you locate a suitable residence," he said.

"Would you?" Ian said. "The hotel is quite nice, but I appreciate privacy."

Edna said, "Do I hear correctly? You, in the country! You're the most urban creature I've ever known."

"And you are the most urbane creature I've ever known, madam," Ian riposted. "If you can adapt, I can, too. At least for a while."

Everyone saw the way he looked at me. "I think I'll turn in early," I said.

They all bid me good night, and I went to my room. "Daisy," I said to my *perra.* "I am seriously and sincerely conflicted." She wagged her tail and that helped. I opened *Jane Eyre* at a random page and found her being taunted by Mr. Rochester, a powerful, worldly man who actually did love poor, penniless Jane. Why was I feeling ashamed when my interlude with Ian had been one of mutual consent?

Still, I was relieved when he did not come to the ranch the next afternoon. Cornelia, Edna, and I had our own pool party. We wanted Winnie to join us but she said she'd rather sit and read.

We made a pitcher of mimosas and played Frank Sinatra and Dionne Warwick songs. I felt a wave of sadness that we could not open the retractable roof to the clear blue sky.

After dinner, Cornelia pulled me from the family room and said, "Ian just called and he's found a party."

"Is Pepper having a party?" Bikers in the daytime are one thing; bikers at night are another.

"No, not Pepper. Some new people."

Cornelia insisted on selecting my outfit. She went through my humble wardrobe and said, "How sad-making." She pulled out the puce dress and said, "Someone hung this rag in your closet," and tossed it on the floor. Then she selected the black chiffon skirt and white beaded sweater. "These will have to do. I'd loan you something, but I don't think my clothes would fit," she said, glancing at my chest.

She did some snazzy tricks to my hair, making it tousled and wild, and applied thick black liner to my eyes. "Don't make me look like a cheap hooker."

"No, you look like an expensive one." She laughed.

I thought that to someone as lighthearted as Cornelia, Winnie might seem prissy. Cornelia didn't perceive the important distinction between being a priss and having a serious and sincere nature.

Sam looked years younger in a black T-shirt and jeans. "What kind of party is this?" he asked Cornelia as we got into the car.

"Does it matter?" she answered.

"Don't Winnie and Oswald want to come?" I asked.

"They've got 'work' tomorrow," Cornelia said disdainfully.

Life seemed much more flexible when you didn't have a job or you ignored your obligations. Mercedes would not approve. I promised myself that I would return to my writing tomorrow.

Ian drove as though he knew the area well. "What I like about the country is that people have privacy. You can do what you like."

"You've mentioned privacy before, yet you're very social," I said.

"All things in proportion, Young Lady." He smiled at me. "You look very beautiful tonight."

"Big hair," I said, and when he laughed, I relaxed.

The isolated old house was painted a dark reddish purple. Now that I knew what puce was, I saw it everywhere. The only light visible was a dim bulb over the porch. "Are you sure this is the right address?" I asked. "It doesn't look like anyone is home." Then I noticed the rows of cars parked in the field.

"I'm sure."

When we got out of the car, I could hear low music throbbing from the house. Ian knocked on the front door and a white-faced waif peered out. He handed her a card, she glanced at it and said, "Welcome, Brethren Vampyres." I could tell she said it with a "y" like that because it was a hard vowel.

Candles didn't do much to illuminate the living room,

which was filled with other white-faced, heavily made-up creatures in interesting black leather and satin costumes. I did not understand the whole American Goth thing, you know, romanticizing death and lugubrious poetry and all that. That's because Mexicans are sort of exuberant Goths. They keep altars to the dead, celebrate *Dias De Los Muertos,* have black hair, and daydream merrily about their funerals.

Ian should have looked out of place in his light-colored suit and snowy shirt, but he seemed perfectly comfortable. "How quaint," he said when he saw the black-clothed table set against a wall with an inverted cross over it. Atop the table were black candles, a knife, a plaster skull, a chalice, and a bell.

"Simply marvelous," said Cornelia.

"Do you really think so?" asked Sam. "Why are we here?"

"Local color," answered Ian. "Wait, they're starting."

The room grew quiet and everyone faced the altar. Some awful John Cage music started, and I wished Mercedes was there to scold whoever put it on. From a doorway on the other side of the room came a woman dressed in a shiny black vinyl halter top and hot pants, black fishnet stockings, and platform boots. A huge silver pentagram hung from a chain around her neck. She was trying to hide her years with makeup and enormous breast implants. No wonder everybody stared.

She began to do a ritual cha-cha-cha of ringing the bell and turning around. Then she picked up the knife and pointed it toward the inverted cross and intoned, "*In nomine dei nostri Satanas Luciferi Excelsi!* In the name of our Master Satan, his High Excellence Lucifer, I call upon the forces of darkness and the infernal foundation of power!"

Ian put his finger to his lips because I had started laughing. His eyes sparkled with mischief, and Cornelia was enjoying herself, too. Sam, however, looked pained. He leaned to me and whispered, "This is grotesque."

The High Breastess did a whole lot more chanting, yammered about the gated community of hell and the forces of Dracul. I spaced out. I'm not big on rituals, and besides, Ian's hand was roaming around my posterior.

A figure came forward in a long, hooded cloak. The priestess declaimed, "I drink from this chalice, drink the *prana,* wellspring of all energy and strength, drink to fill my spirit so that my being can increase and be mighty and awful for all to behold. I drink of the essence of Tiffany," and with that she pulled away the figure's cloak and exposed the hotel girl who looked pasty as dough and really should have known better than to wear a white lace bra and panties if she didn't have a decent tan. I could see the gauze bandage wrapped around her wrist when she picked up the chalice, accidentally sloshing some viscous red liquid, and handed it to the priestess.

"I drink your essence, Tiffany, and you are a mere vessel of my desires, of my power. You are an empty shell and must do my bidding, so say the powers that I command here tonight . . ."

"Speaking of drinking, I'm getting one," I told Ian. He followed me out of the room into the kitchen. It had cute little café curtains with a barnyard scene and a marvelous old O'Keefe and Merritt stove. A huge punch bowl filled with red liquid sat on the butcher-block island.

I sniffed and knew it was the house drink in hell: Hawaiian

punch and cow's blood with a pineapple ice ring garnish. In the fridge I found a six-pack of beer. "Want one?" I asked Ian.

"Thank you. Were you amused by the ceremony?"

"If I wanted to see a bad drama, I'd buy a theater ticket."

"I appreciate their naiveté. The innocent confusion of vampires, I mean vampyres," he said with a smile, "and Satanism."

"Yeah, it's real cute," I said. "Calling upon the devil to increase your own power. When most people want to be immoral and have power, they just get an MBA."

"So young to be so cynical," he murmured.

I shrugged. "When you said party, I expected dancing."

Sam came into the kitchen, pulling Cornelia along with him. "Good heavens," he said, "I think they really did drain the blood out of that poor girl. I can't believe that's legal."

Cornelia caressed his arm. "Sam, you've been hiding in an office too long. She looked fine. But if you're bored, we don't have to stay."

As we were leaving, Tiffany spotted Ian and her dull eyes brightened. I'd bet that she had given him the invitation. "Ian," I said as we stepped outside, "Tiffany has a crush on you."

"I told you, I'm not interested in children," he said. "If you want to dance, we shall dance."

He drove down various roads, meandering back toward the ranch until he saw a brightly lit estate with valets parking cars.

"Who lives here?" Sam asked.

"Haven't the slightest, Sam." Ian pulled into the drive, stopped the car, and we got out. "What is this event, my good man?" he asked the valet, and I saw him palming a bill with his keys to the valet.

The valet checked to make sure the bill was a big one, shoved it into his pocket, and said, "Fund-raiser for the local children's hospital."

"That will suffice."

We were underdressed for the gathering, and I might have said something, but I heard fabulous live salsa music coming from the back of the house. "Let's go," I said, and this time I was pulling Ian along. We passed lemon trees in large urns, olive trees draped in tiny fairy lights, and round tables with guests sipping wine. My preliminary check showed two black couples, one possibly Latino man with a blond woman, and no Asians. A dance floor had been set up on a back terrace and a ten-piece band was playing some really hot rhythms.

Mercedes had patiently spent many evenings teaching me about Afro-Cuban music and how to dance to the heartbeat of the *clave.* I had struggled to learn the moves, but Ian danced them like a Caribbean, effortlessly guiding my steps, twirling me, leading me.

It was exhilarating, but I thought it was too easy. Ian maneuvering me so smoothly that I felt manipulated. Looking over at the other vampires, I saw that Sam was trying not to step on Cornelia's feet and struggling with the rhythm of the music. She was coaching him through the moves. I realized how unreasonable it was for me to take offense at Ian's graceful dancing.

When the song ended, Ian excused himself and found the hostess. I saw him write a check and flash his white, white teeth at her and she nearly wet herself with delight. I thought of Sebastian's accusation that I had been using him.

As the party progressed, Ian and Cornelia made several

new acquaintances and received invitations for exhibits, wine tastings, brunches, golf. I was invited, too, but I knew these people never would have paid attention to me if it hadn't been for the sophisticated vampires.

Though the hour was late, the band played on and we danced, Ian's swarthy face close, his hips directing the movement of mine, his lips nuzzling my neck. "I can't wait to be alone with you," he murmured in my ear. "Let's go."

After searching high and low for Cornelia and Sam, Ian said, "They'll manage to get home. Cornelia's quite resourceful."

Ian expected me to spend the night with him, but I wasn't ready to verify what the others suspected, that I was having sex with Ian. I agreed to go with him for an hour. In that time, he again touched me and stroked me in a way that was exquisitely pleasurable, and, drunk with sensation, I allowed him to make tiny incisions on my shoulder, which he sucked until they closed over.

After he dropped me off at the ranch, I sensed a presence in the darkness on the drive. "Who's there?"

Oswald stepped forward. "You're back late."

"The party just ended."

He simply looked at me. His features were so clear and open compared to Ian's worldly, shadowed face. "Milagro, it's not my place to give you advice, but think twice, hell, think three times before you get involved with Ian Ducharme. You have no idea what he's capable of."

"Actually, I do. Good night, Oswald." I went to bed feeling awful about the expression I'd seen on his face. Why did this damn man affect me so? The sooner he got married, the sooner I'd be able to move on with my life.

twenty-six

pardon my french (panties)

I'd remembered my promise to Mercedes, so I spent the day writing. Later, I caught Edna in the family room as she was watching an Italian comedy in Italian. She said, "The subtitles are missing half the jokes. Come sit beside me, Young Lady."

When the show was over, she turned off the television and faced me. "I dread asking this, but is there anything on your silly little mind?"

"Edna, I know that Sam doesn't approve of Winnie and Oswald having the wedding now because of everything that's going on with CACA, and he's feeling obligated to stay with me while you go off to Prague for the festivities, but I think his mood is upsetting Winnie and Oswald."

"Yes, I would say that it is." Her emerald eyes sparked in curiosity.

"Well, maybe you could say something to him."

She sighed. "Young Lady, I cannot describe to you the anguish it puts me through to see my grandchildren behaving foolishly. However, it is my experience that people must make their own decisions in matters of love and marriage."

"But Sam is not the one getting married! If Oswald and Winnie have made up their minds, then he should respect their decision."

Edna looked to the ceiling for heavenly guidance. "Sam is a very smart man. I am hoping that he will allow his heart to lead him instead of always doing what is responsible."

"Maybe Cornelia can convince him to go."

She paused before speaking. "Cornelia and her brother are charming people and can be very persuasive. I enjoy their company when they visit." She left the rest for me to infer.

I completely agreed with her that Sam should let his heart lead the way. Then I decided that he needed some encouragement. I lurked around until he was alone in the study. "Hi, Sam," I said, closing the door behind me.

"Hi, Young Lady," he answered quietly.

I pulled a chair beside his. "Sam, do you mind if I speak honestly?" He didn't say no, so I continued: "Don't you care for Winnie's feelings? And Oswald's, too?"

My comment took him aback and he sputtered, "Of course, of, I mean, yes, I mean, what do you mean?"

"If we're their true friends, then we celebrate their love,

right? You need to put your preoccupation with CACA aside long enough to show that you're happy for them."

Sam looked gloomy and said, "Yes, I guess you're right."

"And now that you and Cornelia are getting along so well, you empathize with how Oswald and Winnie feel about each other."

Sam fiddled with his pen before speaking. "I've always wanted to marry for love, Milagro. Not because the rest of the family thinks it's a good match, but because I love someone and she loves me and nothing else matters. If I found a girl who felt the same way, I would stand up to the family and demand that they accept the relationship."

Did he mean that the family might not approve of a match with Cornelia? "Sam," I said as I remembered Edna's words, "let your heart lead you." I left him to think about my suggestion.

I had just walked into the garden when I saw Daisy come crouching toward me. "Hey, girl . . . ," I began before I noticed the crimson staining the snowy blaze on her chest. She looked at me with her golden eyes. Bending down, I saw a large gash below her neck. The blood seemed to be coagulating, but the torn flesh looked bad. I said, "It's okay, girl, it'll be okay, girl," as I gathered her carefully in my arms.

I hoped that either Oswald or Winnie would be home as I ran toward the cottage, with Daisy quietly enduring the jolts as I stumbled over the clumps and pits in the field. "Help!" I shouted as I struggled with the gate. "Help!"

Oswald opened the front door and hurried to me. "Oswald, she's hurt! Do something, please." I didn't cry until he took Daisy from my arms and carried her inside.

"Calm down—it's just a cut. I can take care of it." He pushed aside books and newspapers on the long plank table and laid her down. He pointed to his "command center" and said, "Get my bag."

A black leather satchel embossed with OKG leaned against the side of the metal desk. I took it to him.

Daisy whined softly as he tenderly probed the cut. "This is wrong," he said in a worried voice. "But it isn't bad."

"What do you mean?"

"It's a clean incision. Barbed wire or a nail would leave something more jagged. I'm going to clean it and close it up. Infection's what we have to worry about."

He told me to get him a razor and a towel from the bathroom. After grabbing a thick white towel, I went to the cabinet and shoved aside bottles of Swiss skin care products before I found a jar holding disposable razors. I hurried back to Oswald, who had filled a bowl with warm, soapy water.

"I need you to hold her still," he said.

I couldn't watch what he was doing. I turned my head and focused on the room while holding Daisy. The furniture had been rearranged, everything was clean, and there were fresh flowers on a side table.

"You're letting her wiggle," he said firmly.

I tightened my grip on Daisy and pressed my face into the soft fur on her back. To distract myself I said, "Where did you get all this weird furniture?"

"I bought it as a lot in an auction. The auctioneer hinted that it might contain interesting American country antiques and this is what I got."

"Oh. It looks like my old furniture."

He said, "I'm almost done," but several minutes passed before he finally announced, "There."

I looked at Daisy. There was a bare patch on her chest and the wound was closed by tiny black stitches. "It looks awful."

"Awful? This is possibly the best cosmetic surgery that has ever been performed on a canine. I also gave her an eye-lift, and once the swelling goes down, she'll look like a puppy again."

I laughed out of relief. "Why do you do it?"

"What?" He put Daisy on the floor and she waggled her back end gallantly.

"Cosmetic surgery."

He shrugged. "I'm good at it. I told you I have excellent small motor skills. Let me guess—you think it's decadent and self-indulgent."

"I didn't say that."

"You didn't have to," he said with a tight grin.

"My mother Regina has had a lot of plastic surgery. Her face is like a mask."

"Some people would rather wear a mask than show their face to the world," he said as he walked toward the bathroom to wash up.

I heard the water running and I glanced down at myself. My blouse was smeared with bright red blood, but for the first time since I'd been infected, I felt no desire at the sight. I went to the kitchen sink and sponged soap on the fabric so that the stain wouldn't set, and then I washed my hands.

Oswald returned to the room with a damp hand towel. He

began wiping the blood and grime from my face with the same heartbreaking tenderness I recalled from my fever dream. What was wrong with me that I couldn't feel this way toward Ian?

"Milagro," he said, "it's easy to be dismissive of cosmetic surgery when you're naturally beautiful."

"It's not a moral judgment . . . ," I began, wary of his compliment. I knew that his ideal was Winnie. "I don't have to defend my beliefs to you."

"No, you don't. I don't have to defend my profession to you, but I will say that it's not all about vanity. It's about making people feel that they're not outsiders or freaks. It's about fitting in. Yes, I also perform surgeries for spoiled women who have more money than common sense, but that income allows me to do the other work for people who've been in fires or accidents or wars, for those who were born with problems."

I was going to say something about the tyranny of the media in defining a vacuous and unreal standard of perfection, when we both heard a clear "ahem."

Winnie stood in the doorway watching us.

"Hi, Winnie," Oswald said quickly. "Daisy had an accident and Milagro brought her here."

The dog was nowhere to be seen, and Winnie sighed heavily. She looked sallow and unwell.

"Daisy!" I called out, and the dog trotted back into the house with muddy paws.

One glance at her was enough to change Winnie's expression. "Poor Daisy! What happened to you?"

"I don't know. It was a clean incision so she sliced herself on something razor sharp," Oswald answered. "She'll be fine." He went to his desk and took out an amber prescription bottle. He counted out pills into a tiny manila envelope. "Here are some antibiotics. Give them to her twice a day—once in the morning and once at night."

"Okay," I said as I took the envelope from Oswald. "See you later, Win."

As I walked out of the shack, Daisy scampered into the vegetables after a bird. "Make sure to keep that wound clean until it heals up."

Mumbling, "Thanks for all your help with the dog," I took Daisy back to the house, washed her paws with a hose, and led her to my room. I closed the door firmly. Daisy sprawled on the bed as if she was perfectly fine.

I took a shower and put on my cute aqua silk capri pants and shell, did my makeup, painted my toenails a glittery pink, and slipped my feet into leopard-print slides. I parted my hair on the side and dried it slick and straight. I looked in the mirror and noticed that my breasts and hips had returned to their rounder, more succulent shapes. "Welcome back, girls," I said. "I can always use your company."

twenty-seven

we don't need no stinkin' badges

Ian and Cornelia showed up for cocktails. As twilight fell and drinks were refilled, we all enjoyed *espíritu de los cocteles,* except for Winnie, who only played with her drink. She looked like an anemic angel in a pale yellow raw silk sheath. My own ensemble seemed hopelessly gaudy.

While Cornelia openly showed her affection for Sam, Ian sat with Edna instead of me. Glancing at me, Ian said to Edna, "She reminds me a little of you."

Edna rolled her great eyes and said, "Are you insulting me or complimenting her?" and he laughed.

"Maybe he's insulting me and complimenting you," I said.

"She's a dreadful girl," Edna replied with a smile.

"I think so, too. I'd like to take her out after dinner, if it's acceptable to you."

"I'm not her mother Regina," Edna replied.

"I am an adult and can make my own decisions, thank you very much," I said.

"They're frequently dreadful decisions," Oswald offered with a cool smile directed at Ian.

For Winnie's sake, I held my tongue.

Before we left, Ernie brought over a bottle of mutton. I was sitting in the corner, and Winnie came to perch on the arm of my chair. I took a sip of the mutton-tainted drink. It was unlike any other blood I'd had: deep and pungent. It revolted me and I put down my glass.

"It's strong stuff," Winnie said. "But the older members of the family like it."

"Winnie," I said very quietly, "is Edna's husband still alive?"

"Yes," she said softly. "Alive and living in Nova Scotia."

"What broke them up?"

Winnie glanced at Edna, who was chatting with Ian, one languid arm stretched out with a glass of crimson liquid, her sleek legs crossed. "Edna's one of the last great femme fatales," Winnie said, so earnestly that I almost laughed.

"What?"

"Men find her irresistible and do stupid things to impress her. My mother says an infatuated admirer told her he was going to kill Uncle Allen, that's her husband, and she thought he was joking and said she'd be delighted." Winnie's blue eyes grew wide in the telling and we both glanced at Edna again.

"What happened?" I whispered.

"So her admirer challenged Uncle Allen to a duel, and when he refused, the admirer tried to shoot Uncle Allen, missed by a mile, and then committed suicide. It was a huge scandal."

"Well," I said, "Edna shouldn't have been held responsible for one deluded guy . . ."

"It wasn't *one* deluded guy. Men were always falling for her. There was an incident that no one will tell me about, and after that, Uncle Allen said enough is enough."

"I think she still has that effect," I said.

Winnie sighed. "What's it like, Mil, to make men do crazy things over you?"

The question was ridiculous. "I don't know what you mean. I'm generally the one doing stupid things."

"If you say so," she said skeptically.

"Winsome, they may want to boink me, but you're the kind of girl they want to marry," I answered. "You're the one they take seriously."

She thought before speaking. "I don't want to be the careful choice, the cautious choice, Young Lady. I want to be the passionate, irrational choice."

I thought that she should be satisfied by having someone as fabulous as Oswald in love with her. "You've just got wedding jitters." I took her hand—it seemed so finely boned and soft—and wanted to protect her from her own insecurities. "You must be excited about getting married."

"What girl wouldn't be?" She smiled a little, but her tension seemed to spread to others, so I didn't mind leaving after dinner with Ian. "I have a special surprise for you," he said.

"You don't have to buy me things."

"It's not a thing. It's an experience, one that I expect you to find very pleasurable."

When we arrived at the hotel's carriage house, he opened the door to reveal dozens of candles flickering inside. "For you." The room was filled with flowers, their scent heavy in the warm air. It took me a moment to see the girl on the bed, lying in her underwear on a plastic sheet, her watery blue eyes blinking lashes thick with mascara. Sharp implements glittered on a silver tray on the table beside the bed.

"Tiffany?" I said.

"Hi, I am your vessel. Take your *prana,* energy, from me and drink of me and restore your dark power and stuff."

I turned to my companion. "Ian, what exactly do you mean by this?"

"A treat for you. Human blood is so far superior to animal blood and, yours, ah, Milagro." He took me in his arms. "I didn't even know anything like it, like you, existed." He caressed my body. "Of course, this girl's is not nearly the same quality, but still interesting. I would offer myself to you, but the effects might be deleterious."

Okay, all men are perverts. Any man you know, get him comfortable enough and he will reveal some warped desire. Case in point: Sebastian. It's their nature and I understand even if I do not concede to all their demented requests.

Ian went to the bed and picked up an old-fashioned razor. Tiffany quivered and her mouth opened. He was about to slice into her flesh when I said, "Stop it!" and yanked his arm away.

"What are you doing?" he asked, puzzled. "There's no harm in it. She wants it. She likes it, don't you, Tiffany?"

Tiffany bobbed her head in acquiescence. "My dark lord may do what he's into. My only wish is to serve his desires and everything and be his vessel."

"This girl doesn't know what she wants," I said. I took her hands and made her sit up. "Tiffany," I said sternly, "he is not your dark lord. He's just a guy who wants to use you."

Ian poured himself a brandy. "Is this necessary, Milagro?" he asked. "Why can't you face the reality of your role in the world? Some are predators and some are prey."

"It's cool," Tiffany said. "The dark lord can use me to nourish his internal, I mean infernal, power."

"No, it's totally not cool," I said to Tiffany. "One, you could get blood-borne infections. Two, you could get scars," and I saw that I was too late, her arms bore old pale marks as well as fresh scabs. "Three, he doesn't like you the way you like him, *muchacha,*" I said, and finally saw a flash of something in her eyes. "And, four, if you got out of this little village, you might find enough to interest you so you wouldn't have to dabble in devil worship nonsense. And you should find a decent religion. I've heard great things about the Unitarians."

"Are you about done?" Ian asked in a bored voice.

"Yes."

Moving so swiftly that I couldn't stop him, Ian crossed the room and lightly slashed Tiffany's breast with the razor. The blood rose quickly in the cut and he said, "Drink, Milagro, drink!"

I shook my head and he said calmly, "How is this any different than what you've allowed me to do?" He bent over the girl to suck at her blood. I couldn't bear to watch as Tiffany writhed in ecstasy, but when I tried to leave, Ian reached out and grabbed my wrist hard. Her blood was still on his mouth when he drew me to him for a kiss.

"No!" I cried, twisting away and struggling to be free of his embrace.

He released me, and his dark eyes searched my face. "You have no idea what you mean to me. I offer whatever you want. I will care for you and give you all the pleasure you desire, all the things that amuse you. I will treasure you as the rare creature you are. You only have to tell me what you want."

He was charming and persuasive. He was an entertaining visitor. "What I want, Ian, is to earn something on my own. I'm not quite sure what that is yet, but I know I don't want to be treated like a vessel or a vassal, like a possession or a pet."

"If that is what you'd like . . ." He didn't bother looking at Tiffany, but said to her, "Girl, get dressed and go."

She slowly began gathering her clothes. Her face bore the same glazed expression the biker Artie had had.

"Ian, it's not going to happen. I'm saying good-bye now."

Tiffany was fumbling with her boots. I helped her put them on. Ian watched me struggling to shove Tiffany's floppy arms into her sweater.

"My heart," he said finally. "I asked if you would endanger my mind, my body, or my soul. The answer is my heart."

I remembered my dream of listening to Oswald's heart beating; I wanted to feel that perfect unity again, even if it was only a fantasy. "I don't know if you're a bad man, Ian, but I don't think you're a good one."

I opened the door and waited for Tiffany. Her eyes finally focused on Ian, and she whimpered, "Please let me stay, Master."

I left her with him.

On the long and dusty walk back to the ranch, I wondered why I had thought it acceptable for Ian to cut me, while I was upset that he cut a very eager Tiffany. Was it because I saw her as clueless and deluded; was I really so much more aware?

A car slowed down beside me and I glanced over to see Oswald's sedan. The window slid down and he said, "Want a ride?"

I kicked my foot to get a pebble out of my sandal and said, "What are you doing here?" I got into the car.

"There was another attack on an animal and I got worried. I called Ian and he told me you'd left."

"What kind of attack?"

"Sheep two ranches over had their throats slit." He glanced at me and I could see his concern. "Ernie said they were drained of blood."

"Daisy!" I said.

"Looks like that wasn't an accident." His kind of fabulous face looked troubled. "Milagro, what were you doing walking back tonight? Why didn't Ian give you a lift home?"

"Ian was occupied," I said. "I'd really rather not talk about it."

Oswald was good enough to respect my request and left me to mull over the unfortunate scene at the carriage house and the animal deaths. Blood was all around.

twenty-eight

too hot to handle

The day was sunny and lovely, giving no indication of trouble nearby. Sam, Oswald, Edna, Winnie, and Ernie were conferring in the kitchen about the animal killings. Cornelia sat on a counter, drinking something that looked like tomato juice. "Ernie," Oswald said, "put the horses in the small turnout where we can keep an eye on them, and I want the other animals in the stalls."

"Why do you think someone's doing this?" Winnie asked.

"Sadism," Edna suggested.

Sam looked concerned. "I checked with the sheriff's office. They're talking about ritual killings. Satanic practices."

"That's unbelievable," Edna scoffed, and then she saw our guilty expressions. "What?"

Sam was the one brave enough to tell her. "There are some local Satanists, vampire-wannabes," he said. "They looked harmless enough. We stopped in at one of their parties . . ."

"What!" Oswald said. "When you know that CACA is after us? Have you lost your mind, Sam?"

"Don't blame him," Cornelia said. "Ian took us and we had no idea what to expect. It was quite droll."

"Droll?" Winnie said. "They may be killing animals."

"Doesn't that kind of thing happen in the country all the time?" Cornelia asked. "Crop signs, animal slaughter, alien abductions . . ." Her nose wrinkled with distaste and she added, "Bad perms."

Ernie shrugged. "Maybe four years ago, a coupla cats got hung from trees. They figured it was some kids."

"You see, it is of no import." Cornelia turned to me. "Milagro, if I could have a word?"

If she wanted me to go out with her and Ian, I'd have to think of some excuse. "Sure." I poured myself a cup of coffee and we went to the study.

When we were settled on the sofa, I said, "What's up?"

Her smile was sympathetic. "Milagro, Ian's told me that you had a falling-out last night. He thinks it was most unfortunate."

"It was unfortunate," I admitted. "I hope that you and I can remain friends."

Her bony hand reached out and she lightly ran her red nails across my wrist. "I wanted us to be more than friends. This is very sudden, I know, but I've seen how Ian feels about you, and I thought that you and I might be sisters someday."

I shook my head, amazed. "No, that can't be. I will never feel that way about him."

Sam came into the room and we both turned to him. "Sam, darling," Cornelia cooed. "Please try to convince Milagro to give my brother another opportunity to win her affections. She's being very unreasonable."

Sam said evenly, "Milagro is entitled to make her own decisions. If she doesn't want a relationship with Ian . . ."

"How can she know what she wants?" Cornelia demanded, eerily echoing my own words about Tiffany. Cornelia faced me and said, "You will never have this chance again. Ian can give you everything you've ever dreamed of and all you have to do is lie back and let him take a sip now and then."

Her comment took Sam by surprise. He looked at me and I nodded guiltily.

"Now, Milagro," Cornelia continued, "women have always loved him and men, too. Don't tell me that a common Mexican girl is going to deny him?" Her voice was sweet, but her eyes glittered with anger.

"You underestimate the determination of common Mexican girls," I said icily. "I am not going to change my mind."

"Is it because you're jealous?" she asked with a little laugh. "So what if he drank the blood of some tramp? Is that reason for you to run off like a stupid child? Don't be so provincial."

"He did what?" Sam asked, taken aback.

"That hotel girl," Cornelia said dismissively. "She was a willing thrall. He even paid her, which shows his generosity when so many beg to serve him."

"Cornelia, surely you can see how wrong that is?" Sam said.

"In a committed relationship there can be an agreement about some activities, but—"

"Sam, my brother and I are vampires. We are proud to live as vampires. We take whom we desire, when we desire. We may drink animal blood in a barn out of politeness to our hosts, but we don't cower from the world."

He comprehended the full force of her insult even as she did not. "I'm very sorry you feel that way, Cornelia. I do not approve of such selfish, amoral behavior, regardless of its legality."

Seeing that she had gone too far, Cornelia retreated. "Oh, Sam, this is our first argument! We have so much time to reconcile our differing ideas—"

"I'm afraid not," he said firmly. "Cornelia, it was a pleasure to have you and your brother visit us. We do hope to see you sometime in the future."

"But, Sam," she began. When she saw his resolution, she recovered with chilly aplomb. "Yes, it has been a lovely visit. Please tell the others that I've remembered another engagement. Other parties, other resorts," she said, "so many other lovers . . ." She strode out of the room without looking back.

When we heard her sharp heels on the stairs, Sam said, "Sorry about that, Young Lady."

"Are you sure you want her to leave?"

"Yes." He sat on the edge of his desk and massaged his forehead. "I'd heard about their ways, but I found myself compromising because I liked Cornelia's attention. So I ignored that biker in Lower Sky and the party of 'vampyres.' And you, too. That was my fault."

"It happens to the best of us."

"I gather that Ian proffered a long-term agreement."

"If that's lawyer talk for a serious relationship, yes," I said. "He's like a force of nature."

"So are you," said Sam. "That's what he saw in you."

"I think she really liked you, Sam," I said, trying to console him. "Were you falling in love with her?"

Sam shook his head sadly. "I have an idea of the kind of woman I want. Cornelia isn't it."

We stayed in the study until we heard cars come and go, the docs off to work and Cornelia leaving. Then Sam started making phone calls about the animal killings. I took my typewriter outside. The other dogs were locked in the barn, but I kept Daisy beside me in the fenced garden.

I would have liked to talk to someone about Ian, but I couldn't even think of revealing the tawdry details of our intimacy to Winnie or Edna. I kept telling myself that I hadn't done anything wrong.

The day progressed into a quiet evening. Winnie told us that Cornelia had joined her brother at the hotel and would leave tomorrow. I felt everyone's eyes upon me and Edna said, "I told him to be careful with you, but no one listens to me."

The next morning, a horse was found eviscerated at the stables on the outskirts of town. Ernie found out through the Mexican-worker grapevine that the entrails had been arranged in a pentagram. The heart was missing.

A wire report of the animal killings went out and a few reporters started drifting into town, asking questions about ritual sacrifices. Some of the more racist locals were claiming that these were Santeria practices and wanted to round up all the immigrants for questioning. "Stay at the house," Sam said to me. "The last thing we need is for a TV camera to catch you."

Sam met up with me on my walk with Daisy the next morning. "Are you keeping an eye on me?" I asked.

"Safety in numbers," he said. We walked for several minutes in companionable silence. "Are you bored here?"

Ribbons of morning fog hung on the mountains around us. The fields were damp and the air was fresh with the scent of dew. "No, it's so very beautiful here."

"Do you really want to leave?"

"It's not as if I can stay here indefinitely, can I?"

Sam was quiet again for a long time. "You seem to get along with all of us and . . . I just thought, I thought, since we're both alone and in this condition . . ." He paused before continuing. "We don't have to be alone. I know I've been preoccupied by CACA and distracted by Cornelia. I find you very attractive and I hope you find me attractive, too. More important, I think you are a good person. I have an excellent income and I'm a steady worker. I am obliged to tell you that my chances of fathering a child are extremely low. I don't know how you feel about having children . . ." A blush rose in his cheeks.

"Sam, are you proffering an offer?"

He nodded his head. "Milagro, I just ask you to consider that we might have a good chance of being happy together."

It wasn't the most romantic speech I'd ever heard. Nevertheless, it came from a serious, responsible man, a man I could trust who also looked fabulous. "Thank you, Sam. I would like to take your offer under consideration."

He smiled with relief. "Please take your time deliberating. I believe that if we proceed with caution we can avoid some of the hazards common to many relationships."

"Sam, can we keep this to ourselves for now? I don't want to take away anything from Winnie and Oswald's celebration."

I went to bed that night and mulled over everything that had happened. The choice was obvious when I was presented with beach-read relationships, hedonistic Ian Ducharme, and admirable Sam. I had found the happy middle ground. I was becoming the sincere and serious woman I longed to be. I don't know what I dreamed, but I awoke confused and in a cold sweat.

twenty-nine

the icing on the sin cake

The good news was that there had been no animals killed that night. The bad news was that more reporters had come to our little village and I was confined to the ranch.

To amuse myself, I dressed up for dinner. I slipped on the shocking pink dress and beige sandals with shells that I had found at Ye Olde Rose and Grape Consignment Charitee Shoppe. The silky fabric of the dress slithered over my flesh, clinging like a mountaineer to a precipice. Scrunching my hair with gel made it wave a little. I paid special care to smudging the liner and blending shadow to make my eyes sexy.

I scrutinized myself in the mirror, turning this way and that. Odd. I seemed to have acquired a tan. I had been so preoccupied in looking out for intruders on my walks that I had forgotten to wear sunscreen. Self-condemnation wasn't easy when my tan was so yummy.

It was time to give Daisy her antibiotic, but I couldn't find her anywhere in the house. I went to the back door and called to her, imagining the worst. I dashed to the barn and Ernie gave me a serious once-over and said, "*Dios mio,* but you're looking *muy* juicy, *mamacita,*" before he told me that he'd seen her near the cottage.

I ran across the field, shouting, "Daisy, Daisy!" but I couldn't see her shaggy-dogginess anywhere. When no one answered my knock at the cottage, I opened the door, saying, "Hello, Winnie?"

Oswald came out of the bathroom, a towel wrapped around his waist. His stomach was flat and his chest had just the right amount of hair running between his well defined pectorals. His gray eyes were shining and his skin was flawless.

I stared stupidly before pulling myself together. I looked this way and that, anywhere but at Oswald. "Is Winnie back?"

"Not yet. She's on her way, though."

"Oh, I can't find Daisy anywhere." I tried to keep my voice light, but it cracked and my eyes began to well.

He clapped his hands and I experienced a moment of panic that the movement would shake the towel off his body, which was absurd since it was snugly wound around his slim hips. "Daisy, come!" he ordered. I heard the patter of her nails on the hardwood floor and she skittered out of the bedroom.

"Bad girl, bad girl," I said, bending over to ruffle her fur, relieved to see her whole and safe.

"That's a topic you should know something about."

"What do you mean by that?"

"What the hell do you think you were doing with Ian Ducharme?" he said sharply.

"Ian's single and at least he really wanted to have a relationship with me. Not that it's any of your damn business whom I date."

"Dating? Is that what you call it?"

His attitude was really detracting from my enjoyment of his belly button and my happiness about Daisy. "Yeah, dating and scorching, depraved, bloodsucking sex." I came close to him and looked him straight in the eyes. "Would you like me to describe it? What he did to my body?" I said huskily. "How incredible it was when he . . ."

My effort to taunt Oswald only succeeded in getting myself all worked up. We stood but a few inches apart and it was as if we were playing a game of chicken.

I flinched first and broke eye contact. "Damn it, Oswald, you have never apologized for what you did to me."

"Wanted to, couldn't," he said, and stepped back.

"You couldn't? You lack the power of human speech?"

"I *couldn't.* Sam told me not to."

My particular method of processing this information consisted of my rapidly spitting out, "What? What? What?"

"Apologizing admits liability."

"You *are* liable for what happened. Sam knows that."

Oswald walked into the bedroom and came out with a shirt. "He's a lawyer. More important, he's one of my lawyers."

I struggled to compose myself. "Oswald," I said in as calm

a voice as I could manage, "lawyers give advice. You don't have to take it."

"You're right. I'm sorry, Milagro. Are we square then?"

I considered telling him that we should seal our truce by licking each other all over. Instead I said, "Yes, we're square."

We both jumped at the sound of footsteps. "Oswald," Winnie called. She came into the room and saw us standing there.

I didn't want her to know that we'd been squabbling again. "Hi, Winnie. I was looking for Daisy, and she was here."

"Daisy again," she said skeptically. This time the dog in question was in clear view.

"Okay, I'm taking her back to the house."

Winnie's stare turned clinical. "Milagro, do you have a tan?"

"It's possible," I said.

Both of them said, "Hmmm," in that ominous doctor way. "I'd like you to have another exam tomorrow," Winnie said.

I felt fine and didn't want another exam, but I wasn't going to argue with her now.

Walking back with Daisy, I thought about how I always misinterpreted every interaction with men as sexual. Sure, it was a fun thing to do when you were drinking gimlets and gossiping with your gay friends. I loved my gay friends with a passion; however, even I had to admit that they were occasionally wrong. Not every stunning actor was a homosexual and not every encounter with an attractive person was sexually charged.

Just as I was missing the advice of gay friends, Gabriel's

truck came down the drive. He hopped out and gave me a big hug before observing, "Girlfriend, how did you get that tan?"

"The medics have already been alerted." I hooked his arm in mine. "How are things going?"

"Since it's almost done, you may as well know. We've almost hacked into CACA's accounts. Then we'll have those bastards. They've got more shady deals than a queen's got attitude. But the real dirt is I hear you made a conquest of Ian Ducharme!"

"Gawd, does this family do anything but gossip?"

"Lawdy lawdy, Miz Milagro, what a sexy dark lord he is. Mad, bad, and dangerous to know."

The smile froze on my face. "Why do you say 'dark lord'?"

Gabriel shrugged too casually. "Just an expression, you know, his dark coloring and whole lord-of-the-manor way. Many have tried to capture him, but only you have succeeded. He's still in town, you know, until tonight."

"And I'm still not interested."

"I'd do him in a heartbeat."

"You're welcome to him." Laughing, we went into the house.

Gabriel had hardly said hello to everyone when Ernie brought us the news that a coop of chickens had been discovered mutilated on a property in town.

The location increased people's fear that a human would be the next victim. Helicopters began circling overhead and the media covered the animal slayings nonstop. We left the television and radios on, listening to the coverage. I thought of Cornelia when a local woman with a bad perm was interviewed about Satanic practices and instead rambled incoherently about her alien abduction.

Journalists went to Lower Sky, where one Ernest Culpepper, aka Pepper, told them that his biker *compañeros* had long renounced devil worship and were good churchgoing men.

The moon was full that night. Winnie was locked in her room, grimly going over final wedding details, and Sam and Gabriel were working in the study. Edna was in the family room watching the news. I couldn't stand it anymore, so I decided to dangle my feet in the pool and stare at the sky.

A man was walking in the shadows from the direction of the barn. I assumed it was Ernie and said, "*Hola, guapo.*"

Oswald stopped short and said, "Milagro, what are you doing out here?"

"I'm going to the pool." I hope he didn't know I'd just called him handsome.

"You shouldn't be by yourself." Oswald lifted his arm and I saw the glint of a bottle in his hand. He took a long pull. "I'll go with you." He held out the bottle.

It seemed rude to turn down a drink. I took the bottle and lifted it to my mouth, not knowing what it was. Rum warmed my throat. It tasted so good I drank again.

The moon shone brightly as we walked to the swimming compound. We entered the gate, and it swung shut behind us. Oswald opened the roof panels, and the night sky appeared. The lights came on, illuminating the azure pool. Small spots lit up along the compound's periphery.

Oswald took another drink and walked to the side of the pool as I trailed behind. "Are you going to swim?" I asked him.

"No, but I might consider drowning myself." He passed the bottle to me and I took a long, slow swallow. "Stay with me awhile." He sat down sideways on an oversized chaise longue.

It is not easy for a lady to sit upright on cushy outdoor furniture. Especially when said lady was beginning to feel the effects of potent potables. I contemplated my dilemma as I had another swig. Perhaps the answer was in letting my feet brace me as I tried to keep my spine straight.

"Young Lady," he said, passing me the bottle again. "I'm going to be a married man very soon."

"I know, Oswald. Congratulations."

We both drank to his upcoming nuptials and then he said, "She doesn't love me."

The statement was suspended between us like a spider in a web. "I thought you two had great sex."

The sound he made was not a laugh. "Not to my knowledge."

I tried to recall what Winnie had told me. "I remember exactly. Winnie said you were very compatible in one important way."

He smiled that devastating crooked smile. "You misinterpreted. What's important to her is our fertility levels. She and I are very compatible in the probability that we will, with the help of modern medicine, eventually be able to have children."

"Oh," I said, pondering this news. "So no great sex?"

"No sex at all. Ever. She cringes when I touch her and makes excuses."

I felt great sorrow for both Oswald and Winnie. I had to lean against Oswald to think about this, and because the nature of the chaise dictated relaxation and also because Oswald and I were sharing our final *espíritu de los cocteles.* His body was strong and I thought that a girl could trust him to keep her upright.

It seemed that Oswald expected some comment so I said, "That is so, so, so sad, Oswald."

"Yes, it is." He cleared his throat with another drink and held the bottle up for me to take a swallow. "Why Ian?"

"Are you still stuck on that? It's not like you're available."

"No," he said. "I wish I was. How was the sex with him?"

It seemed an invasive question, highly impertinent. I would have told him so except that "impertinent" seemed too complicated to pronounce at that moment. "Physically amazing, but emotionally very confusing. Do you know what I mean?"

"No, not really. I was afraid you had fallen in love with him."

"We seem to be talking about the absence of love tonight," I observed, and thought I was being very profound.

We drank a little more and he said, "That night in the hotel, if we had, you know, what do you think it would have been like?"

Maybe it was our camaraderie, but I admitted, "Oswald, even kissing you was the most damn satisfying thing I've ever experienced. And that is why I hate you."

"Same here, except for the hate part." he said. "Why do you hate me?"

"Because I mean nothing to you. You're engaged to a very dedicated and wonderful woman who is your physical and spiritual ideal." I suddenly remembered Sam. "Do you know that Sam and I want to develop our relationship? We're like that. We share common values and respect. I need to learn how to play chess."

"You do mean something to me," Oswald said as he put down the bottle and turned to me. "And I respect every damn inch of you." His breath was warm and somehow, who knows how these things happen, it's one of those unfathomable mysteries of the universe, we were facing each other and his arms were around me.

"Milagro," he said, low and hoarse, "I wanted to stop it, but Winnie wouldn't agree. She said we have to follow through with this wedding. And I . . . I will never again be with a woman who wants me, a woman who takes pleasure from my touch . . ." As he said this, his fingers were moving down my bare arms, sending delicious tremors through me. "All I am asking for is one night with you . . . something I can remember."

His mouth was on mine and he had the same intoxicating effect as before. I didn't think of caution or appropriateness or morality; all I thought of was that I needed to touch Oswald and I needed him to touch me. Oswald tugged off my clothes and showed proper appreciation of my fancy undergarments. In fact, he stood me before him and ran his hands all over me, saying, "Beautiful, beautiful."

He unclasped my bra and slipped off my panties. I was acutely aware of the fact that I was naked in front of a man used to gravity-defying, synthetic breasts, liposuctioned stomachs, and surgically enhanced fannies and thighs. My hands flew up to cover my breasts.

"No, no," Oswald murmured, moving my hands away. "They're perfect, real," and his own hands covered them. The chaise was too unstable, so he threw the mattress onto the cement. Our arms tangled and fingers fumbled as we struggled to remove his clothing. When we finally succeeded, I decided that Oswald was not sort of fabulous, he was truly fabulous.

Then we were on the mattress and, oh, la, he was a man who was going off to war and I was a grateful girl who was giving him his last hurrah. I lost all perception of time as we rolled and moved together, shifted positions, and explored each other. I didn't feel like Milagro anymore, but part of whatever he was, what we were together, and this was the way we were supposed to be.

"Oswald," I said, "I had a dream about you when I was sick." I adored his crooked smile.

"It wasn't a dream," he said. "It was the only way I could think of to save you, jump-starting your immune system."

We were kissing and our lips were tender from small nips and bites. "I wish we could stay this way forever," he murmured in my ear.

"I can't believe this!" a woman shrieked.

Oswald and I both looked to see Winnie and Sam staring at us in shock.

"Oh, my God!" Winnie cried out. Sam's mouth was open and his eyes were wide.

Oswald and I sprang away from each other, grabbing desperately at our clothing. I needed to cover my nakedness, so I yanked on his shirt and pulled on his boxers. I didn't want to look at Winnie and Sam, but I did.

Oswald clutched his pants to his crotch and said, "I can explain," which was riduculous because there was no justification for our crime. I had done the worst thing possible, betrayed my friend Winnie. Ruining my chance with Sam was nothing in comparison. I hated myself.

"Really?" said Winnie. "Because I came to tell you that I'm pregnant."

Grabbing my dress, I said, "Winnie, I'm sorry, I'm sorry, oh, please, I'm so sorry." And like a coward, I ran.

Their raised voices became indistinguishable as I stumbled down the path. The sharp stones hurt my bare feet, but I deserved the pain. I crept around the house like a thief. To my great relief, the kitchen was empty. I slipped into my room and Daisy jumped off the bed and greeted me with a thumping tail. I stroked her furry head and said tearfully, "Sorry, girl, sorry."

I was crying as I pulled on underwear, jeans, a sweater, and sneakers. I found a backpack in the closet and shoved whatever clothes would fit inside. In the bathroom, I grabbed the basics and crammed them into my handbag. Then there was the typewriter.

It was mine. Oswald had given it to me. I jammed my manuscript into a paper bag, slipped the backpack over one shoulder, my handbag over the other, and picked up the bag and typewriter case.

When I slinked into the kitchen, Edna was standing there as if she had been waiting for me. "What exactly is going on?"

"I have to leave, Edna. I'm . . . thank you for everything." I was sniffling and crying.

She looked at me sadly. "Whatever it is, we can fix it."

"We can't, Edna. I'm awful. I did something unforgivable."

She reached out to me. "Milagro," she said, but I jumped away. "It will be all right, Young Lady. Stay and we'll make sure everything works out."

"No, it won't. I'm sorry. Tell everyone I'm sorry." I couldn't bear the disappointment in her great emerald eyes.

I dashed out of the house. Fueled by rum and anguish, I couldn't drive safely. There was the old bicycle with a basket that had once been stored in the maid's room. I shoved the typewriter case into the basket and rode clumsily down the tree-lined lane.

The vampires' dossier on me had been right. I was a foolish, unreliable, irresponsible tramp. The gates opened automatically and I gracelessly departed Count Dracula's country estate, the kind friends I had betrayed, my ruined future with Sam, my dog, my chicken, and my garden.

thirty

mi sofa es tu sofa

I leaned the bike against the wall of the Kwickie-Mart and went inside. A hefty woman with a crew cut was standing in front of the chip display. The skinny dude behind the counter looked at me with curiosity. "Can I help you?" he asked.

"Do any buses go by here?"

"Not tonight. In the morning."

"Like what time? Or is there a train?"

"Where you going?" said the rough voice behind me. The woman had selected a bag of Cheez Doodles. I was going to hell eventually, but now I told her I was heading for the City.

"I can take you most of the way there, princess, *no problemo.*"

She told me her name was Sierra Madre, so I told her my

name was Dolores. I left the bicycle where it was and got into her battered pickup. As we headed over the mountain, the forest obscured the indigo sky that had witnessed my sins.

Sierra Madre sang along with folk songs on the radio, songs of desolation, survival, hope, and lost love. I tried not to cry. It was still dark when we entered a small city. She dropped me off at a bus stop in front of an open diner and said, "Nice knowing you, doll. It'll get better. From the look of you, it couldn't get any worse, right?"

"Thanks. You're a treasure."

I'm sure she'd heard it a hundred times before, but she chuckled anyway as she drove off. I bought a cup of burnt, watery coffee from the diner and drank it while I waited for the bus.

The bus was slow and the ride jarring. How could I have believed Oswald's blatant lie that he'd never had sex with Winnie when I should have noticed that she was pregnant? I was a low-down selfish bitch. I was beneath contempt.

Cunning, insidious sleep overwhelmed me. My respite was short. Forbidden, erotic images of Oswald came to me, but then he was not Oswald—he was Sebastian and he was Ian and this composite creature was ravishing me in impossible, hideous, wonderful, horrible ways.

When I arrived in the City, the smells and noises hit me like a wall. It was not yet morning, but big rigs and delivery trucks rumbled by spewing exhaust. A police siren wailed in the distance, and voices shouted down the road. There was an ambient buzz that I had never noticed before from millions of gadgets and appliances. A Dumpster reeked of rotting garbage, and the bitter odor of roasting coffee beans hung heavy in the foggy air. I shivered a little. I'd forgotten how chilly the City was.

I thought about going to Nancy's, but I didn't want to inflict myself on Todd, who was in contact with Sebastian and had never been a member of the Milagro Fan Club. Another bus took me within a few blocks of Mercedes's house on the edge of the Latino district. The narrow older structure stood shoulder to shoulder with similar houses. Mercedes had the neatest house on the block. Her steps were swept clean, the gray and white paint was fresh, and on the landing, two big pots held bright orange geraniums and ivy. Tenants lived on the first floor, and she lived in the tidy one-bedroom upstairs.

The sky was beginning to grow lighter and I realized that I hadn't brought sunscreen. I pressed the buzzer for her flat and stood away from the door so I would be visible from upstairs. After a minute, I saw the amber velvet drapes on the second floor move. The lock buzzed and I opened the door and walked up the narrow stairs.

My pajama-clad friend stood at the top, looking both annoyed and curious. "Milagro, what the hell are you doing here at this time of the—"

I put down my backpack, the typewriter case, and the paper bag. When I fell into her arms, she immediately tried to comfort me, patting me firmly on the back, saying, "Get hold of yourself, *mijita.*"

Trying to compose myself, I released her and struggled to stop sniffling. Mercedes shook her head. "You're a disaster. Maybe we need some coffee." She led me through a small living room into a smaller kitchen. I sat down on a wooden chair in front of a table pushed against the wall. The kitchen was painted a cheerful aqua and gleaming pots hung from a rack. Shelves displayed pretty souvenirs from her parents' homelands.

"May I use the bathroom?"

"You know you don't have to ask," Mercedes answered gruffly. "Go ahead and take a shower if you want. The towels are in the closet."

In the mirror, I saw the face of a selfish bitch. Poor, poor Winnie—why had my own transient pleasure been more important than her happiness? Poor, poor Sam—why had I forgotten him so easily? Turning the shower on so hot I could barely endure it, I scrubbed myself harshly, trying to clean away any traces of lying, treacherous Oswald.

When I returned to the kitchen, Mercedes had made strong, sweet Cuban coffee. She poured a cup for me. "Okay," she ordered, "spill it."

So I did. I told her everything from the beginning and I didn't hold back. When I said "vampires" the first time, her hazel eyes widened, but I continued with my story. I told her how both Sebastian's family and the vampires had come from towns with unspellable names and had once been allies. I told her about CACA's plan to exploit the vamps' DNA, about how my skin healed and how I lusted for another woman's fiancé and why I adored Edna. I described the layout of the garden, Ernie's blood tastings, and the way the sun rose above the mountains. I told her the sordid details of my liaison with Ian, the vampyre party, the slaughtered animals, and my ugly, selfish behavior. I concluded with, "And then I took a bus here."

We were on our third cup of coffee and I was shaking with nerves and caffeine. "Do you really expect me to believe that?"

"No, but I needed to tell someone I trust."

"I think what you really need is to sleep," my *amiga* said. She made up the sofa for me. The room was dark behind the thick drapes, and I let her fuss over me, tucking a comforter around my feet, putting on a recording of Cesaria Evora's plaintive crooning.

Self-loathing and despair are exhausting. When I awoke in the afternoon, Mercedes had gone to My Dive. She left me a note telling me she'd be back late.

I didn't expect Winnie to ever forgive me, but I wondered if she would, if she could, forgive Oswald this time. Would she have to for the sake of their child? Why had Oswald lied to me about their relationship? Was I one last fling or one in a series of flings for a man who could have had any number of women? It was humiliating to know that he had used me so easily.

At least Sam had been saved last night; now he wouldn't be trapped in a relationship with a cheap harlot.

I was too depressed to get up. The hours passed and I wondered what the vampires were doing. It seemed impossible that they could be sitting on the terrace, drinking and chatting. But then, what did I really know about their lives?

thirty-one

artist in (ratless) residence

Early the next morning, Mercedes pulled the drapes open and yanked the comforter off me. "Your grandparents didn't work in the fields just so you could feel sorry for yourself," she said inaccurately, since my grandparents had worked in canneries, textile factories, and a welding shop.

I sat up and said, "I feel horrible about what I did."

She pulled a big plastic clip out of her jeans pocket and snapped it around her frizzy auburn hair. "You should. That was really low."

I got up and we started folding the blankets together. "Why did I act like such a selfish *puta*?"

"Let's not psychoanalyze you just yet." She took the pile of bedding to her bedroom and returned with a sheaf of papers.

"You know how I think you're irresponsible and unmotivated?"

"Um?"

"Okay, you've never struck me as especially neurotic. You're kinda stable, considering your mother Regina." Mercedes had once insisted on meeting my mother Regina because she said that it was impossible that any Latina could be as heartless as my description.

"Thanks, I think."

"Anyway, I did some research yesterday and found out lots of interesting stuff." Mercedes's own dark secret is that she had been a hacker in her youth; if anything had ever been entered in a computer, she and her renegade buddies could find it. She'd explained her skills to me by saying math and music were intimately connected.

Now I joined her on the sofa and she put the papers on the coffee table. "Look," she said, "there is a genetic disease that causes extreme photosensitivity. It doesn't cause cravings for blood, the pica you mentioned, but it isn't weird to guess that a variant of this condition or a similar genetic condition might have that symptom."

"They kept telling me they weren't vampires," I said.

"Of course not," she said. "There's no such thing." Mercedes waved a few stapled pages. "Myths about blood-drinking demons show up on every continent. We've got our own *chupacabra.*"

"I've always liked the *chupacabra.* I mean, what's not to love about a goat-killing flying monkey?"

"Milagro, *focus,*" said Mercedes. "Okay, those vampire stories developed out of ignorance. But your mutant friends might have crossed paths with the mythology somewhere in the Old World, and we got the whole Bram Stoker Count Dracula thing out of it."

"I've never read Stoker, but I did see *Blacula* at a film festival."

"You're hopeless. Read the book. It kicks ass." While Mercedes brewed up a pot of java, I sorted through the papers and found Sebastian's photo.

Mercedes glanced at it and said, "That's the CACA guy who came to the club looking for you. There's a secret society that came before CACA—I think that's the Old World connection between Beckett-Witherspoon's family and your vampires. CACA's just the latest political tool of this group."

I read aloud: "'It has long been speculated that the founders of CACA are members of a secret society that can be traced back to a ninth-century clandestine alliance called Chalice of Blood. This alliance between pagan and Christian clans was in violation of the schism between the Eastern Orthodox Church and the western Roman Church.'"

Mercedes said, "That must be the alliance the vamp doc told you about. Go on."

I continued to read: "'Chalice of Blood was disbanded during the occupation of Serbian territories by the Austrian Hapsburgs in the early 1700s, but was resurrected in the United States. While the reformed Chalice of Blood rejected most pagan practices, they continued to conduct initiations on. . .'"—and here I paused—"'. . . on the Eve of St. George's Day, April 22 on the Julian calendar.'"

"What?" Mercedes asked.

"Nothing," I said. My one-night romance with Sebastian had been on April 21. I continued to read: "'The initiate was abducted by members and subjected to gruesome physical and mental tests. If he passed, he swore a blood oath of fealty to Chalice of Blood.'"

"What a bunch of nuts," Mercedes said. "They excavated some of the old ceremonies for a new rich boys' club and then they went after your bloodsucking pals."

"'Bloodsucking' is such a limiting definition, Mercedes. That's just a part of who they are. I mean, that's as demeaning as calling me a 'tortilla eater.'"

"You *are* a tortilla eater."

"Yes, but I'm more than that. Back to the subject of Sebastian, what do you think I should do?"

We decided that I should stay with her until the vamps and CACA hashed out their differences. Mercedes suggested that I call the vampires just to tell them that I was okay.

"I'm sure they wish I was dead instead of just undead or whatever I am," I answered.

"From what you've told me, it sounds as if they liked you," Mercedes said.

"Maybe they did for a little while. Before I ruined everything."

Mercedes gave a huff of exasperation, so I said quickly, "Okay, I'll call them. But not yet. I need more time."

The highlight of the next few days was making a midday meal for Mercedes and myself. I cooked the dishes that Edna taught me, but they didn't taste quite the same. To my great relief, I didn't crave blood anymore.

I decided to test my photosensitivity and went out on

Mercedes's back stairwell for a few minutes. My tan deepened, but I failed to find solace in the outdoors and suffered from the aggressive noises and smells of the City.

When Mercedes was at home, she spent much of her time in front of one of her computers in her bedroom. When I asked what she was working on, she said, "Mostly spying on CACA. Knowledge is power."

I set up the typewriter on the kitchen table and tried to write. I was unhappy with the optimistic tone of my story. I started it all over again. This time my tale was mournful and grim. The zombies had a nameless yearning for a life well lived. However, they could not escape from the nothingness of their existence. It became a Jamesian tale.

Mercedes was always gone at cocktail hour, so I would pour a glass of wine for myself and stare out the window. A feeling I had never known came over me. It took me a long time to identify it: I was homesick.

The night sky was a dullish, reddish nothing color, a puce, at the edges. Thousands and thousands of city lights and the dense covering of fog blocked the stars. I slept on the sofa and left the television on to drown out my thoughts, especially those tempting images of Oswald. My desire for him was part of my moral corruption.

I was miserable. I deserved to be miserable.

I couldn't stay with Mercedes forever, so I decided to ask Nancy for help. I hadn't talked to her since her party, but I didn't dare call her. I waited for a Wednesday morning, when she had her weekly manicure and pedicure at a Vietnamese salon across town.

I was soaking my feet in hot water and feeling bad about enjoying the vibrations of the massage chair when Nancy swished in. She was wearing darling purple sandals, jeans, a snug F.U. T-shirt under a leather jacket, and giant sunglasses, as if she was expecting a stampede of paparazzi at any moment.

She grabbed a bottle of shell-pink polish from the display and was slipping off her shoes when I said, "Hey, Nancy-pants, fancy-pants."

Turning toward me, her mouth made an "O" of delight. "Mil, I am about to completely kill you! Where have you been? I'm unbelievably furious that you left my tea so presciently."

"Precipitously," I said.

"Exactly. Do you like this color, or should I go for something more pearlescent?"

"That color is nice, and you know I'm trying to stay away from Sebastian."

Nancy rolled up her pants legs and sat in the chair next to mine. Her sandy curls had been cut and styled into a chic crop. She turned her head to the right and to the left. "Critique, please."

"Too marvelous for words."

Nancy waited for the manicurist to turn off the water that was filling the foot bath before she continued. "I saw Sebastian last week at a fund raiser for children or animals or endangered diseases. He said wonderful things about you and how he's so crazy to see you again and just be good friends, but not to tell Tessie because she's insanely jealous."

"'Crazy' and 'insane' being the operative words. Nancy, he's out of his mind and friendship is the last thing he wants."

"I think he probably meant he wants to be good friends with your boobs, which are looking quite boobalicious by the way, and I can see why Tessie would be mental. Also, Sebastian looked *fabulous.* I was completely smitten. You told me he'd gone to hell."

"I think I meant that he should *burn* in hell. Anyway, have you ever heard of a group called Corporate Americans for the Conservation of America?"

Nancy tilted her head charmingly. "Natch. What color are you choosing?"

I loved Nancy, but it seemed to me that ever since she had quit her job so that she could concentrate full-time on wedding plans she had become really silly, and not the good kind of silly. "Scarlet—it's so classic. Sebastian is a top-level member of that group."

"Strong colors look good on you, Mil. It's fab that he's so established with CACA. He's going places." She winced and pulled her foot away from the young woman sitting by the bath. "I *told* you before, not so rough!" she said sharply before turning her bright smile to me. "These people can be so careless."

I could see the manicurist's embarrassment at Nance's rebuke. I gave my F.U. friend the benefit of the doubt; perhaps the woman had been rough. "Nance, I don't think you understand everything CACA does. They aren't interested in conserving anything but their power. They see the earth as their private treasure trove and all third-world people as merely chattel for exploitation."

She gave me a patronizing smirk. "Mil, you mix up patriotism for bigotry. You're always hyper-oversensitive like there's this big conspiracy or something, and you know how I adore your whole ethnic thing, but let's not overaccessorize. Be a dear and pass me the new *Cosmo*."

It was no use trying to have a serious conversation with Nancy while she was getting a beauty treatment, so I pretended to read an ancient copy of *Good Housekeeping*. When our nails were done, Nancy suggested we get potstickers at the dinky Chinese restaurant next door. She kept peering at our feet under the table. "Next time I'm going to get something more puce, I think. You haven't even asked me about house hunting."

"How's that going?" I said politely.

"Todd and I found a fantastic place across the bay. A three-bedroom, one-bath on four acres."

"I thought Todd wanted a gargantuan house."

"Who doesn't? We can't wait to tear it down and build something amazing. Once we clear out a boring old oak grove, we'll have oodles of room."

"You might want to check the city ordinances before clear-cutting. A lot of places have restrictions on removing old trees."

Nancy snatched the last dumpling with chopsticks. "Really, Mil, you are becoming *quel* major drag. Todd won't have any problems because he knows people in the planning office. In fact"—she looked up at me with a challenge in her eyes—"the city planner is a member of CACA and Todd just joined."

I practically spat out my jasmine tea, even though I should

have seen this coming. That explained Todd's renewed relationship with Sebastian. Todd had always talked about ethics while justifying anything that increased his personal portfolio. "And that's okay with you, Nance?"

She smiled brightly. "I support anything that helps the Toddster in his career and I *j'adore* my country, except for the flag, which is too busy. Stars *and* stripes—what were they thinking? CACA *cares* about this country, Mil. Don't you?"

"Nancy, you know I am all about the let-freedom-ring thing, even though I agree about the flag," I said defensively. I sadly realized that my friend had gone over to the dark side. "Nancy," I said, "promise that you won't tell anyone that you saw me."

"Why?"

"Just promise. I won't ever ask for anything else."

"Sure, whatever," she said breezily. "But if you really love me, you'll work out things with Sebastian and Tessie so there won't be any nasty fighting at my wedding. Todd's asked him to be one of the groomsmen."

"Sure, Nance," I said despondently. We promised to call soon, even though she didn't ask where I was staying, and then exchanged air kisses and parted ways. I wondered if I'd ever see Nancy again.

The city commotion and clutter assaulted me. Gusts of wind blew grit and papers down the sidewalks and everyone seemed to be in a rush. Like a forgotten temple, a branch library stood solid and neglected in the chaos. I walked up the steps, past the Doric columns, and pushed through the tall, heavy brass-trimmed doors. The room was high-ceilinged, serene, and silent, with the glorious scent of paper and ink.

Running my fingers over the book spines, I saw familiar and loved names. I found myself by Faulkner and I remembered Dena Franklin. I walked backward until I discovered Franklin's slim collections of stories and something I hadn't seen at the ranch: a full-length Franklin novel titled *Chalice of Blood.*

I flipped to the back inside jacket and there, in black and white, was a photo of a younger Edna. Dark hair waved around her perfectly oval face, eyeliner accentuated her magnificent eyes, and her lips curled in a naughty grin. I experienced a "Duh!" moment. The bio said that Dena Franklin traveled extensively, had published several short stories, and enjoyed "icy cocktails, dashing escorts, and witty repartee."

The book was a first edition published decades before. After searching through ancient microfiche, I discovered a lone reference to Franklin, a mention in a social column. "Devastating Dena Franklin was spotted in the company of several handsome companions at a late-night hot spot. The author of the audacious *Chalice of Blood* laughed off critics who are offended by the novel's madcap sexual escapades. " 'Darling,' " she purred to yours truly while sipping an appropriately crimson cocktail, 'a girl's got to have her fun.' "

And that was it. Dena Franklin had disappeared from public notice. I found a comfortable chair in the corner of the library and started reading *Chalice of Blood.* It was a raucous love story between a vampire girl and a lusty novitiate born into families once bound together by a secret order. Franklin's vampires enjoyed copious blood drinking, robust sex, slaughtering enemies, and the latest fashions. The novitiate's sanctimonious clan professed chastity in others, but secretly indulged in orgies and sadomasochism.

Edna had just been taunting her enemies with this novel. I don't know how she had dared.

I put the book back on the shelf and thought about the vampires' last names: Grant, Harding . . . Why hadn't I noticed before? They were trying to fit in with classic American names, trying not to be freaks. I remembered what Oswald said about helping those who wanted to be normal. Of course he would understand what it was like to be an outsider.

My thoughts were all in a muddle as I left the library. Nearby, a dusty Victorian box tree was in bloom, but its heady fragrance was barely discernible under the stench of the street. I heard a voice calling, "Young lady! Young lady!" and my heart leaped. I turned around to see the librarian bustling after me. "You forgot your handbag," she said.

"Thank you." She returned to the library, but I was frozen on the sidewalk. I couldn't believe that I would never be "Young Lady" again. I needed to apologize again and again and again even if the vampires never forgave me.

On the corner, I found a working pay phone. Although I had never dialed the number at the ranch, I knew it by heart. The phone rang once and I felt so jumpy I almost hung up. Then a man said, "Hello?"

"Hi, it's me," I said nervously. "It's Milagro."

"I thought you'd call eventually," said the man, and a chill ran down my spine.

"Who is this?" I asked.

"You know who it is," answered Sebastian. "Once Kathleen

spotted you, we knew where to start our search. We have your friends in custody."

"How can you do that?" I said, stunned.

"We worked with local authorities," he said. "You'd be surprised at how flexible they became when all the rumors about Satanism began. The most amusing thing is that some of these yokels were actually worshipping the devil! All we had to do was encourage a few animal sacrifices and offer a sympathetic ear to misunderstood locals, and we were able to flush out your vampire allies."

What would he do to the vamps, especially pregnant Winnie? I had to get them out. "Sebastian, let them go and you can have me."

"That's not much of an offer, Milagro," he said smoothly. "I don't want you. I have never wanted you."

Thanks to Tessie, I knew he was lying. "Yes, you did, Sebastian," I said seductively. "You want me still. I know because I want you, too. Let the women go and you can have me again." I could hear him breathing heavily at the end of the line. "You know I can provide you with more pleasure than an old lady and a pasty stick."

He was silent so long that I thought he had hung up. "Sebastian?"

"I'm here," he said. He paused again, then asked quietly, "Why did you keep all those things? My letters, theater programs, ticket stubs . . ."

So he *had* found my mementos when he'd ransacked my flat. "They mean a lot to me. You mean a lot to me." I became flustered, so I said, "I'll call you later," and hung up.

thirty-two

classless reunion

"Absolutely not," Mercedes said when she came home. She'd left the club early to deal with my crisis. "There's got to be a better way."

"What way? You saw the news report—'suspects in custody.' What happens when the word 'vampire' comes out?"

The latest news reported that a local girl had gone missing, although the sheriff's department had not found any signs of foul play. "Foul play" made me think sadly of both Oswald and my chicken. When the television screen showed a photo of the missing person, it took me a moment to recognize Tiffany without the heavy makeup and dyed hair. Surely, Ian wouldn't have harmed her.

"Winnie's pregnant and Edna's older and I'll be okay," I said. "I always am."

"You aren't going without taking some precautions and having a plan."

"The vamps had a plan and what good did it do them?" I was frantic and wearing a rut in the carpet with my pacing. "They were trying to hack CACA's accounts, as if that would stop them. What a waste all my great forgeries are!"

"Milagro, go clean the kitchen. I've got to think." I would have argued with someone else, but I trusted Mercedes implicitly. Her giant brain would figure a way out of this.

At one point she asked me for a detailed description of Gabriel and to tell her absolutely everything I recalled about his activities. When I asked why, she answered, "International Brotherhood of Hackers. I'm going to work backward and see if I meet his hackers coming from the other direction."

Several excruciating hours later, while I was scouring the grout around the sink with a toothbrush, Mercedes emerged. "Okay, you can call Sebastian now. You offer yourself up in a fair exchange for the women in a public place. I'll have you and the others out soon after that."

She connected the phone to the computer so we could record the conversation. "See if you can get him to fess up to something sexual. Hell hath no fury like a pissed-off fiancée, and Tessie Kensington's uncle is a senator."

Sebastian picked up the phone on the first ring. "Yes?"

"It's me, babe," I said in a sultry voice. I called upon the great Latina femme fatale, Rita Hayworth, to help me in this hour of need. "I hope we have a deal. I've missed you so much. I want you so much."

"Milagro," he said in a rough voice. "I, I, um, yes, we have a deal. Where will you be?"

I named the biker bar in Lower Sky. "Meet in front, tomorrow at eleven o'clock. Release the women and I'll give myself to you . . . again and again and again." I sounded cheesier than a daytime soap, but my gay friends had assured me that you could say any outlandish sexual comment to a man and he would believe it. "That's what you want, Sebastian, isn't it?"

"You have no idea," was his response.

Waiting was the hardest part. Mercedes worked at her computers while I altered a dress of hers to make it more revealing. When she saw me lowering the neckline, she asked, "You're not going to have sex with him, are you?"

"I hope I'll just be able to lead him on," I answered. "But if I have to, it won't be the worst thing I've ever done." The worst thing was betraying Winnie.

"Stall as long as you can. I'm hot on Gabriel's trail in the CACA accounts, but I need more time."

Our drive to the township of Lower Sky was awful. Just getting out of city traffic was difficult and I panicked that we wouldn't be on time. Mercedes was anxious to get back to her hacking.

When we arrived at the bar, I immediately noticed a huge, shiny SUV parked down the block. I got out of Mercedes's car and stood on the sidewalk. The back door of the SUV opened and Edna and Winnie stepped out, accompanied by the gorilla, Peters.

"Hey, Milagro," a voice boomed behind me. I turned to see Pepper. "I'm here like you axed. Where's Ian and everyone?"

"Hi, Pepper," I said. "Wish I could party hearty with ya, but I got some business to take care of. I'd appreciate it much if you and your buddies could escort me to that SUV, then make sure those ladies down the street are treated good. I'll owe you."

"Hell, you don't owe me for nothing," Pepper said. "We're still in debt to Ian for getting Artie to shut the fuck up, pardon my French. What is this, a hostage exchange?"

"Yeah, afraid so."

Pepper glared at Peters. "We can take them easy. Might be able to piece out the car for some beer change."

"Thanks, Pepper, but we're still in negotiations."

"Your call," said the biker, with a shrug.

The cluster of bikers gave me confidence as I walked to the SUV.

"Milagro," began Winnie.

Peters snapped, "No talking!" His beady eyes took in the contingent of animals behind me. If he had been thinking of keeping Edna and Winnie and grabbing me, too, he'd have a hell of a fight. "They can go now and you come with me," he said.

"Come on, ladies," Pepper said to my former friends. "You gonna be okay, Milagro?"

"You know it," I said just as Peters clutched my arm.

Edna's and Winnie's eyes were wide with concern, but I glanced at Peters and said, "Don't ruin the merchandise or your boss will have your lumpy ass."

I was pushed into the car and the door slammed shut. "You filthy vermin," Sebastian's thug muttered. A more compact version of the same unappealing model was in the driver's seat.

"Hi, Peters," I said. "I hope we can let bygones be bygones. You kidnap me, I shoot you—it evens things out. Years from now we'll be laughing about this whole crazy mess."

"*I've* got the gun this time," he snarled, and pulled his jacket back to show me an intimidating hunk of metal.

Mini-Peters cackled at his partner's great wit.

Peters snapped a pair of handcuffs onto my wrists. "Does Sebastian go in for this kinky stuff?" I asked. "Where are you taking me?"

"That's for me to know and for you to shut the hell up," said Peters.

"Your kind makes me sick!" the little one spewed.

"What kind? Sexy babes who wouldn't give you the time of day, you loser creep?"

"I could . . . ," he began, but Peters shut him up with a hard look. Neither of them spoke for the rest of the journey to a nearby town. They drove into the back parking lot of a blocky institutional building. There were few cars in the lot and the day was so warm I could see the heat rising off the asphalt.

Even though I walked willingly, Peters and mini-Peters felt the need to jostle me as we got out of the car. We entered the building through an industrial metal door and went along an L-shaped hall. Another door led to a main hallway and Peters hollered, "I got her, boss! I got the bitch!"

Lo and behold, there was Sebastian before me. He stood on the dull green linoleum floor wearing the establishment uniform of a navy suit, immaculate white shirt, and red power tie. An enameled American flag pin decorated his lapel.

"Hello, Sebastian," I said with an enticing smile. "I came just like you wanted me to. I'm so glad you wanted me."

He nervously cleared his throat. "I'll take over from here, Peters. Thank you."

Peters and his puny cohort gave me hateful looks before leaving us standing under the fluorescent lights. "You're not going to try to run away?" Sebastian asked.

"I wasn't the one who ran, remember? You were the one who abandoned me."

He took my elbow and guided me down a hallway of doors with reinforced glass windows. At the end of a corridor was a large oak paneled door that he unlocked. We went through a reception room and into a large windowless administrator's office. The room contained a bare desk, a leather chair, and a matching sofa. At the far wall was a door.

Sebastian stepped toward me, his whole body so tense that I felt sure he would strike me.

I waited for his hand to come at me. I would step on his insole, and then knee him. I would bring the handcuffs up hard under his nose and at about that time the security guards would tackle me and crack my skull open.

"I thought you'd be dead by now," he said in a gentle voice that hurt me more than a blow. It was the voice he'd used to read sonnets to me, the voice that spoke to me as he explained a museum exhibit or recommended books, the voice that made me feel loved. "You kept everything. Despite the way I cut you off, you kept everything."

"Sebastian, why don't you tell me what's really going on?"

His beautiful face became sorrowful as he dropped onto the sofa. "I'm sorry I was so rough on you at Kathleen Baker's and that night in the car. I had to be with Peters there. They expect me to behave a certain way, especially with the lower levels."

"Other people's expectations can be a burden. Not that I know. No one ever expected anything from me."

"I know," he said. "Everyone else at school knew just how to behave, and you were in your own world. You made up your own rules as you went along."

"I was clueless," I said with a little embarrassment.

"You were wonderful. You always made me laugh. No one makes me laugh anymore." The color of his eyes reminded me of the sky beyond these walls.

"Sebastian, why did you leave me for Chalice of Blood? Didn't it matter how much I loved you? How much you loved me?" I'd forgotten about being seductive. I was fighting to keep from crying.

He jumped up and ran his hands through his golden hair. "So the vampires told you about Chalice of Blood, did they? Did they tell you how my life is controlled?" he asked bitterly. "The Chalice decides what I do and when I do it. They told me to join CACA, pick a suitable wife, take leadership positions . . . They didn't even want me to write fiction, but I fought them on that one and they gave in."

"Why can't you leave them? Why can't you lead your own life, make your own decisions?"

"The Chalice does not accept resignations, Milagro.

Punishment is severe. Conversely, the rewards for compliance are enormous."

"Accept the punishment, reject the rewards," I pleaded. "We've both made some terrible mistakes, but we're still young. Don't you think there is time for redemption?" The years dissolved, and I was speaking to the golden boy again.

"Milagro," he said, "my favorite girl." He took me in his arms and we stood together.

"You broke my heart, Sebastian."

He brushed a tear from my cheek. "Didn't you realize how impossible it was for us to ever be together?"

"No," I said honestly. "Why was it impossible?"

"I am my father's son. I was born to greatness," he said, pleased with his entitlement, his position, his unearned wealth. "You were born to . . ." He stroked my arm. "Is this a tan?"

"Yes, I can tan now. I'm over that infection." I was my mother Regina's daughter. I was born to survive, I thought. "How are the others? Are they all right?"

"We're not the animals, Milagro. They are."

I held up my hands. "Then please take these off?"

We stared at each other and I tried to make my look convey all the dirty thoughts I'd had since puberty, which were considerable. When he reached into his pocket and took out a tiny key, I felt a jolt of power. Milagro De Los Santos, femme fatale!

Sebastian put the key into the lock. "Are you sure you're not contaminated?"

"Would I be here if I was? Would my skin look like this?" I shrugged and the dress slid off one brown shoulder.

He turned the key and removed the handcuffs. I rubbed my wrists and did not give in to my strong desire to scream bloody murder and begin choking this man. I let him put his hands on my hips. I arched my neck back and gave a small moan.

He pressed his face between my breasts and groaned, "You don't know how often I've replayed that night together."

I stroked his thick hair and said, "Me, too, baby," and debased what had been one of my dearest memories.

When he raised his face, Sebastian's cheeks were flushed and his pupils had expanded like an addict's. "When I come back, we will share something special together."

"I know we will," I answered. I wondered if I'd always dread "special" presents from men. Knowing that Sebastian had willingly given me up for a club was worse than thinking that he had never loved me. Ian's depravity did not compare with Sebastian's moral abyss.

When the door clicked shut, I whispered softly, "Mercedes, please come quick!"

I sat on the desk and tried to think. What I needed to do now was keep Sebastian in that conflicted place where he desired me but couldn't justify it. Ian was right: there were predators and prey; when forced to decide between the two, I knew which I wanted to be.

I snooped around the office. The desk drawers were empty and the mysterious door led to a restroom, but I didn't think I could attack anyone with a roll of toilet paper. I tried to pry the towel bar off the wall, but it was industrial grade and held firm. Eventually, I fell into a bleak mood of boredom and terror.

I heard the outer door open and close, then footsteps approaching, and then the door to the office opened. Mini-Peters entered carrying lunch on a tray, a garment bag slung over his arm. He banged the tray down on the desk. "The boss said to get you Cobb salad," he spat out.

There was an appetizing salad, a bottle of mineral water, a cookie, a cloth napkin, and a fork. "That's so sweet. Are the fellows getting the same great food?"

"You mean those creatures from hell? All they get is oatmeal."

What was it about Oswald and oatmeal?

Mini-Peters came close to me and I could smell beer on his breath and the stink of sweat coming through his polyester suit. A gun bulged at his waist. "You think you're smart, huh? You're not smart. Sebastian's smart. He's got those vampires next to a bunch of hemophiliacs. When those demons go for the defectives, we'll have some dead bodies to prove that none of you is human."

Sebastian could wait forever, I thought, because I knew my vamps wouldn't hurt anyone for blood.

Mini-Peters threw the garment bag at me. "You dress in this now. Boss's orders."

I cautiously unzipped the bag and saw a black satin and lace bustier, a black leather miniskirt, black stockings, and black leather boots.

Mini-Peters took out his gun. His eyes shone dangerously and his breath quickened. "Do what I tell you. Get changed."

While I undressed, he watched. He gave a grunt when he saw my fancy red lace bra and *chones.*

"You filthy whore!" he snarled, and moved toward me. I knew exactly what was on the mind of this woman hater. I picked up the boots, one in each hand. I swung at his head with one boot and bashed the gun from his hand with the other. Before he recovered from the blow, I dove at his knees and he fell, his head making a solid thud as it hit the floor.

I'd scrambled for the gun and was ready to threaten him before I realized that he hadn't moved. He was still breathing, but his eyes were closed. I needed to make sure he wouldn't attack me again. I ripped my dress into shreds and used them to gag and tie him.

After taking the keys from his jacket pocket, I dragged him to the bathroom and closed the door. I knew I couldn't thwart all the guards by myself, but at least I could investigate the situation. Having no other options, I dressed in the vampyre outfit and picked up the gun.

I cracked open the outer door and peaked out. I'd stepped out to the empty hallway when I heard a terrified scream coming from past the set of double doors. I dashed toward the sound and pushed one door open a few inches: Sebastian was coming out of a room carrying a bloody knife. When he turned into another corridor, I ran to see what awful thing he had done.

In a barren exam room, I found a pale and scrawny young man trying desperately to staunch the flow of blood coming from his wrist. "Help me!" he whispered weakly. "Someone help me!"

"I'm here," I said.

When he saw me in my vampyre get-up holding the gun, his eyes opened wide and he cried, "Don't kill me!"

"I'm not a vampire," I said, "I only play one on TV." I crouched down to look at his wrist. "We've got to get a doctor."

"They put me here and that man, that man . . . I'm a hemophiliac and I need my treatment . . ."

He began to pass out and I knew I needed to act fast. I remembered what Ian had said about my blood tasting like life and death and life again. "I'm going to try something," I told the young man. "I don't know if it will work."

He was muttering now and I could barely make out his words. "I'm going to die without ever feeling a woman's tits."

"Go ahead," I said. It was about time I used the power of my *chichis* for good and not for evil. I bit down on my lip until I tasted the sharp metallic tang of blood, and then I put my mouth to his wrist. He reached over and curled his free hand into my bustier, releasing first one and then the other breast. As I kept my lips on his wrist, I felt his attentions to my nipples grow more and more enthusiastic and then heard him say, "Hot damn, baby, what a great rack!"

I couldn't feel the flow of blood anymore and I pulled my mouth away from his wrist. As fascinated as the young man was with my anatomy, he became even more astonished with his own. "How did you do that?" he asked, looking at the flesh that had formed a rough scab.

"I'm not just a girl with a great rack," I said. "I am Milagro De Los Santos, the miracle of the saints." Shoving my breasts back into the bustier, I said, "We gotta get out of here. What's your name anyway?"

"Hugo. So would you like to go out sometime?"

"Hugo, we have other things to worry about at the moment. Have you seen some guys locked up here? One looks like a math professor, one's a darling redhead, and the other, well . . ."

"Was there a snotty old lady with them for a while?"

"Yes, and a pretty blond woman."

"They're here with my medical study group of hemophiliacs," said Hugo. "I don't understand what's going on. We were told that they were developing a new treatment . . ."

"You were being used as bait," I said as we ventured into the hallway.

"They have guards on all the doors."

"The cavalry should be here soon, but we've got to lay low until then," I said. I took him back to the office and locked the doors behind us. Hugo was still gazing lovestruck at my boobs when I shoved him in the bathroom and said, "Stay there and keep quiet."

"Hey! There's a guy tied up here!"

"Yeah, and there'll be another if you don't shut up." I had barely closed the door to the bathroom when I heard someone coming into the office. I slipped the gun into the desk drawer and sat atop the desk as if I'd been relaxing.

Sebastian came in. He'd changed his clothes, and I wondered if Hugo's blood was on his other suit. He gave me a glassy-eyed smile that made my gut churn. "You look incredible," he said.

Prostitutes always claimed that many of their clients just wanted someone to talk to, so I said, "Sebastian, tell me why you're so fanatical about the vampires. You know that it's only a genetic anomaly."

"It's an exceedingly profitable genetic anomaly. The old guard in the Chalice are stuck in old economic models, old technologies, old ideas. They hated the vampires on principle instead of realizing the financial opportunities they present. If my group can jump on this opportunity in the genetic engineering sector, we'll be able to amass enough money and power to drive the organization."

"What of the vampires themselves? What of their rights?"

"Individual rights are subservient to the needs of our organization. I accept that my personal rights are subservient to those of the Chalice." He looked at me the way a hungry dog looks at a plate of barbecue. "Just as your personal rights are subservient to mine."

"I'm willing to accept that to be with you. But what are your plans for me? How do we go on?"

"I've got it all figured out," he said eagerly. "I'm buying an apartment for us. You can live there and I'll come when I can. There'll be a guard, of course, just as a precaution. You can go out as long as you're escorted. You won't need to work, so you'll always be free when I want you, when I need you."

Sebastian's hands were on me before I could really process the idea of being a full-time sex slave. He began grinding his hips against me and clutching my breasts, my ass. He stared straight at me and I tried to hide my revulsion and panic. I kept thinking of the gun in the desk drawer.

I heard voices outside and improvised. I massaged the front of his slacks and said, "But what about Tessie?" The office door began to open and I stepped away from Sebastian and repeated loudly, "Won't Tessie be upset if you keep a mistress?"

He frantically yanked down his trousers and said, "I don't give one damn about Tessie."

Tessie herself stood staring at Sebastian. Her scream instantly deflated his excitement. Behind her was a tall, dashing patrician man—and Edna. While Sebastian quickly pulled up his pants, Edna said, "Oh, Frederick, this is really intolerable. I insist that you do something about this wretched boy immediately."

Sebastian blanched and choked out, "Gramps, this isn't what you think."

Frederick Beckett-Witherspoon, confidant of presidents, commander of a vast financial empire, and participant in international affairs, strode forward and faced his grandson. "What the hell do you think you've been doing?"

I ran to Edna, who took me in her arms. "I told you not to leave," she said into my hair as I clung tightly to her. "You see why I don't trust your clothing choices?"

Sebastian desperately tried to regain his composure. Brushing back his shining hair, he looked at his audience. "Tessie, there is a reasonable explanation." Addressing the older man, he added, "Sir, you have come at an untoward moment . . ."

"Boy, your whole damn life has been one untoward moment after another," boomed Frederick. "Deciding you wanted to be a pansy writer and then trying to take CACA off in a 'new direction.' You're not Chalice of Blood material, boy."

"A highly profitable new direction—" Sebastian started to say.

"I saw what direction you were taking," shrieked Tessie.

She marched to Sebastian and slapped him hard across the face. Glaring at me, she said, "You're a slut and I hate you!" Her mascara was so good that it did not run with her tears.

"I'm sorry, Tessie. You were always decent to me, but honestly, you can do better than Sebastian."

I saw the hurt in her eyes, and then she ran out of the room.

"Chalice of Blood?" asked Edna, releasing me from the hug but keeping her arm around me. "Frederick, I remember when *you* were a young man in Chalice of Blood."

He winked at Edna. "Edna, you and that damn book were very nearly the end of me." They shared a warm smile before his face turned grim. "This younger generation, they think they know everything. They're green and greedy and don't want to pay their dues."

I had been watching the interaction, and I wanted a few answers. Looking from Frederick to Edna, I asked, "You two know each other?"

"Oh, we're old friends," Edna said.

"Old enemies," Frederick chuckled. "Keep your friends close and your enemies closer, especially when they're so irresistible. Ah, Edna, why wouldn't you ever run away with me?"

"Because you were quite evil, Frederick," she said with a laugh. "But you were *very* handsome and tremendously fun."

Frederick turned to Sebastian and said, "And you, boy, did you actually think you and your fellow young bucks would wrest control of the Chalice and put our administration out to pasture? I've brought down governments for less reason than your insubordination."

"Gramps, this effort was absolutely not a power play! I

thought you'd appreciate the way we'd use the vampires to expand our assets and—"

"That reminds me, boy," said Frederick. "Siphoning CACA funds into your personal offshore accounts was damn stupid. I'm pulling in major chips so that your spoiled ass doesn't fry. Those monies are going to be returned and the interest is going to come out of your trust fund."

Sebastian shook his head in confusion and said, "But, sir, I haven't done anything like that! I never—"

"If that wasn't enough," Frederick said, "someone got into all our financial records and is threatening to expose them if we don't release Edna's family."

"Frederick, if you were honest and aboveboard, you would have nothing to hide," Edna said.

Frederick burst out laughing. "You amuse me, Edna. God, how I've missed that."

Sebastian's face took on a calculating expression. "This situation can be remedied, Gramps. Perhaps I did begin this project without your approval, but that doesn't mean I can't hand it off to you. I've had my operatives collect important historical documents that will allow us to hold the vampires indefinitely." Sebastian yelled out, "Peters!"

"This better be good, Sebastian," said Frederick.

Peters hurried into the room and Sebastian told him, "Bring those letters here now!" Peters ran out and Sebastian smiled nervously at his grandfather. "You will see how these documents can expedite our containment of the vampires. I'd like to move these creatures ASAP to non-U.S. territory for experimentation."

Peters rushed back with a metal case. At Sebastian's nod, he unlocked it and handed it to Frederick.

I inhaled Edna's fragrance of lemon verbena and enjoyed this closeness to her. Frederick removed a sheaf of papers from the case and slowly went through them. Then he stopped and studied one sheet. He took off his glasses, brought the page close to his face, and squinted. Then he put on his glasses again. He held the sheet of paper to his grandson, who was smiling with expectation.

"Boy," Frederick barked. "Benjamin Franklin did not sign his name with tiny little hearts over the i's!"

"But—"

"Shut up, boy," Frederick said, and ripped the letter to shreds. He let them flutter to the floor and then gave a long, lecherous look at my outfit. "Edna, this girl reminds me of you. Is she one of yours?"

Edna's arm was firmly around my waist. "Yes, she is as a matter of fact."

"You don't hate me?" I asked her.

"You really are ridiculous, Young Lady."

The bathroom door creaked open and Hugo peered out. "Can I come out now, babe?" he asked plaintively.

epilogue

There was a tense hour of negotiation between Sam and Frederick before the rest of the vampires were released. I learned that we had been kept in an unused wing of a research hospital. Edna and I sat in a small waiting room. She told me how the sheriff had appeared at the ranch and taken them into custody. They'd been treated decently, but were concerned about Winnie.

"Is she okay?" I said. "Did she work things out with Oswald?"

"You know I don't meddle in the affairs of others," Edna said. Changing the subject, she said, "I called Frederick as soon as you got me out."

"So he acted out of his affection for you," I said.

"Men like Frederick never let affection get in the way of their grand schemes. He was already on his way here. He needed to put Sebastian in his place and maintain control of Chalice of Blood."

"I guess it's time for me to go now," I said.

"No running away anymore, Young Lady," Edna ordered. "You sit right here and wait."

So I sat and thought about all that I'd been through since that night at Kathleen's party. I'd wanted to be seen as a deep and sincere person, I'd wanted to write, and I'd wanted a serious relationship. Despite my clear goals, I had lost my apartment, all my possessions, my part-time nursery job, and Nancy's friendship. I'd had an affair with a decadent vampire and a one-night stand with a philandering one. I'd let my psychotic old flame grope me. I'd ruined Winnie's life and made Tessie miserable. I had a morbid zombie story and a useless ability to forge historical letters.

I was beginning to regret turning down Hugo's offer to move into the basement of his mother's house with him, when everyone showed up. Oswald, Gabriel, and Sam came from the conference room, and Mercedes and Winnie arrived with a motorcycle escort provided by Pepper.

Edna's grandsons rushed to her, hugging her and covering her with kisses. Then Oswald saw me. He took me in his arms and, while I stood stock still in astonishment, he tried to kiss me right in front of everyone.

I shoved him away. "What are you doing?"

"You know I don't meddle in others' affairs," Edna said. "But you may want to know, Young Lady, that Winnie is just fine."

Winnie came over and took my hands in her own. "You shouldn't have left. Sam and I are together. I'm pregnant with his baby and we're getting married and it's all because of you, you and your precision clock–like influence."

When I recovered from the news, my heart rose with hope. Oswald put his arm around me and then everyone began chattering. I was giddy with happiness as I introduced Mercedes to everyone.

She was especially pleased to meet Gabriel. "Your hackers rock," she said. She had helped them solve the maze of CACA finances, including their illicit payments, bribes, and tax evasion.

"Did you do the skimming into Sebastian's accounts?" Gabriel asked.

"The classics are classics because they work," Mercedes said with a grin.

We didn't get back to the ranch until late. As we drove through town, we saw the media vans leaving. On the radio, we heard the sheriff's statement that a mountain cat responsible for the animal deaths had been captured. The mystery of the missing girl was also solved. Tiffany had called her parents from Las Vegas and said she was going to stay there and train to be a card dealer.

Once we were on the tree-lined drive, the dogs came barking to greet us. Ernie stood on the hood of a truck, waving and hollering. I was home.

I moved into the cottage with Oswald. Ian was right about the importance of privacy, but we had enough room for Daisy and my chicken, Petunia, too. "I loved you from the first moment I saw you," Oswald told me. "You were trying to act demure, trying to fit in, but you had this attitude, and I could see it whenever you looked around the room . . ."

"What kind of attitude?" I asked.

"Kind of a 'bite me!' attitude," he said.

Oswald had taken graduate classes in anatomy, but I had a degree in creative writing from F.U., and I think we both taught each other fabulous things. We also made each other laugh.

Dr. Winnie gave me a medical exam and confirmed that I had developed immunity to their condition. Well, Sebastian had said that my people had the ability to adapt and he was right. Arrangements were made for a few vials of my blood to be sent to Hugo's doctor for research purposes and the results showed nothing out of the ordinary: I was a common Mexican girl and that was exactly what I wanted to be.

The Beckett-Witherspoons paid a huge settlement to Hugo so that he wouldn't press charges against Sebastian. He bought a house of his own and a few fancy cars. The last time I phoned him, I couldn't hear a word he said over the squeals of girls attending his pool party.

Oswald decided that since I fulfilled his most important cravings, he could resist others. He told me that he'd stopped drinking blood altogether. Sometimes in the throes of passion, he nipped a little hard, but a swift slap to his taut bottom usually brought him under control. I wanted to be a trusting partner, so I tried not to be skeptical when he suddenly remembered an important question he needed to ask Ernie in the middle of the night.

It seemed to me that the vampires had a fair amount of

control over their blood drinking, and I foolishly suggested that they end this practice.

"Tradition is the basis of civilized behavior," Sam said with an awful lot of decorum, considering that he was defending siphoning blood from farm animals.

I responded that tradition is doing something just because it's been done before. The vampires were not swayed by my logic.

"We are what we are, Young Lady," Edna said. "Heaven knows I try to accept you."

"Are you referring specifically to my ethnicity?" I asked sharply.

"No, I'm referring generally to your nuttiness."

Winnie tried to make me feel better by telling me that there was a chance her baby would be born without the craving. So now I could look forward to evenings of babysitting while the *niño*'s parental units sipped *los cocteles de sangre.*

We did what families do: learned to ignore those things you can't change. I would like to say that I had no disagreeable traits that the vampires had to endure.

One day I went outside and found a little green pickup truck with a big red bow on the hood and a bed filled with gardening tools. I set up a small garden consulting business that left me time to write.

Despite all my efforts, I couldn't find a living (or undead) soul interested in my novel, so I put it aside. Edna asked me to collaborate with her on a book, a guide to country life. I did the gardening chapters and she wrote the cooking sections. We found a publisher, and *Spirit of Country Life* is expected to have modest but respectable sales.

Sebastian was dispatched to a small private college in the hinterlands of Nebraska where he teaches creative writing. Chalice of Blood quietly disbanded CACA, but it is to be expected that the Chalice has already started forming another public group to promote their agenda.

Cornelia sent an enigmatic postcard to Winnie. It seems that she has decided to explore the United States. The postmark was from Nebraska, but everyone else seems to think it's just a coincidence. As for Ian, every now and then a package arrives for me from exotic locations. Inside I find lovely presents: ruby earrings, exquisite old books, smooth river stones, fountain pens . . . There's always an unsigned note that says, "I can wait." I tear up the notes and hide the gifts in a corner of my closet.

Mercedes, who loves to ride, visits often and has become good friends with the family and Ernie. When she comes, we females commandeer the pool for night swims and conversation. Beautiful Winnie floats on the water, her belly as round as the moon above, and Edna reminisces about her family and children. Sometimes we can even get her to talk about all the men who fell at her feet.

Mercedes told me that Nancy had been asking after me, wanting to resume our friendship. She's even set back her wedding date. I need a little time, but I'll talk to her again. We all make mistakes and I miss her madly.

Every morning, I wake beside a fabulous man and love him more and more. The main house is filled with noise and laughter and family, and soon there will be a child, too. We are none of us alone anymore and the sky above us is endless.

acknowledgments

I would like to thank those who made writing this book even more fun. My wonderful agent, Julie Castiglia, was always available for advice and chat. Maggie Crawford, my brilliant editor, made rewriting a delight. Thanks to my brother, Marlo, for helping me with ridiculous plot ideas. Dan Sonnier, MD, a scholar and a gentleman, provided me with medical terminology. I'll aways be grateful to columnist Leah Garchik for her kindness and encouragement.

Special thanks to the Gough family, who graciously invited me to spend time writing and relaxing at their ranch.

None of this would have been possible without my parents, who took me to the library.